THE
SISTERHOOD

ALSO BY TASHA ALEXANDER

Death by Misadventure
A Cold Highland Wind
Secrets of the Nile
The Dark Heart of Florence
In the Shadow of Vesuvius
Uneasy Lies the Crown
Death in St. Petersburg
A Terrible Beauty
The Adventuress
The Counterfeit Heiress
Behind the Shattered Glass
Death in the Floating City
A Crimson Warning
Dangerous to Know
Tears of Pearl
A Fatal Waltz
A Poisoned Season
And Only to Deceive

Elizabeth: The Golden Age

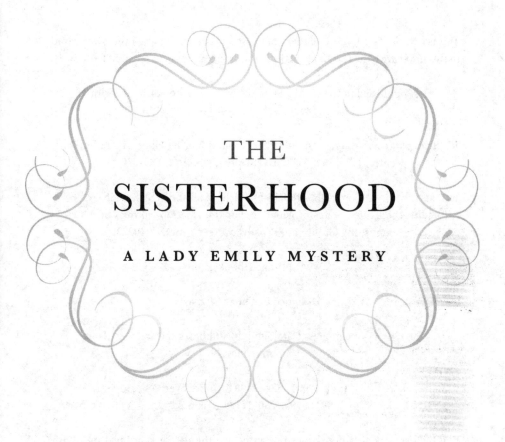

THE SISTERHOOD

A LADY EMILY MYSTERY

Tasha Alexander

MINOTAUR BOOKS
NEW YORK

This is a work of fiction. All of the characters, organizations, and events portrayed in this novel are either products of the author's imagination or are used fictitiously.

First published in the United States by Minotaur Books, an imprint of St. Martin's Publishing Group

EU Representative: Macmillan Publishers Ireland Ltd, 1st Floor, The Liffey Trust Centre, 117–126 Sheriff Street Upper, Dublin 1, DO1 YC43

THE SISTERHOOD. Copyright © 2025 by Tasha Alexander. All rights reserved. Printed in the United States of America. For information, address St. Martin's Publishing Group, 120 Broadway, New York, NY 10271.

www.minotaurbooks.com

Designed by Omar Chapa

The Library of Congress Cataloging-in-Publication Data is available upon request.

ISBN 978-1-250-37498-1 (hardcover)
ISBN 978-1-250-37499-8 (ebook)

The publisher of this book does not authorize the use or reproduction of any part of this book in any manner for the purpose of training artificial intelligence technologies or systems. The publisher of this book expressly reserves this book from the Text and Data Mining exception in accordance with Article 4(3) of the European Union Digital Single Market Directive 2019/790.

Our books may be purchased in bulk for specialty retail/wholesale, literacy, corporate/premium, educational, and subscription box use. Please contact MacmillanSpecialMarkets@macmillan.com.

First Edition: 2025

10 9 8 7 6 5 4 3 2 1

For Robbie, who should have her own book

I would have girls regard themselves not as adjectives but as nouns. —*Elizabeth Cady Stanton*

Woman must not depend upon the protection of man, but must be taught to protect herself. —*Susan B. Anthony*

So long as we have not votes we must be disorderly. —*Christabel Pankhurst*

Courage calls to courage everywhere, and its voice cannot be denied. —*Millicent Fawcett*

Deeds not words. —*Emmeline Pankhurst*

THE
SISTERHOOD

Prologue

Harrington House, London
June 1907

Victoria Goldsborough was wearing white that evening, satin shimmering like pearls. Her grandmother had initially objected to the extravagance. The color would show dirt too easily. It wouldn't wear well. She changed her mind, however, after Peregrine proposed. When a girl catches a marquess so soon after her debut, the world around her becomes a magical place. Now, extravagance was encouraged.

The enormous ruby, set in Welsh gold and surrounded by diamonds, still felt heavy on her hand. It caught on the frilly net edging the bodice of her gown. Untangling the prongs nearly made her trip as she climbed the stairs of Harrington House, her future home. She laughed as she regained her balance.

"Do focus on dignity tonight, my dear." Her grandmother wouldn't rest easy until the wedding was over. The family's future depended on this marriage. "It's bad enough we're arriving late. There's no need to draw further attention to yourself by behaving as if you were an uncouth American. Laughter should be discreet, delicate, and only dispensed when absolutely necessary."

Victoria's sister Portia shot her a look and pulled a funny face. It took great effort not to laugh more, but she managed. They'd reached the ballroom at the top of the marble stairs. Crystal chandeliers glittered, illuminating the dancers on the floor. Huge arrangements of white roses filled the space with their sweet aroma, mingling with countless French perfumes and a hint of tobacco. The orchestra, brought from Vienna, played in a minstrels' gallery above it all.

"You look divine."

"Like a princess."

"Who designed your dress?"

Every young lady she passed had a compliment; none of them was sincere and none gave Portia more than the barest acknowledgment. They'd all hated and envied Victoria in equal measure from the moment her engagement announcement appeared in *The Times*. Yet they would become integral to her life, the friends required by expectation. As a marchioness, she would outrank them all. In theory, that should make the situation more bearable, but in practice, it would only mean she'd never be free from them. It was what she'd wanted, though, so she could hardly complain.

"Darling!" Peregrine was at her side almost as soon as she'd entered the room. Her grandmother spoke before she could.

"Lord Harrington, where is your mother? I must apologize for our tardiness. We had every intention of arriving early—"

"It is of no consequence, I assure you, Lady Goldsborough. She was speaking to Cook a moment ago. There's a problem with the jellies she meant to serve tonight. I told her it was irrelevant because my darling girl doesn't like them."

"You remembered that?" Victoria asked.

"Of course. I hang on your every word."

She looped her arm through his. Tugging on it gently, she led him to a quiet corner of the room, not bothering to take leave from her grandmother or sister.

"I'll get an earful about behaving inappropriately, but I can't resist, not when you prove so considerate," she said. "It bodes well for our happiness." Her eyes darted from side to side. She bit her bottom lip and then kissed him, ever so quickly.

"Blimey, I'd no idea jellies could prove so significant. *I have drunken deep of joy, / And I will taste no other wine tonight.*"

"Is that Shelley?" Victoria asked, wishing she could blush on command.

"It is. I'll send you a book of his poems first thing in the morning. What would you say to a quick turn in the garden? It's already oppressively hot in here. Fresh air would be a delight."

Victoria doubted it was fresh air he was after, but she didn't object. In fact, she had no time to reply. Her grandmother's voice intruded from behind.

"That's quite enough. You're both destined to be pillars of society from the moment of your marriage and it's never too early to set a proper example. You ought to be dancing."

"There's nothing I could better enjoy," Peregrine said. They were waylaid, however, by a Mr. Morgan. Victoria waited in the ballroom for the gentlemen to finish with their business, and then, at last, Peregrine took her hand and they spun across the floor to one of Strauss's waltzes, the tempo so fast Victoria felt as if she were flying. Her fiancé gripped her waist firmly, guiding her and keeping her secure. They moved beautifully together. When a second waltz started, they continued on, without taking a break to catch their breath.

"'Voices of Spring' is one of my favorites," Victoria said. "It's the sound of perfection. I—" She stopped.

"Are you all right?" Peregrine asked.

"Yes, of course, I just—" She gulped. "My stomach doesn't feel quite right. I think I ought to—"

And that was all. Her knees went weak. Her muscles convulsed. She fell to the ground. Peregrine was kneeling next to her, but she could hardly see him. He was speaking, but she couldn't make out his words. A horrible pain gripped her abdomen. She tried to cry out, but no sound would come. Then, there was darkness, relentless darkness, an oppressive silence, and finally, nothing. Nothing.

1

London
1907

"I never doubted it would come to this, Emily, you disgracing the family. It was inevitable that eventually we would witness the nadir of your eccentricity. Your categorical refusal to behave the way you ought. Your lack of consideration. Victoria Goldsborough would be alive today if it weren't for your selfishness."

I'm not foolish enough to expect compliments from my mother and consider myself well armed against her frequent barrages of criticism. However, her words that day cut me, despite the utter absence of truth in them. I'd harbored nothing but fond feelings for Victoria, the eldest of four sisters, each beautiful and accomplished in her own right. The Goldsborough Girls, as everyone called them, were widely considered exemplars of all that is good about Britain. Much was expected of them, and Victoria's triumphant debut that season had not disappointed. Crowds of ordinary people (lower-class people, according to my mother) gathered before her grandmother's house daily, hoping to catch a glimpse of her. Fleet Street reported with breathless delight the girl's every move. Had it been natural, her shocking death at the Dowager Marchioness of Harrington's ball would've filled their pages for weeks. That it was murder ensured even greater coverage, far more than her society wedding would have garnered.

"Do not look at me in that tone of voice, impudent girl. You daren't deign to argue." My mother stood over me, her arms crossed as her eyes attempted to pierce the depths of my soul. "This is the culmination of decades of your poor behavior. Of your flouting the rules of decent society. Of your believing that you know better than those around you. When I think of the grief you have caused that poor family—"

"Lady Bromley, I must insist that you stop." My husband, Colin Hargreaves, rarely allowed emotion to creep into his voice, but anger was evident in his baritone. "Your accusations are egregious at best, cruel at worst, and I shan't allow my wife to be treated in such a manner."

"Mr. Hargreaves, you speak out of turn. Emily—"

"This is my house, and I shall not allow it."

"Well." She pulled herself taller and very nearly smirked. "It's good to see one of you behaving as you ought. An English gentleman is indeed the king of his castle and I shall respect your wishes. One can only hope you continue to do your duty, acting the righteous husband and reining in your spouse's outrageous manner of conducting herself."

"Miss Goldsborough's death was a tragedy," Colin said. "No doubt your long-standing friendship with her grandmother has colored your view of the situation. You want justice, as do we all, but blaming your daughter for the girl's murder—"

"Civilized people don't go around killing each other at society balls, Mr. Hargreaves. It simply isn't done. If Emily had been in attendance that night, as she ought to have been, Victoria would still be with us."

I tried to ignore the burning sensation in my abdomen. I was not at fault, but violently wished there was something I could have done. "Mother, my presence wouldn't have made the slightest difference," I said. "Yes, I'm an investigator, but that hardly means I was in a position to have prevented the attack."

"Don't think me imbecilic enough to believe you are capable of any such thing. What I mean to say is that if you had been at Harrington House the night of the ball, your husband would not have refused the invitation either. No murderer would've committed a crime with Mr. Hargreaves looking on. Everyone knows the Crown relies on his skills when it comes to . . . well . . . the fewer unsavory details spoken about his work the better. The material point is that your selfishness in keeping him home is no different from having handed poor Victoria the poison yourself."

Colin's cheeks colored and he opened his mouth to speak. I silenced him with a look. Nothing could be gained by correcting my mother's wild untruths. "I shall do everything possible to identify the perpetrator and bring him to justice."

"You'll do nothing of the sort," she said. "It's bad enough Victoria is gone. The last thing her family needs is the scandal that would come from a lady of supposedly good breeding traipsing about doing the job of a man. I do wonder how I went so wrong with you, Emily. You weren't raised this way. I'm thoroughly ashamed." She turned away from me, without her usual dramatic flourish. Her hands, clasped behind her back, were shaking ever so slightly, an indication of how upset she was.

"Lady Bromley, we're all devastated by this," Colin said. "Forgive me if my words have caused you additional pain."

"Victoria's demise is a blow to every decent person. Society will not soon recover from it. And when I think of the poor marquess . . ." She sighed, then kissed my husband on the cheek. Only one; two and people might mistake her for French. "It's too much to be borne. I must return home. The earl will be in desperate need of my consolation." She glided out of our sitting room without acknowledging me.

Earl Bromley, my father, shared sensibilities far closer to my own than that of his spouse. It was fortunate I'd inherited more from him than her. He'd always encouraged my love of reading and study and, even before my twin brothers fell victim to influenza, had never treated me differently because I was a girl. It was he who had brought us the horrific news of Victoria's death, soon after she'd suffered a fatal collapse while waltzing with her fiancé, the Marquess of Harrington. My mother blamed the dance; she'd always considered the waltz borderline obscene. Only later, after the Goldsboroughs' physician expressed concerns and insisted upon an autopsy, was the truth revealed: Victoria had died after ingesting poison brewed from yew leaves. There was no question of suicide. She'd never displayed the slightest sign of melancholy. She'd only recently accepted Lord Harrington's proposal, and no one could deny her excitement about their upcoming nuptials. It was the match of the Season. This was a girl cut down in her prime, on the cusp of greatness, about to be elevated to the rank of marchioness.

"We'll have to find the perpetrator," I said. "It's the only way she'll stop blaming me."

"That's not your motivation." Colin touched my cheek. "You're incapable of standing idly by when a murderer is on the loose."

"This is a murderer stalking high society. Perhaps we ought not act too quickly. He might have his eye on my mother next."

"Perhaps we ought not act at all."

That, unfortunately, was not an option.

My aptitude for catching criminals dated back nearly two decades, after the death of my first husband, Philip, Viscount Ashton. After a wildly erroneous—and thankfully brief—suspicion that Colin, Philip's dearest friend, had dispatched him, I exposed the murderer. The experience gave me a taste for bringing criminals to justice.

"I wish I'd known Victoria better," I said. "Our families spent time together when I was a girl, but I haven't seen much of them in eons. I liked her well enough, but never felt much of a connection. She always seemed . . ."

"A tad frivolous?" Colin asked.

"Perhaps, although she was far from a vapid socialite. She liked to read. I should have tried harder with her."

"You're too old to have been her friend and too young to have mentored her."

"I don't much like you applying the phrase *too old* in reference me."

"I use it relatively, my dear. She was barely older than you were when we first met. We didn't marry for a further four years and now have children who are eleven years old." Our twin boys, Henry and Richard, were a few months younger than our ward, Tom, who was as dear to us as any son could be. They were all happily ensconced at Anglemore Park in Derbyshire, where they would spend the summer running about the estate's extensive grounds.

"Whom do you suspect of killing Victoria?" I asked.

"Given that we know none of the specifics, her fiancé is the likeliest, statistically speaking. Murderers tend to be those closest to their victims."

"Peregrine, Marquess of Harrington, doesn't seem the sort, but I've always thought he was too perfect."

"I don't much like you describing another gentleman in such terms." His eyes danced, telling me he was teasing.

"He's not perfect in any way I find appealing. He's a caricature of the English aristocracy. Careful not to be seen as clever, he received the gentleman's third at Oxford. He's endlessly passionate about the hunt, heaven help the nation's poor foxes. Rumor says he won't let a lady go without a partner at a dance. What kindness! Is there anything more us ladies might dare desire? Personally, I suspect he rises every morning infinitely satisfied by the knowledge that the sun never sets on the British Empire."

"That sounds about right."

"They claim it was a love match," I said.

"He's already in possession of a fortune and a title. The Goldsborough family are only barely solvent. Was Miss Goldsborough fond of him?"

I shrugged. "I haven't had a meaningful conversation with her in ages. My mother could probably answer the question."

"I doubt the police will ever ask," he said.

"We owe it to her to find out the truth about what happened. Do you think you could take care of things?"

"With the king? So that we handle the investigation instead of Scotland Yard?"

I nodded.

"I've no doubt he'd be delighted by the prospect. Less chance that sordid details will be leaked to the press."

"My mother would be grateful for that."

"Yet you persist nonetheless."

"For Victoria," I said. "Only for her."

2

Britannia
AD 60

I wasn't the only one who'd believed they were our friends. The Romans, that is. Not that anyone would think I meant someone else. Who else was there? We Iceni knew our enemies. At least we used to.

And now we do, again.

It's wrong of me, there's no question about that, but sometimes I miss those days, back when we liked them. When we welcomed them, more or less. When exotic pottery and underfloor heating were more seductive than pretty words. Gaius Marius Aquila, a senior officer, had plenty of those. The words. Both in Latin and in our language. It's what first made me notice him.

That, and his height.

I'd never expected to see a Roman man so tall. Not for any reason in particular, only because, before him, most of the ones I'd met were similar in size to us. Or rather, to our warriors. So when my brother Solinus walked toward our house with someone a head taller than him, I made a mental note. Otherwise, his looks weren't out of the ordinary for his people. He had the usual dark hair, the usual dark eyes, and the usual complexion, the kind that grew pale away from the Italian sun. I supposed that he, like the rest, would complain about the weather. They always did. He was fit, as all soldiers are, and cut a fine enough figure even in his ridiculous uniform, with its pteruges, leather strips that formed a skirt hanging below the metal cuirass protecting the chest.

"This is my sister," Solinus said after he'd introduced the newcomer. "Vatta. She'll break your arm if you trifle with her and sing for you if you don't."

I whacked him. "I don't sing."

"I believe I understand," the Roman said. *"Aut non rem temptes aut perfice.* Either don't try at all or make damned sure you succeed. It's from the poet Ovid."

"I know your language." I crossed my arms and met his eyes.

"So your brother tells me, but I always like to verify facts for myself."

"Abundans cautela non nocet," I said. You can't be too careful. "I don't know your poetry."

Why did I utter those words? In the moment, they gave every appearance of being innocuous. Isn't that always the way? The most innocent things can wedge open the door to evil. As I sit here now, when it seems three lifetimes later, I can't help fixating on them, probably because now there's no denying all is lost. All is destroyed. There's no hope, no path away from annihilation.

But it wasn't so that day. Then, there was only possibility along with a glimmer of temptation. Who can resist either?

3

London

It all happened quickly, once Colin spoke with the king. Bertie, as I still thought of him, or rather, Edward VII, was well familiar with my husband's work, which dated back to his mother's reign. Colin had long been called upon to serve the Crown whenever matters requiring more than a modicum of discretion popped up. It took no convincing for His Majesty to agree that the investigation into Victoria Goldsborough's death would be better served by his trusted agent than the police. Whether Scotland Yard disagreed was irrelevant to the king. I was delighted they wouldn't stand in our way.

So confident was I in the outcome, I hadn't waited for Colin to return from the palace before sending a note to Victoria's sister Portia. It is always a delicate matter, questioning the family of a murder victim after the sad event, but I knew how critically important it was to do so as quickly as possible. Portia was only a year younger than

Victoria, and the two were as close as twins. At least that's what my mother claimed.

I hadn't wanted to call on the Goldsboroughs before I'd spoken to Portia on her own. It would be better to talk somewhere more private, so I'd invited her to come to me at her convenience. I never dreamed she'd appear on the stoop of our house in Park Lane half an hour after receiving my message. She was swathed in black from head to toe, a single strand of jet beads hanging around her neck. Her eyes were red and swollen.

I received her in the library, the most comfortable room in the house, with its well-worn leather chairs and sofas and my collection of ancient Greek vases. Cherry bookcases soared to the ceiling. A long marble mantel dominated one wall. This being summer in England, a fire roared in its hearth, taking the chill out of the damp air. We sat in front of it, silent for a moment after I offered my condolences.

"I know you have questions," she said. "I can't bear the thought of speaking about any of it—about her, but it must be done if we're to catch the man who—" She choked back a sob.

"I'm so dreadfully sorry. It's awful to have your grief compounded by the pain of an investigation."

"At least it's you rather than some awful policeman. We might not be all that close, but you're an old family friend. You knew Victoria and cared about her."

"Had she been acquainted with Lord Harrington long before he proposed?" I asked, deciding it was best to jump in without delay.

"They met briefly in Yorkshire last autumn, when he came to a shooting party at an estate near our grandmother's. Victoria didn't take much notice of him at the time, but that changed when they encountered each other again, two days after her presentation to the king and queen here in London. She was riding on Rotten Row and her horse got a stone in its hoof. Peregrine, who was standing nearby, saw the animal was in distress. Swooping forward without hesitation, he told her the days of knights in shining armor carrying swords are long gone and lamented that his only weapon was a penknife, which he pulled out of his pocket and used to remove the offending object."

"Their courtship was quick, then?"

"Rather, but who in her right mind would delay making such a match?" Portia asked. "He's quite the catch. She couldn't have done better."

"Did she love him?"

"Would it be possible after so brief a time?" Portia's nose crinkled and her cheeks colored.

"Did she at least fancy him?"

"There was a definite spark to her when she talked about him. He gave every appearance of being wholly besotted, but that's no surprise. She was a beauty, all vivacious energy. Who could resist?"

"Were there other suitors?"

"She had a steady stream of gentleman callers, but none made much of an impression. Once Peregrine made his interest clear, she pushed everyone else away. No one could compare to him."

"Did any of the others take her rejection badly?"

"And become jealous?" She shook her head. "Wouldn't they have gone after Peregrine then, not Victoria? It would've made for a perfect story. Girl loses fiancé to violent death. Boy steps forward, ready to console her and heal her wounded heart. Of course it rather falls apart in the last chapter when she learns he killed her original love."

"So she did love him?" I asked.

"Yes, I suppose she did in her way, whatever that means. Victoria wasn't much of a romantic. She had reasonable expectations and the prospect of marrying excited her. She wanted to be a wife. Peregrine was more starry-eyed. That amused her. I don't mean to give the impression that she didn't care for him. She wouldn't have agreed to take him on if that were the case. His situation is entirely different from ours. He's a peer of the realm with an enviable fortune. My grandmother has to cobble together dowries for four girls." She bit her lip. "Three, now."

The girls' parents had both died young, their mother shortly after giving birth to her fourth daughter, their father succumbing to influenza less than a year later. It was left to their grandmother to raise her son's progeny. There was no other family. Allegra Goldsborough had enough to live comfortably as a widow, but not much more. She'd long been a stalwart matron of society, respected by all, a lady of impeccable taste and manners. Caring for her granddaughters only enhanced her standing. There's little so appealing to those in the highest social circles as the impoverished gentry. Not that it's something they aspire to for themselves. Rather, they like the idea of being seen to appreciate their less fortunate brethren.

There was nothing cynical in Lady Goldsborough's decision to take in the girls. She had adored them from the moment each was born. When their parents were still alive, she did what she could to improve their station. She paid for tutors and drawing masters and dancing lessons. She bought them clothes their mother couldn't afford so they'd never have the appearance of poor relations. Most of all, she spent loads of time with them, making herself available as confidante and friend to them all. She was as comfortable giving serious consideration to what ought be served to dolls for their tea as she was consoling a twelve-year-old when her friends turned on her. A more ideal grandparent could not be imagined.

Portia dabbed her eyes with a black-hemmed handkerchief. "Poor Grandmama. Peregrine had brought her such hope. She'd joked that Victoria marrying him was akin to Jane and Mr. Bingley in *Pride and Prejudice*. Her good fortune would throw the rest of us in the way of other rich men. We might not have to survive on the income from Grandmama's handful of properties in the city. Now we're all tainted by murder. I shouldn't be surprised if none of the rest of us find a husband. I certainly shan't. Things might improve by the time Seraphina and little Winnie are ready to come out, but odds are we're ruined."

"It feels like that now because your grief is so raw," I said, "but things will improve. No one is going to hold your sister's death against the rest of you."

"We both know that's nothing more than a pretty lie. A lie I appreciate, but a lie nonetheless. Who in society wants to associate their family with a victim of murder?"

I leaned forward and took her hand. "That is a problem for another day. For now, all that matters is uncovering the truth about what happened to Victoria. My mother always says you were more like twins than ordinary sisters. Did she have other close friends?"

"Every young lady of marriageable age claims a friendship with her, but she kept most of them at arm's length."

"Why was that?"

"She couldn't trust them. She went from being a regular girl to the toast of London in the span of about forty-eight hours."

This was true. First, the king and queen took special notice of her when she was presented to them. Later that night, she appeared at a ball in an ethereal white gown, looking more like an ancient goddess than a debutante. She glowed from within. It wasn't merely her beauty that made her stand out, however. Victoria possessed a sharp wit and enough charm to make everyone around her take note. She didn't sit out a single dance that evening. By the next morning, the papers had already anointed her as the queen of the Season.

"Given the attention she was getting, I can imagine her popularity soared," I said.

"Precisely. Every girl in town wanted to be seen with her. They gained cachet from association. How genuine can friends be who are so clearly using you?"

"Surely she had true friends from before her debut?"

"We've always spent more time with family than anyone else," Portia said. "Grandmama prefers it that way. She doesn't approve of many young ladies, but you're well aware of that. She and your mother are the best of friends and share the same sensibilities. They only associate with the best. There is Frances Price, however. She and Victoria have been close for ages. Other than that, I'm afraid I won't be of much help. I can't think of anyone else my sister considered a true confidante."

"Did you notice anything out of the ordinary at the ball that night?"

"No, it was just as I'd expected it would be," she said. "Victoria was in her element, being feted by all of society. Her fiancé took her in hand as soon as we arrived."

"What time was that?"

"We were late leaving home. Victoria was wearing a set of jewelry Peregrine gave her. Diamond and rubies. Her maid had difficulty getting the tiara to stay in place. Grandmama was livid. It must have been after ten o'clock before we reached the ballroom at Harrington House."

"Was the Dowager Marchioness upset?"

"Not in the least," Portia said. "I don't think she noticed."

"Tell me more about the girls who tried to befriend her, despite their selfish motives. Did any of them show signs of jealousy? Or inappropriate affection for Lord Harrington?"

"Peregrine was everyone's target from the moment the Season opened. He's the Holy Grail of bachelors. Beau Brummell and Lancelot rolled together." She frowned. "Maybe not Lancelot, given that he was in love with a married woman, but you take my meaning. Peregrine's proposal broke hearts throughout the empire, but no one suffered more as a result than Cressida Wright. She's been desperate to catch him for two years. Can you imagine? Two years out and she's still not engaged. She was focused on getting him and him alone. Obviously, he was never interested. I can't say I'm much bothered. I've never liked her. She's pushy."

I knew Miss Wright only by reputation. Like Victoria, she was beautiful and vivacious. Unlike Victoria, she came from a wealthy family. Beyond that, I'd heard nothing about her character or her interests. Given the superficial nature of society, her prospects would be bright regardless. I was surprised she wasn't already married. I can't imagine her parents were content for her to waste so much time on Peregrine. Most mothers started to despair halfway through their daughters' first Season if a proposal wasn't imminent.

"How fixated was she on Lord Harrington? Did she do anything to make you believe she was jealous enough of Victoria to harm her?" I asked.

"No, I can't say she did, but then I can't think of anyone who would've wanted to . . . to . . . to do anything bad to her. Victoria wasn't the sort of girl to draw attention to herself. Before the start of the Season, I doubt anyone gave her much thought. Grandmama is an icon, of course, so there was talk about Victoria's debut, and mine as well, but it's not as if great things were expected from either of us. Peregrine's interest came as a welcome surprise. It solved countless problems. Now I can't help but wonder if it caused them, too. Would she have been killed if she hadn't accepted him? We'll never know. It's all too, too tragic. I can hardly bear it."

Her voice was trembling and she wouldn't meet my eyes. I didn't press her to continue, despite the fact that I had the distinct impression she had much more to say. Something was holding her back. Could it be her sister's social success ignited jealousy in her?

4

Britannia

A glimmer of temptation. Not from Gaius Marius himself but from his poetry. Rather, Ovid's poetry, recited by him. We Iceni had nothing like it. Which is not to say our culture wasn't rich or valuable or worthy of praise. Just that it was different. Solinus would have called it less sophisticated, but he became one of them. A Roman. Even then his bias was evident. We were farmers, our lives shaped by work. Sheep. Barley. Wheat. Horses.

Especially horses, for me, at least. My father said I could ride before I could walk. The truth of this claim was debatable, but I'd always had an affinity for the creatures. Anyone who watched me with them saw I could understand them without words and they could do the same for me. When I was six years old, I favored one of them, a pure white stallion that I named Aesu who made himself mine. He'd buck off anyone else who tried to ride him, but was endlessly gentle and patient with me. Whenever I was upset, he'd seek me out, no matter where I was in the village. Once, he pushed through the door of a neighbor's house and came inside, where I was being brutally teased by a boy my age.

That was the usual way for me, being brutally teased. I never quite fit in anywhere. I didn't take to the things I was supposed to take to. Like spinning wool or cooking or looking after the hordes of children running through our village. For a long time, Aesu was my only friend.

By the time I'd turned ten, I'd learned to drive the wicker chariots our warriors deployed in battle, easily managing the two horses that pulled them. Before I was fifteen, I was better at it than any man in the village. They laughed at me at first, but then started looking at me differently. Not in a better way, mind you, but like they were suspicious. Like I shouldn't be good at it. Like I ought to focus on other things. Things women were supposed to do.

But I'm getting ahead of myself. Poetry was the problem at hand.

My mother was the one who wanted me to learn to read. Latin, obviously. We had no written language of our own. She thought it would benefit the family for one of us to be able to communicate with the Romans. When the emperor Claudius's legions invaded what they called Britannia, we Iceni did not fight them. Other tribes resisted, but we were left unmolested. Those who live on our marshy land like to say we do different. Our village was safe. The Romans called it Venta Icenorum, Market of the Iceni. I thought that made it sound loftier than the motley assortment of round houses and other buildings that formed it. There was a spot of bother some years later when a new governor was appointed by Rome. He threatened our right to arm ourselves with anything other than weapons specifically used for hunting. We objected. Vehemently. His armies defeated us in a relatively minor face-off, yet, somehow, we managed to maintain our independence. That's where Prasutagus came in. He was our leader at the time, and happy to become a client king. Loyal to them. Loyal to the emperor. An ally of Rome.

> *Cede repugnanti; cedendo victor abibis.*
> Yield to the opposer; by yielding you
> will obtain the victory.

Ovid could make even losing seem tolerable. Poetry has that effect. Our defeat didn't sting the way it might have. We had our king, we had our customs. Prasutagus befriended our invaders. It improved our lives. We experienced no noticeable change in our freedom, but made strides culturally. At least I thought so. See above. Reading poetry.

"I notice you have an affinity for literature." Gaius Marius had come to our house, invited by my brother, to dine. The night was foul, cold and wet, but, unlike most Romans, he didn't comment on it. That endeared him to me. I never liked people content to discuss the weather. It showed a depressing lack of imagination. We were gathered inside, seated around the fire, while the rain pounded the thatched roof and the wattle and daub walls. The room was smoky. It felt to me like comfort. Warmth. Love. Everyone knows smoke prevents disease and strengthens the body. I liked being enveloped in it.

"Literature?" I laughed. "That might be taking things a bit far." It's true, I loved to read, but that didn't amount to much. There weren't scads of books lying around waiting to be picked up. Solinus borrowed some from the Romans on occasion. I couldn't help noticing he always gave them to me first. He read them, too, eventually, but I had suspected for a long time this was only so I'd have someone to talk to them about. No one else in our village was interested. I guess the truth is Solinus wasn't all that keen either. Except in Caesar's *Commentaries*. But that came down to their subject.

"I've been watching you since we finished eating and the storytelling began. You're more engaged than the others."

We always told stories at night. It's how we learned our history. Our religion. Our mythology. More than that, though, it was how I discovered deep truths about the people around me. They revealed more about themselves than they realized when they spoke, especially when their tales were fiction, not fact. Their guard dropped and they spoke without worrying they might let their own secrets slip out. To be fair, most of the others never noticed when they did. So far as I could tell, I was the only one paying close attention.

"I'm not sure what that has to do with literature."

"Your culture may be oral rather than written, but I would argue the merits are the same either way. There was a time when the Greeks didn't write either, when poets traveled through the country singing their stories. It's how Homer started."

"Homer?"

"The greatest poet who ever lived. You've not heard of his *Iliad* or *Odyssey*?"

I looked toward the ceiling and shook my head. "No." I'd thought him to be a reasonably intelligent man until then. Only a fool would think I might have access to Greek poetry. My skin prickled. Was this his way of insulting my people? Pointing out the inadequacies of our culture while pretending he was complimenting it?

"It's fascinating to think about," he said, draining his beaker of wine. "Had the Greeks not turned to writing, I suspect you would know the poems, because someone would have eventually come here and sung them to you. Once things are written down, there is perhaps less of a sense of urgency to make sure people hear them. Instead, it's assumed anyone who is interested will read them. But doesn't that result in the exclusion of huge swaths of people? Not everyone has the opportunity to learn to read, but we can all listen to a song. Writing makes ideas accessible only to the elite."

"It also makes it possible for a person to immerse herself in works that don't appeal to those around her. Assuming, of course, she has access to scrolls. Otherwise, she's at the mercy of what everyone else wants to hear."

"Access is the problem." He frowned. "You give me much to think about, Vatta. The world is improved when more people are exposed to ideas. It's part of what I love about Rome. We bring civilization to far-flung places."

"*Roman* civilization," I said. "Not everyone finds it preferable to their own."

He met my eyes. "I suspect you don't feel that way. You're the kind of girl with a hunger for knowledge, who understands that expanding her horizons doesn't require rejecting her way of life. Not altogether."

"Would you have me believe Caesar left the surviving Gauls to live as they liked after he massacred the rest of them? That's not what I gleaned from his commentaries on the wars."

"You've read Caesar?"

"It's the only book we have. Solinus got a copy."

"I'm impressed."

"It should be required reading for everyone when you Romans arrive. A preview of what's to come."

I'm sure he didn't consider it a fair accusation. He didn't turn away from me, but sat silent for some time. My father started to tell a story. Only after he'd finished did Gaius Marius speak again.

"*Candida pax homines, trux decet ira feras.*" Rage is for beasts, but shining peace for man.

5

London

After I'd bundled Portia back into her carriage, I considered our conversation. It came as no surprise that Victoria's fiancé was more enthusiastic about the match than she was. He was in a position to choose what he wanted, and had done just that. She would have felt enormous pressure to accept the best possible offer, regardless of the gentleman making it. Yet Portia made it sound that her sister was pleased with the idea of the marriage, which made me suspect there was something more in it for her than simply doing her duty.

"You didn't even wait for me to return before you summoned her, did you?" Colin asked, coming into the library. "Davis told me you were sequestered with her and advised me to leave you alone. He said the expression on her face when he opened the door to her suggested she had something critical to share about her sister's death."

Davis, our indefatigable butler, could not be said to rejoice at my involvement in criminal investigations, but he had long ago given up all hope of dissuading me from my work. He'd been with me from the time of my first marriage and stood by me despite what he viewed as my eccentric habits.

"I'm inclined to agree with him, but she didn't share anything revelatory," I said, and went over every detail of the conversation.

"What are your thoughts?" he asked.

"We must speak to Lord Harrington, of course, and Frances Price, Victoria's closest friend. Also Cressida Wright."

"I'm acquainted with Miss Price's father. Do you know the family?"

"No."

"He leans to the radical, politically. A solid bloke, with the right sort of ideas, even if sometimes he takes them too far."

"And his children?"

"One daughter and three sons, all of whom are in the army. Two in India, one I can't recall where."

"His wife?"

"A suffragette and supporter of Emmeline Pankhurst."

"Lady Goldsborough would never approve," I said, "but Portia didn't say her grandmother objected to Victoria's friendship with Frances."

"She would have, except Miss Price doesn't share her mother's views."

"That's unexpected."

"People often rebel by choosing a path opposite that taken by their parents. You, for example."

"My father's politics are beyond reproach," I said. "My mother holds views any enlightened person must reject out of hand."

"I couldn't agree more, although when she expressed hope that

I would continue to act as a husband ought to, it made me want to throw you over my shoulder and carry you upstairs."

"She would've been horrified."

He took my hand, raised it to his lips, and kissed it. A knock sounded on the door. After a brief pause, it opened.

"Sir, this just arrived from the coroner." Davis entered and handed Colin a thick envelope before ducking back into the corridor.

"Already?" I asked, astonished.

"This is what happens when we're officially in charge. The palace has made it known we are to get whatever we request as quickly as possible. His Majesty asked that you thank him for his assistance."

"He would," I said.

"You will thank him, won't you?"

I sighed. "If I must, but I promise he'll be disappointed. It won't be in the manner he prefers."

"Given his lecherous predilections, I should certainly hope not." He picked up a silver letter opener from his desk and sliced the envelope. Together, we read the report.

Yew's toxicity is well known. It's also easy to get, particularly as it's found in nearly every churchyard in England. Most people believe that cutting them down was forbidden after Agincourt, where Henry V's army emerged victorious because of its archers, armed with longbows fashioned from the trees' wood. It's a pretty story, but while the Church of England does require its vicars to apply for permission before getting rid of yews, so far as I can tell, there's no truth to it. A pity, really. Perhaps I could suggest to Bertie that he consider pushing for such a law. The French, after all, are only just across the Channel. One can't be too careful.

Given the time of Victoria's death, the coroner estimated she must have drunk the poison sometime between nine and eleven o'clock the evening of her death.

"Which means we don't know whether she was given it at home or at the ball," I said. "The Goldsboroughs didn't arrive at Harrington House until after ten."

We decided to start by calling on the Harringtons, whose house was a short walk from ours in Park Lane. As well as interviewing the marquess, his mother, and their servants, we would have to get from them the guest list for the ball. The number of potential suspects was daunting, easily numbering in the hundreds.

"Fortunately, the ballroom is not as large as in some houses," I said as we set off. The rain had stopped and the sun was doing its best to peek through the slate gray clouds in the sky. "The Duchess of Devonshire sends out seven hundred invitations at a time."

"Bertie was in attendance that night and said there were approximately three hundred guests."

"Dare I hope he's our murderer?"

"No, you may not," Colin said. "In fact, when you see how much easier it is to conduct an investigation with his blessing, you may wholly revise your opinion of His Majesty."

"Highly unlikely."

"He's much improved since his mother died. A far better king than any of us expected. She didn't do him a service keeping him out of politics while she was alive. It left him nothing to do. Is it any surprise, then, that he turned to debauchery?"

"You would've found a more useful way to occupy yourself."

"The perks that come from being in the royal family don't often inspire greatness." We turned into Curzon Street and followed it until we reached the imposing edifice of Harrington House. The butler, wearing a black band on his arm, opened the door and took us to an enormous sitting room before fetching the marquess. The grandfather clock in the corner was stopped, the mirror over the fireplace draped in black cloth, and the curtains were closed. We'd been transported back in time to a Victorian household in deep mourning.

"This is more depressing than I'd expected," Colin said. "I don't miss the previous century."

Lord Harrington arrived a few moments later, his face pale. He couldn't have been older than twenty-seven and looked very much as I expected he would: a vision of the perfect English gentleman. His clothing was well tailored, his hair perfectly cut. He invited us to take a seat and asked if we'd care for any refreshments. His manners could not be faulted. He didn't sit but rather stood in front of us, hands clasped behind his back, and straightaway turned to the matter at hand.

"His Majesty alerted me to your role in the investigation and I, of course, told him I'd do anything I can to offer my assistance," he said. "Nothing's more important to me than catching the miscreant who murdered our dearest girl." He clenched his teeth and started to pace.

"It's a terrible blow, Harrington," Colin said. "How are you holding up?"

The marquess glanced at me and then looked away. "The less said, the better. I'm afraid I'm in no state for polite conversation."

"Of course not." I rose from the sofa and placed a hand on his arm. "Don't feel it's necessary to censor your words on my account. The more candid you are, the better."

"His Majesty mentioned that you're something of a force of nature when it comes to this sort of thing, but I don't want to offend your sensibilities. You are a lady, after all."

"You won't," Colin said. "She'll have heard worse, I promise you that."

"Worse than what we're going through? How is such a thing even possible?" He drew a deep breath, pressed his hands hard against his forehead, and started to pace again, walking in a small circle. "Are there so many murders in society?"

"Not always in society, but, yes, there are many," I said. "My husband and I both realize how difficult it is to discuss personal relationships with mere acquaintances, particularly after so recent and so violent a loss, but I'm afraid it's necessary. The more we know about you and Victoria and everything you can recall that happened that night, the quicker we'll be able to bring her killer to justice."

Lord Harrington stopped walking. "I must admit it's difficult to speak candidly in front of you, Lady Emily. I don't mean to denigrate your skills, but perhaps it would be preferable if you spoke to the ladies involved in this, er, situation, and Mr. Hargreaves handled the gentlemen."

"My wife is in possession of an incomparable instinct," Colin said. "If we were to exclude her from our conversation, we'd likely miss something of critical importance that would never escape her notice. If you care about seeking justice for your fiancée's death, you will not suggest any more modifications to our methods."

"I say, Hargreaves, I'd no idea. Forgive me, Lady Emily. I know not of what I speak." He dropped onto a chair. "Where do I start?"

"Let's go over the details of what occurred at the ball. What time did Miss Goldsborough arrive?" Colin asked.

"I'd asked her to come early," the marquess said. His voice was measured, careful. He gave every appearance of taking this very seriously. "Mother had wanted to speak to her about wearing some family pieces for the wedding and thought it would be a bit of fun for her to see them that evening, before the party began. Ironically, Victoria wasn't able to because of some difficulty her maid had securing the tiara she was planning to wear to the ball. It was part of a suite of jewelry I'd given her in honor of our engagement."

"Were you aware she was running late?" I asked.

"Yes. She sent word and, in the end, reached the house around nine thirty."

"You're certain of the time?" Colin asked.

"No, I'm bloody well not, Hargreaves," he said, snappish, but only for a moment. He quickly reined himself in. "Forgive me, Lady Emily. I'm afraid I'm not at my best right now and the veneer of good manners isn't sufficient to get me through. I didn't look at my watch, but have a vague memory of hearing it chime on the half hour shortly before I saw her."

"Could it have been half ten?" I asked.

"No, no I don't believe so. That would have been noticeably late."

I nodded. Portia had said they hadn't arrived until after ten o'clock. Either one of them might remember wrong. Either one of them might be deliberately misleading us.

"I didn't know I ought to be paying careful attention to such things," he said, shooting back to his feet, agitated again. "I was under the impression it was an ordinary night, an ordinary ball. If someone had suggested to me that the slightest detail might make all the difference in catching this man who—who . . . well, I would've made a point of being more aware."

"That's quite all right," Colin said. "There was no reason at the time for you to have done otherwise. Did Miss Goldsborough arrive on her own?"

"No, her sister Portia and her grandmother accompanied her. I had gone into the ballroom only a few moments before they came. Until then, my mother and I had been on the stairs, greeting our guests. She stayed behind to discuss with our butler something about supper. I believe there was a sort of problem with one of the jellies Cook planned to serve. I only recall this because Victoria isn't fond of jellies and I thought it wouldn't matter if we didn't have them at all. I told her as much the instant I saw her, and she—" He paused for an instant and looked at Colin, as if asking for permission to continue. My husband nodded. "Well, she took my hand and pulled me into a quiet corner, leaving her sister and her grandmother behind without a word. She had the most fetching smile on her face and her eyes! They were dancing like she'd never been happier in her life."

"This gives the impression that she had an astonishingly strong dislike of jellies," I said.

"She was delighted that I'd taken note of how she felt about them. Said it boded well for our marriage and kissed me under a potted palm, right there, in the ballroom. Not that we were in plain view, mind you. Then she laughed and told me her grandmother would be mortified. As you, no doubt, are as well. I promise you I wouldn't usually reveal such a thing."

"These circumstances require it," I said. "I know Lady Goldsborough well enough to agree with your assessment. She and my mother are the best of friends. You'd be hard pressed to find more fearsome dragons in London."

"I've been lectured by your mother more than once," he said. His voice sounded less strained. "She's terrifying. Apparently the cravat I wore to Ascot last year was tied sloppily and in danger of spoiling the entire event."

"That sounds like her."

"She found it appalling beyond measure that a gentleman of my rank could employ a valet who would let me leave the house looking such a mess."

"So far as I can tell, no one other than herself has ever managed to meet her exacting standards."

Lord Harrington visibly relaxed during this little exchange. His shoulders sagged and his brow smoothed.

"What happened after the kiss?" I asked.

"I asked her to take a turn with me in the garden," he said. "We ought to have danced, but I wanted to speak with her privately."

"About what?" I asked.

"Er . . ." Once again, he looked to my husband.

"I presume you're using *speak* as a euphemism for wanting to be alone with her," Colin said.

"Yes. I must come across as a dreadful beast, Lady Emily, but I assure you I had no inappropriate designs on her. She was my future wife and I unreservedly adored her. I'd never have done anything to compromise her reputation. That being said, our connection to each other was still new, still fresh, and I wanted her all to myself, even just for conversation."

"So the two of you went to the garden?" I asked.

"No. Her grandmother had followed us and made it clear that she expected us to dance. Immediately. She was rather severe, if you must know."

"A fearsome chaperone," Colin said.

"I don't blame her. I ought not have been so thoughtless," Lord Harrington said. "It's easy for a gentleman to forget how fragile a lady's reputation can be."

"So you danced?" I asked.

"No. We were waylaid en route to the dance floor by Lionel Morgan. We had some business to discuss, so we ducked into my study. I left Victoria in the ballroom. She was still there, waiting for me when I returned about a quarter of an hour later."

"What was the business?" Colin asked.

"A private matter. Financial. He's a second son who's suffered rough treatment from his family. The less said about it the better."

"That's never the case in the midst of a murder investigation, Harrington."

The marquess grimaced. "If you must know, I'd loaned him some money. He informed me he wasn't yet in a position to pay it back."

"How much money?" I asked.

"A hundred pounds."

"That's an extraordinary amount," Colin said.

"He'd got in a bit of trouble in Monte Carlo."

"Gambling?" I asked.

The marquess nodded. "If you could keep that to yourselves, it would be much appreciated."

"Of course." Colin crossed his arms. "Has this been a long-term problem?"

"You could say that."

"You must be very close friends," I said.

"We met at school."

"After you spoke with Mr. Morgan did you and Victoria dance?" I asked.

"Yes, we did. Two Viennese waltzes in a row." He managed a thin smile. "I requested them specially as they're her favorite. Halfway through the second, she collapsed. You know the rest."

"I'd like to hear the details from you nonetheless," Colin said. "Did you see her drink anything?"

"No," he said. "When it all happened, I initially thought she'd fainted, although that would've been out of character. It was quite warm in the ballroom, though, so not impossible. I dropped to my knees next to her. She convulsed briefly and then fell still. I thought she was only unconscious, and called out for someone to fetch a doctor. A lady handed me her smelling salts. I'm not sure who she was; I didn't see her face. They had no effect. Victoria's skin had an unnatural pallor and her eyes were open, but it was obvious she couldn't see. That's when I started to realize that she was gone." He choked on the last word.

"I'm so sorry," I said.

"I hate that it happened, but if it had to, I'm glad I was there with her."

"I'm certain that was a comfort to her." I didn't really believe that, but it wouldn't hurt to make him feel a bit better.

Before I could say anything else, the door opened and his mother entered the room. I knew her better than her son, but not well. Her reputation was sterling, and her generosity legendary, but we did not move in the same circle. She and her late husband had run with the Marlborough House set in the then Prince of Wales's wildest days.

"Mr. Hargreaves, how good of you to come." She crossed to him and offered her hand, which he raised to his lips. "Dearest Bertie explained the moment he knew what had happened he sent for you and insisted you handle the dreadful business yourself. It's so good of him to take matters into his own hands. And so clever for him to include you as well, Lady Emily. You'll be able to get all the young ladies to confide in you. I've no doubt one of them is behind the whole thing. Jealous of poor Victoria, they were."

"I shall, of course, do my best to—"

"Yes, yes," she interrupted. "I assumed nothing less. Something else has come to light, however, that may change the course of things.

I didn't notice it until today, which I realize is most unfortunate. With all the fuss over poor Victoria, I didn't return to my jewelry room after the ball. Obviously, the servants should have picked up on it, but they're all in a state of utter discombobulation. Probably afraid one of them will be blamed for the murder." She took her son's hand. "Forgive me, darling, I ought not speak of it so directly."

"I can assure you it makes no difference, Mother," he said. "Words cannot alter the horror of what occurred and I know you never mean to cause me harm."

"What a dear boy you are, so strong, even in the face of such a terrible loss." She was beaming, her expression and manner incongruous to the grim state of the room, the black armbands on her servants, and her son's obvious grief. "I couldn't be more proud."

An odd thing to say in the moment. "Was something missing from your jewelry room?" I asked.

"Yes. The tiara I intended for Victoria to wear at the wedding. It's vanished without a trace."

6

Britannia

I've never been naïve enough to believe the Romans were after shining peace or any other kind. They wanted land and power and wealth. They mined our silver. Our lead. Our salt. Our gold. Anything they could find in the ground. They dotted our lands with fortified garrisons and filled them with soldiers ready to subdue anyone who objected to being Romanized.

We Iceni preferred to keep to ourselves. We didn't mingle much with other tribes. We wanted to be left alone. To be treated with respect. That's how Gaius Marius started to worm his way in with my brother. Respect. We all want it.

Solinus was a soldier. All our men were, but he stood far above the rest, a born warrior. His courage, his strength, and his determination made many wonder why Prasutagus was our king. I didn't wonder. I knew my brother too well. Solinus wasn't interested in governing, only battlefield tactics.

"So you've studied Caesar?" Gaius Marius asked my brother one afternoon. I'd ridden in the wagon with him to the Roman fort, so we could trade. That's how he got his copy of Caesar's *Commentaries* in the first place.

"Who better to learn from, Solinus?" Gaius Marius asked. "We've touched on this subject before, but I must bring it up again. You're made for the military. I've never seen anyone else with such a natural proclivity for it. We both know there's no army like the Roman army. Join us. Watch those tactics be put to use."

"Against his family?" I asked.

"Of course not, Vatta," Gaius Marius said. "We'd never station a provincial soldier near his hometown. Half the reason a man enlists is to see the world, is it not? The empire encompasses nearly every mile that's interesting on the entire planet. Imagine how you'd get on in Hispania, Solinus, where the sun shines all day every day and you'll never suffer through a cold rain."

"The weather has never troubled me," my brother said.

"It's more than just that. You'd be exposed to the most brilliant tactical minds of your generation," Gaius Marius said. "With study, you'd take your place among them. I guarantee you'd work your way up at an unheard-of pace."

"*Unheard-of* sounds to me more like *never going to happen*," I said. Solinus glared at me.

"It's only natural that you worry about your brother." Gaius Marius smiled. I couldn't decide whether it was patronizing or sweet. More likely the former. He turned to Solinus. "We have the finest army in the world. The best equipped, the best trained. A man like you is exactly what we're looking for. Gone are the days of the conscripted soldier. We want professionals, men who will dedicate their lives to service and work their way up the ranks. It's not difficult to picture you as a general."

"Next thing you know you'll be suggesting he's destined to be emperor," I said. "It's not helpful. You Romans make a hard distinction between citizens and noncitizens. As a noncitizen, Solinus would be taken into the army as a member of the *auxilia*, would he not? He wouldn't be a legionary." The *auxilia* supported the legions. Their members were paid less, carried different-shaped shields, and wore their own colors. I'd gleaned all of this from watching the *auxilia* in Britannia.

"Auxiliaries can become full Roman citizens," Gaius Marius said.

"How long does that take?" I asked.

"It varies."

"Vatta, stop," Solinus said in a clipped tone that signaled he would take no more of my interference. "I'm capable of making my own decisions."

"Promise me you won't decide without giving the matter lengthy, serious thought," I said. "Months, not days."

"That I can promise you. Now go inside and get what you can for our barley."

I would do as he asked, because there was no use arguing. He'd always done what he wanted. Nothing would stop that now. Still, I couldn't resist taunting him, just a little.

"They'll never ship you to Hispania," I said. "If you do enlist, I'd prepare for snow and mountains. That's where they send Britons."

The expression on Gaius Marius's face told me I was hitting closer to the mark than he would like.

I smirked at him. "*Res domesticas noli tangere.*" Stay out of other people's domestic affairs.

7

London

Lady Harrington led her son, Colin, and me up a flight of magnificent marble stairs and down a long, wide corridor lined with a well-worn Axminster carpet to her jewelry room, where she pulled out a key and unlocked the door. The lock was large and imposing, difficult to pick. I'd not before seen anything quite like it. The chamber was approximately twelve by twelve feet, with cabinets built into the walls from floor to ceiling. Each cabinet contained drawers of varying heights, but all of them relatively shallow. A square table with a dark blue velvet–covered top stood in the center, a single chair in front of it and a large mirror in its middle. A heavy diamond necklace with matching earrings and a brooch were neatly arranged by the mirror.

"It's much easier to have things organized this way," Lady Harrington explained. "I like to try things on in front of the mirror before deciding what to wear."

"All of your jewelry is here?" Colin asked.

"It wouldn't do much good to have any of it elsewhere," she said.

"I've told her more times than I can count that she ought to have the more valuable pieces in a bank box," Lord Harrington said. "Or, at the very least, in a safe."

"Each drawer locks."

"A thief of even moderate skill could make quick work of them," Colin said. He pulled something out of his pocket, bent over, and in fewer than twenty seconds, he tugged the drawer open.

"Mr. Hargreaves, you ought not to have done that. Now I'll be wondering constantly if you'll return to steal my pretty things."

Lord Harrington's eyes bulged. "Mother, you ought not suggest he'd do anything of the sort."

"I'm only teasing, Peregrine."

"Where was the tiara before it was taken?" I asked.

"On the table," Lady Harrington said. "I wanted Victoria to try it on."

"That might have been a challenge, given that she was already wearing a tiara that evening," I said.

"Yes, yes, I'm well aware of the difficulties she faced. A competent lady's maid would've had no trouble securing it. Evidently, Victoria's girl had little cause to learn how to handle such basic tasks."

The implication, of course, was that Victoria had never before owned a tiara. I doubted that was the case; her grandmother certainly was in possession of several. Lady Harrington was giving the impression she was not altogether thrilled with her son's choice of bride. Not that she would ever be so ill-mannered as to state her opinion openly. She chose her comments deliberately.

I crossed to the table and examined the jewelry laid out on it. "Was the tiara part of this set?" I asked.

"It was," she said. "The parure was a gift presented to the third marchioness on the occasion of her marriage in the eighteenth century." She'd managed to neatly remind us how old her son's title was. Rank mattered to her.

Colin stepped forward. "Have you moved any of the pieces since the theft?"

"No. They're exactly where I left them that night. Except for the tiara, of course."

"Are you certain, Mother, that it mightn't have been misplaced?"

"I'm more than certain," she said. "I locked the door behind me after I'd arranged the set. No one else has a key."

"I have a key," Lord Harrington said, sounding exasperated.

"You don't count. You're incapable of stealing anything."

"Do you know where your key is, Harrington?" Colin asked.

The marquess removed it from the pocket of his waistcoat. "I always keep it on my person, as directed by my mother."

"You see I'm not so lax as you all thought when it comes to securing my possessions," Lady Harrington said.

Colin went to the door, knelt next to it, and examined it. "There's no sign that the lock has been tampered with." He moved next to the room's single large window. He tugged on it, but it was locked. "No evidence of interference here either."

"How on earth did the murderer get in, then?" Lady Harrington asked.

"I'm not sure the murderer and the thief are one and the same," I said.

"My dear lady, to suggest we had two criminals in the house on the same night is . . . well . . . I hardly know what it is," she said.

"To admit one criminal, Lady Emily, may be regarded as a misfortune; to admit two looks like carelessness," Lord Harrington said.

"Oscar Wilde would admire the way you've altered his words to fit the occasion," I said. The marquess gave a quick, little bow. It all seemed most peculiar. Less than a quarter of an hour ago he was visibly grieving the brutal death of his evidently beloved fiancée. Now he was making humorous quips?

"Have you specifically checked each of the drawers to see if anything else is missing?" Colin asked.

"I did just that this morning, twice," Lady Harrington said.

"Did you find anything in them that didn't belong?" I asked. "Another piece of jewelry or perhaps a note?" Colin looked at me, his eyebrows shooting to the top of his forehead.

"No, there was nothing of the sort," she said.

"We shall do all that we can to locate the tiara," Colin said. "In the meantime, I need to ask you some questions about Miss Goldsborough. We've already done the same with your son. Where were you when she collapsed?"

"I was standing with Lady Goldsborough, watching the happy couple dance. Your mother was with us as well, Lady Emily, although I can't say she was enjoying it. You know how she feels about the waltz. It's bad enough in any form, but she particularly objects to the Viennese style."

"Did you see Victoria fall?" I asked.

"No, I must have been looking away," she said. "I don't remember at what, but I didn't see her go down."

"Did either of you notice anything unusual immediately thereafter?" Colin asked. "Perhaps someone who wasn't invited to the ball or someone rushing out of the room?"

"No," Lord Harrington said. "I had eyes for nothing but Victoria." His mood had darkened again. I wondered if his brief show of wit had been an attempt to keep his mother from worrying about him.

"Nor did I," Lady Harrington said. "That is, I didn't see anything out of the ordinary. We all initially believed she'd fainted. There was no reason to be searching the crowd for a murderer."

We spent three more hours at the house, much of it questioning the servants. No one admitted to seeing anything suspicious.

"It's no surprise," I said, as Colin and I stepped down from the stoop into Curzon Street. "There's no reason to assume she was poisoned at the ball. It just as easily could've been done before she left home." We'd pressed the marquess on the issue and he insisted he hadn't seen her drink anything after she arrived.

"She could've had something when she was waiting for Harrington to return from speaking with Lionel Morgan," Colin said. "There were refreshment tables throughout the ballroom. At this point, we can't rule anything out."

"Neither anything nor anyone," I said. "We've a list of two hundred and sixty-three guests."

Both Peregrine and his mother had marked anyone they thought disliked Victoria or was jealous of her. Soon, we'd have to ask the Goldsboroughs to do the same. Before Portia left my house, I'd warned her that we'd come by later in the day. I wasn't looking forward to it.

"The list will be useful primarily to see if any names stand out." Colin stopped walking and stared into my eyes. "You asked if Lady Harrington found anything she didn't expect to in with her jewelry. Tell me you don't believe your old friend Sebastian Capet is involved."

I looped my arm through his and pulled to start him walking again. "One can't help but wonder, given the circumstances. An entire parure of eighteenth-century diamonds left on a table and only one of the pieces is stolen?"

We'd dealt with Sebastian, who styled himself a Thief of Refined Taste, and his eccentric habits more than once. The first time, before Colin and I were married, he was putting to use his skills as a cat burglar in order to steal objects that once belonged to Marie Antoinette. He claimed to have a deep affection for the tragic queen. Since then, he'd made a habit of appearing out of the blue on occasion, as he did when he had embarked on a project that involved removing works of art from the collections of individuals he thought incapable of appreciating them and delivering them to people he considered more worthy. Maddening—not to mention utterly unrepentant—as he was, I privately admired his motives, although I wished he would find a way to satisfy them without committing crimes.

"Have you heard from him?" Colin asked. This was the crux of the matter, so far as he was concerned. One of Sebastian's multitudinous errors was imagining himself to be in love with me. To compound things, he had a habit of sending me romantic notes—usually composed in ancient Greek as a nod to my intellectual interests—and sometimes included small gifts with them.

"I haven't heard a peep out of him for years."

"You've not received any strange messages?"

"None."

"Nothing written in Greek?" Most everything about Sebastian infuriated Colin, but he particularly objected to his use of Greek, feeling that it exploited my passion for Classics.

"I already told you, I've received no strange messages." The instant the words left my mouth I felt in my gut that there would be one waiting when we returned home. That would be just like Sebastian. I had to stop myself from looking around to see if he was lurking somewhere nearby in some sort of ridiculous disguise.

"Capital." Relief swept over his handsome face. "Let's not leap to the conclusion he's back, then. Whoever took the tiara might have intended to steal the entire set, but was interrupted."

I raised a single eyebrow. "You cannot possibly believe that."

"I shall choose to unless we find evidence to the contrary." I thought it best not to point out the word *until* was more apt than *unless*.

The rain hadn't returned and the walk through Mayfair, with its elegant homes and exclusive shops, was pleasant. Before long, we reached the Goldsboroughs' house, the smallest in Berkeley Square, across from where I'd lived during my first marriage. The exterior was beautifully maintained, its stucco bright white, and its window boxes overflowing with a riot of red blooms. When the butler brought us inside, however, I noticed the interior looked a bit shabby. Some of the wallpaper in the foyer was starting to peel. None of the wall sconces in the main corridor had been converted from oil to gas, let alone to electricity, and the runner on the stairs was threadbare in spots. I doubted Lady Goldsborough had made any repairs or improvements since she took in her granddaughters.

The butler ushered us into a cozy sitting room where I was shocked to see my mother beside Lady Goldsborough.

"It's so good of you to call," Lady Goldsborough said, standing to greet us. She looked frailer than I remembered, and older. Although she and my mother had always been close, I'd not had much occasion to spend time with her of late. Her face had aged at least a decade since we were last together. "Portia told me to expect you. I do wish you'd come for a gentler purpose, but I suppose it can't be helped."

"The sooner we ask the difficult questions, the sooner we will be able to identify the person who . . ." I didn't finish the sentence. My heart broke for her. She adored all her granddaughters, but anyone who knew her could see Victoria had been her favorite.

"This is an absolute scandal," my mother said. "You cannot possibly think it's appropriate to interrogate the family so soon after their tragic loss. I'm thoroughly ashamed of you, Emily."

"Your daughter is not here on her own, Lady Bromley, and I agree with her that asking difficult questions is what must be done," Colin said. "Should you wish to be helpful, you can let us speak to your friend without your interference. Giving her some privacy might make it easier for her."

"Yes, Catherine," Lady Goldsborough said, dabbing her swollen eyes with a handkerchief. "You could pop upstairs and check on the girls for me. That would be helpful beyond belief."

My mother had little interest in what would help other people. She knew what she wanted; nothing else concerned her. "I was only a few yards away when Victoria collapsed," she said, "and neither of you has bothered to question me about it. Perhaps your sense of urgency only surfaces when it suits you."

"We've just come from Lady Harrington, who told us you were there. Had we realized earlier that you witnessed the event, we would've asked you about it when we saw you last," Colin said.

She pursed her lips as if she were tasting something bitter, but her eyes were shining. She'd got what she wanted: to be the focus of our attention and to control what we were doing. "One moment she was dancing in her fiancé's arms, the next she was on the floor. It happened so quickly that at first I wondered if she'd tripped."

"I wasn't watching," Lady Goldsborough said, her voice small. "Lady Harrington had asked me a question about the wedding. I turned away and was facing her, but I'm almost glad I didn't see. Not only because it would've been too dreadfully painful, but because it might prove to have been a stroke of luck. I noticed a man in the distance, behind Lady Harrington, who was running along the wall as if he couldn't get out of the room fast enough."

"Did you recognize him?" I asked.

"Sadly, I didn't see his face, but he must have been one of the guests. He was wearing full dress. I remember thinking his behavior was odd. One doesn't race through a ballroom. Then I heard you gasp, Catherine, and looked your way. Victoria was already on the floor." She grasped my mother's hand.

"What color hair did he have?" Colin asked.

"Brown, I think." She crinkled her brow. "Yes, brown. A very ordinary shade, unfortunately. I'm sorry to say there was nothing about his appearance that stood out, so far as I can recall. It's probably not even worth mentioning, but I've read in numerous detective novels that it's best to never ignore even something you're convinced is insignificant."

"You're quite right on that count," Colin said. "We're grateful you're taking such a methodical approach. Perhaps you could tell us, step by step, everything you and your granddaughters did before leaving for the ball that night?"

"Nothing unusual occurred. We sat down for tea in this very room around four o'clock. That ought to have given Victoria, Portia, and me adequate time to dress."

"Winnie and Seraphina were with you as well?" I asked, knowing they were too young to attend the party that night.

"They were. It's our habit. Whenever they were to be left home for the evening, the rest of us made a point of ensuring tea was a specially festive occasion. We didn't want them to feel entirely left out. We'd speculate about who we'd see that night, what they'd be wearing, that sort of thing. The youngsters would tell us whose outfits they were most interested in so we'd be sure to come home with a full report. That day, I'd ordered extra tea cakes and double the quantity of Devonshire cream. It's a particular favorite of Winnie's. We each had a glass of champagne as well. A little splash of bubbles never hurts."

"What time did tea finish?" Colin asked.

"Victoria excused herself first, around six o'clock," Lady Goldsborough said. "She needed longer than usual to get ready. You already know about the trouble with her tiara."

"Was this the first time she wore it?" I asked.

"Heavens, no, but she has a new maid, one who is not nearly so competent as I would have liked. Not that it matters now." She swallowed hard and looked at the floor. "So very little matters now. I suppose I should take you to her room. You'll want to see where it all happened."

8

Britannia

Time passes in such strange ways, almost without us noticing, until all of a sudden it vanishes like mist evaporating as the sun rises. The months after Solinus and I were trading at the Roman fort went by in a flash. *Pereunt et imputantur.* They pass away and are charged to one's account. So I was taken by surprise when, one morning, my brother announced to the family that, after months of consideration, he had enlisted in the army.

My father bellowed in rage. My mother took a step back and ignored him. It was the only reasonable way to cope when anger fired in her husband, as it often did.

"You misunderstand," Solinus said. "This will bring honor to us all. The Romans are not our enemy. Our king can tell you that. The world is changing and I want to adapt, not to cling mindlessly to the old ways. My success will benefit all of us in the family. The whole tribe, even."

Whether or not this was true was irrelevant to me. I didn't want him to leave. That's obvious. But I understood his wanting to be part of the future, not the past. I shared the sentiment. Rome was the greatest power in the world. It would do what it wanted with Britannia, its people, and its resources.

That didn't mean, however, that we had to accept it graciously. Like my brother, I, too, admired much about the Romans. Their culture, that is, not their military. Given that I already wanted to bring some parts of their civilization into my life, was it wrong for me to deny Solinus the same freedom?

"You will fight against your people?" my father asked.

"No. I've been assigned to one of the cohorts called Brittanorum. They are not stationed here."

"They're not stationed in Hispania, either, are they?" I asked.

"Why this obsession with Hispania, Vatta?" Solinus asked. "It may appeal to you, but I don't like hot weather. Never have."

"You've never experienced anything like it, so how could you know?" I asked.

"I've heard enough about it to conclude it's not for me." He looked at our father. "You raised me to be a man capable of making good decisions for myself. Decisions that are not selfish but that will enhance the lives of everyone I care about. Have I ever given you cause to think I would act otherwise?"

"You have not," our father said, shaking his head.

"Then I ask for your support."

"No final decision will be made until I speak to Prasutagus," he said. "If he objects, you will stay here. If he does not, you will have the support of all of us." He left the house, headed for the palace. My mother followed.

"I wish you would reconsider," I said when we were alone.

"It's already done," Solinus said. "Father may believe otherwise, but he's wrong. I've made a commitment. I cannot comprehend why you, of all people—someone who has struggled to find a place in our village—would stand in my way. I have always done what I can to make things happier for you. It was I who taught you to ride when you were still too young to go near a horse. I who encouraged our mother to have you learn to read. I did those things because I know you well enough to see that you've never been the sort of person who can be content in a small world. I did it without considering how it might affect me. I did it solely for you."

I stared at the floor.

"I can't stay here forever and look after you," he said.

"I didn't realize I was such a burden."

"You've never been a burden," he said, "but it's time for me to pursue my own ambitions. The ways our world is changing are primed for you. Writing matters more than ever, and you have an affinity for it. The Romans appreciate that. Their women—"

"Their women run households just like ours do."

"Yes, but you can't claim you prefer our thatched huts to a heated villa."

"I'm a long way from living in a villa."

"Gaius Marius thinks highly of you."

"Is that why you started bringing him around? Are you trying to persuade him to marry me so you can leave without feeling guilty for abandoning me?"

"That never was my intention," he said, "although I don't object to the idea in principle. Worse things could happen to you."

"I doubt he'll be here much once you're gone."

"I wish you could show a little excitement for me. This is what I've always wanted for my life."

I didn't reply. I regret that, now. I should have encouraged him, bolstered him. I should have been proud of him. Instead, I stalked out of the house, flinging at him a feeble excuse about the sheep needing me.

Our father might have hoped our king would keep Solinus home. I never entertained the possibility, and, of course, Prasutagus didn't. He was nearly as Roman as the Romans. Their reliable ally. A man who would never irritate the emperor. And so, just like that, my brother was gone from my life.

9

London

Victoria's bedroom was one of six that lined the corridor on the second floor of her grandmother's house. It looked more like it belonged to a young girl than to the most successful debutante of the Season. There was a visibly worn cuddly rabbit propped up on her pillows, along with three dolls; and a dog-eared copy of *Alice's Adventures in Wonderland* sat on the bedside table. A small shelf contained a handful of more children's literature: Frederick Marryat's *The Children of the New Forest; The Water-Babies: A Fairy Tale for a Land-Baby* by Charles Kingsley; George MacDonald's *The Princess and the Goblin; Friend and Foe; or, The Breastplate of Righteousness,* whose author was identified only as A.L.O.E. (a Lady of England); and William Makepeace Thackeray's *The Rose and the Ring.*

This last volume stood apart from the rest. Thackeray did not ordinarily write for children; and this book, ostensibly meant for Christmas, satirized conventional ideas of love and marriage, of society's ideals. When I was eleven, my own mother had forbidden me to read it. Either Lady Goldsborough was far less concerned about the corruption of her granddaughters or she had no idea what the story was about. On the surface, it might come across as nothing more than an entertaining pantomime. It made quite a contrast to *Friend and Foe; or, The Breastplate of Righteousness*, which, although I hadn't read it, I imagined represented an entirely different viewpoint.

Most young ladies in the midst of their first Season made a habit of saving their dance cards from balls. In my day, we stuck them in the mirrors above our dressing tables. There were none visible in Victoria's room. Nor were there any cuttings from the papers, lauding her beauty and success. This reflected well on her, I thought. She had not been obsessed with her popularity.

She had stored her modest collection of jewelry in a small box atop her dresser, and the only art on her walls was a somewhat crude watercolor depicting Boudica driving her chariot, holding her spear high above her Roman enemies.

"I don't know how she could abide it," Lady Goldsborough said. "There are far better representations of Britain's favorite warrior queen, but a close friend gave it to her and she kept it out of a misguided sense of loyalty."

"Which friend?" I asked.

"Frances Price. She's a dear, sweet thing, despite her mother's best efforts to corrupt her."

"Mrs. Price is a suffragette." My mother nodded as she spoke, as if to indicate that we would understand the horror of this information. "Fortunately, her daughter is not so foolish as to fall for their outrageous claims."

"It is trying," Lady Goldsborough said. "I cannot imagine any responsible parent wanting to convince their children they're part of a society that wants to harm them. Most people understand women don't need the vote. The entire system has been set up to ensure our men take care of us."

"Which is exactly as it should be," my mother said. She looked down her nose at me. Now was not the time to remind her that I, too, was a suffragette. Not that she needed reminding. Her comments were made specifically to acknowledge how misguided my own opinions were.

"Frances spent most of her time here, with us," Lady Goldsborough said. "It was a relief for her to be away from her parents' radical household. I don't mean to criticize women wanting to better their lots in life. Not everyone is so fortunate as we have been. Some of Mr. Price's causes are admirable and I quite agree with his views on child labor."

"No one could object to those," my mother said. How the world was changing! I could well remember a time when most of Society believed limiting children's roles in the workplace would lead directly to the fall of civilization. Perhaps someday in the future, women voting would be something no one could object to either.

There was nothing else in Victoria's room that shed light either on her or the events of her final day. We talked to her younger sisters, but were careful not to press them too much. As we expected, they had little to add to what we already knew. After that, we returned downstairs and Lady Goldsborough called for tea. We asked her about Victoria's other compatriots who might have been jealous.

"Frances was Victoria's only close friend other than Portia. Beyond the two of them, there were loads of acquaintances, but no one who stands out. I never saw any young lady treat her ill. There was some talk last Season about the marquess and Cressida Wright, but nothing came of it, so there was no need for ill feelings between the girls."

"Miss Wright never had a chance with him," my mother said. "Lord Harrington is the quintessential Englishman. He respects God and king and empire above all else. He's perhaps too tolerant when it comes to lazy servants, but that is a fault one can accept. He's even-tempered and fair. Miss Wright is high-strung and outspoken. He may have been temporarily drawn to her—she's a beautiful girl and rampant enthusiasm often temporarily tempts young men—but his mother never would have allowed the match."

"You can't think Miss Wright is responsible for Victoria's death," Lady Goldsborough said.

"No, no, of course not." My mother shook her head with vigor. "Even with Victoria out of the way, she wouldn't have stood a chance."

"They do say poison is a woman's weapon."

"You must stop reading detective novels, Allegra. They'll ruin your mind."

"What about other suitors?" Colin asked. "Was anyone else vying for your granddaughter's hand?"

"She had an astonishing number of gentleman callers starting the day after her presentation, but none of them held any appeal to her," Lady Goldsborough said.

"Did they all accept that with equanimity?" I asked.

"If not, they wouldn't have shown so to me," she said. "There were a few more persistent than the others, but Victoria's engagement happened so quickly, I can't imagine any of them felt stung by rejection."

"Who were the persistent ones?" Colin asked.

"The Earl of Fraser's youngest son, but he had to know there never was hope for him."

"Forgive me for pointing it out, Allegra, but he's in dire need of a fortune," my mother said. "He couldn't have been all that serious."

"You're quite right. Mr. Charles Bradfield came around quite a bit, as did Mr. Lionel Morgan."

"I've always had a soft spot for Mr. Morgan. His manners are impeccable."

"Indeed they are, Catherine," Lady Goldsborough said. "And by all accounts his fortune is more than adequate."

"The family are one of the best in the country," my mother said.

Colin and I looked at each other, but kept quiet about Mr. Morgan's gambling problems. "Is there anyone else you think we should speak to?" I asked.

"Perhaps Victoria's maid," my mother said. "Young ladies do have a dreadful habit of sometimes confiding in them."

"Unfortunately she had not been long with us," Lady Goldsborough said. "She only came to us a fortnight ago."

"Who did she replace?" I asked.

"A wonderful girl, Ida Davies, who sadly has emigrated to New South Wales. She wasn't the sort to encourage gossip, though, so not being able to speak to her won't be much of a loss."

"Is there anything else you can tell us about your granddaughter's habits or her interests?" Colin asked. "Was she involved in any charity work or any other sort of organization?"

"No, she was only just out, Mr. Hargreaves. She'd had no time yet to decide where she wanted to . . ." She stopped speaking and dabbed her eyes with her handkerchief.

"I understand," Colin said. "It's likely, however, that there is something in the specific details of her life that will lead us to the person responsible for her demise. If you can think of anything that might be pertinent, please do let us know. It's of critical importance."

We interviewed all of the servants before quitting the house. None of them could be described as helpful. It wasn't that they were obstinate, but rather that they were guarded. I suspected Lady Goldsborough ran as tight a ship as my mother. The new maid was saddened by the loss of her lady, but couldn't even remember Lord Harrington's name. She and Victoria had shared no confidences.

That finished, we took our leave. We hadn't made it halfway down the block when a voice called out to me from behind. It was Portia. "I debated whether to share this with you, but after speaking with you earlier, I decided I couldn't live with myself if I withheld any information that might prove important." She handed me a slim, leather-bound volume. "It's Victoria's diary. I've not read it myself and I don't think any of us in the family should. She meant it to be private. I wouldn't want them to know I took it from her room. Perhaps you could read it, Lady Emily, and you alone. I know it was an important part of my sister's life. She was always scribbling in it and kept it hidden. I only knew where to find it because I came in right as she was squirreling it away one afternoon. She scolded me, but not too fiercely, for she knew I would never violate her privacy by looking inside."

"I couldn't agree more that there's no need for anyone other than Emily to read it," Colin said. "We're grateful to you for trusting us with it. If I may ask, where did she hide it?"

"Under a loose board in the base of her armoire. There was nothing else there. You'll tell me if there's anything I ought to know within its pages, won't you? I don't mean details of her life, but rather information that might help us find whoever did this to her."

"Of course." I squeezed her arm and she ran back to the house.

"You ought to read that immediately," Colin said. "I can call on Fraser's son and Charles Bradfield."

"What about Lionel Morgan?"

"I'll invite him to lunch at my club tomorrow and take his measure. From there, we can decide how best to proceed. I'd like you to speak to him as well."

We parted just as it began to rain again. A nasty gust of wind shredded my umbrella, so by the time I reached home, I was drenched. Not wanting to delay reading the diary, I rushed upstairs and changed into dry clothes, denying myself the pleasure of a hot bath. Then, installing myself in the library in front of the fire, I started to read. My butler interrupted me almost at once.

"I have taken the liberty of bringing you refreshments, madam," he said, removing a teapot, milk jug, cup, and saucer from a silver tray and laying them out on a table near my chair. There was also a plate of caramel biscuits.

"I'm perfectly content with port, Davis. It will warm me better. I don't see the decanter, though. Do you know where it is?"

"Port is meant to be enjoyed after dinner, madam. It never would've occurred to me to have it at the ready for afternoons in the library."

We went through variations of this ritual daily. Davis had long since given up hope that I would ever behave like a lady ought, but that didn't stop him trying to nudge me in what he viewed as the right direction.

"It's also meant to be enjoyed exclusively by gentlemen. We both know I've no interest in what it, or anything else, is meant for."

"Very good, madam. I'll fetch the decanter as soon as you've had a cup of tea."

I humored him. The tea, a strong bespoke blend I ordered from Fortum & Mason, warmed me well enough and was eminently satisfying, but I knew the port would work its way into my bones. Ah, summer in England. I poured a second cup of tea, opened the diary, and started to read.

The first entry dated back almost a year and the last had been penned the day before Victoria's death. Her early writings dealt primarily with recounting daily activities: walks in the park, taking her sisters to the zoo, and detailed accounts of dinner menus. Starting not long after Christmas, she began to focus more on her social life outside her family, but, as Portia and her grandmother had told us, this primarily revolved around Frances Price.

It was disheartening to read her thoughts about her friend's family. She found Mrs. Price's involvement in the suffragette movement shocking and vowed she would never ally herself with such a cause. While she never directly addressed the subject, it was clear she craved a traditional life. She complained about her drawing master (too fierce) but adored her dancing teacher (winningly handsome) and recorded lists of gentlemen she and Frances thought would make good husbands. The Marquess of Harrington was at the top.

There was an extensive passage about the first time she met him, and it utterly contradicted what Portia had told us about the occasion. Far from it having had no impact on Victoria, she wrote that she knew the instant they spoke that they were destined to marry. She recorded how many birds he'd shot, what he was wearing, and every opinion he shared with her. Fortunately, there weren't too many of them, and they were limited to underwhelming views on things of no importance. He thought rabbit preferable to pheasant for dinner. He believed most ballrooms were inadequately ventilated. A keen cricketer, he would rather watch a test match at Lord's than be in the Royal Enclosure at Ascot. The last, perhaps, verged on the controversial, but one could hardly call it revelatory.

Victoria never mentioned why, exactly, she was so drawn to him. I didn't know her intimately, but had conversed with her enough through the years to believe she wasn't an ordinary, vapid Society girl. A talented pianist, she was eccentric enough to refuse to play anything but Beethoven, even when Chopin would have been more appropriate to a social situation. She went with me twice to the British Museum and expressed great interest in the Lewis chessmen. The next week, she sent me a copy of an article called "Historical Remarks on the Introduction of the Game of Chess into Europe, and on the Ancient Chess-men Discovered in the Isle of Lewis" written by Frederic Madden, a former assistant keeper of manuscripts at the museum.

No glimmer of this part of her character came through in her journal. Instead, she had filled page after page with descriptions of gowns she'd either noticed other girls wearing or seen on fashion plates. Her words came across as rote rather than passionate. It was as if she were doing her best to sound like a frivolous young lady obsessed with appearance.

In the weeks immediately preceding her debut, the tone of her writing changed. Genuine excitement reverberated, even in her penmanship. The letters were formed with more fluidity, more confidence. She'd pressed the pen harder into the paper as she detailed every bit of her court dress and train, of the jewelry she planned to wear. She decided she wanted to put her hair in a Gibson girl pompadour—the style I had long ago adopted—but worried that it might make her look too American.

American girls are rather too free with their opinions. They expect too much out of life. They are not prepared for the challenges of running a household in competent fashion. They complain far too much. Yet their country gave us the Gibson Girl. No one could argue that my hair isn't perfection in a pompadour. Frances has encouraged me to wear it that way, regardless. She assures me that hardly anyone at court would make the connection to Charles Gibson's drawings and the look I'd chosen. After all, he started doing them so long ago, they've taken on a life of their own.

This read as altogether odd. If she was deliberately trying to come across as frivolous, she wasn't succeeding. The door opened. I looked up, expecting to see Davis with the port. It was my butler, but instead of the decanter, he was carrying an envelope. I let out an exasperated sigh when I recognized the handwriting.

ἔλθε μοι καὶ νῦν, χαλέπαν δὲ λῦσον
ἐκ μερίμναν, ὄσσα δέ μοι τέλεσσαι
θῦμος ἰμέρρει, τέλεσον, σὺ δ' αὔτα
σύμμαχος ἔσσο.

Come to me now and loosen me
from blunt agony. Labor
and fill my heart with fire. Stand by me
and be my ally.

10

Britannia

Solinus was gone. I only wished Gaius Marius was, too.

"I don't know why you keep coming around," I said, watching him approach me. I was standing near a stream two miles from the village, ostensibly keeping an eye on our sheep. It didn't require much effort, which meant I could spend the day lost in my thoughts. I didn't welcome his interruption. "You've already got what you wanted. My brother is yours."

"Your brother is his own man," Gaius Marius said, "as he always has been. I'm sorry you think I manipulated him. Nothing could be further from the truth. I liked him as soon as I met him. He'll be happy in the army. It's where he belongs."

"Tell yourself whatever you want. It makes no difference to me."

"I didn't seek you out to talk about Solinus. I wanted to give you this." He handed me a papyrus scroll. "Some of Ovid's poetry. I thought you'd like to read it and then, perhaps, we can discuss it."

"Why would I want to discuss it with you?"

"Because, Vatta, you don't know anyone else who can."

I hated that he was right.

"Tell me where he is," I said. "I know it's not Hispania."

"The Danubian Limes."

I threw my arms in the air. Did he think that meant anything to me? "A little explanation, please? I'm sure it's nothing like our *natale solum*."

"Not entirely like your native soil, but not unrecognizable either," he said. "He's stationed in a fort on the river Danubius. You may recognize the name from Caesar. It's on the northern border of the empire."

"So he's cold and miserable."

"I thought you don't like talking about the weather."

"How would you know?"

"Solinus told me."

"He should keep quiet." I turned away from him and pretended to focus on the sheep. "You don't need to bring me poetry."

"No, I don't, but I want to. Isn't that enough?"

"I'm not interested in talking to you about Ovid or anything else."

"This is a gift, Vatta, not a business transaction. You can read or not read, talk or not talk. That's entirely up to you. Enjoy your sheep."

He walked away. I watched him go, which made me mad at myself. I sat on a rock. I stood and paced. I sat back down. Eventually, I unrolled the scroll. I almost closed it again when I saw the title, *Amores*. Loves. Then I read the preface:

> *We who before were Ovid's five slim volumes*
> *Are three: he thought it better to compress.*

THE SISTERHOOD

Though reading us may still give you no pleasure,
  With two removed at least the pain is less.

It made me laugh. I wasn't naïve enough to believe Gaius Marius wasn't after something, but I decided I didn't care who gave it to me or what he wanted. I didn't owe him anything. If he was stupid enough to bring gifts, I was smart enough to enjoy them without feeling the slightest tug of guilt.

11

London

Sebastian. No one else would have the audacity to anonymously send me a fragment of Sappho's poetry. I crumpled the sheet of paper and was tempted to fling it into the fire, but thought the better of it. More than once, I had tried to reform Sebastian. Colin had even succeeded in persuading him to occasionally offer his expertise, such as it was, to the Crown. Yet now, here he was again, sending me inappropriate messages just at the time when a single piece of jewelry from a set had gone missing. He may as well have left a signed note confessing to the crime.

I sighed. I didn't believe for an instant that he had anything to do with Victoria's murder, but few others would turn a blind eye to the coincidence, my husband included. I would have to contact Sebastian, and there was only one reliable way to that. I crossed to my desk, sat down, and penned a message to place in *The Times*.

"I presume it is that rogue Mr. Capet who sent the note, madam?"

"Yes. How did you know?"

"I've seen his handwriting enough to recognize it as well as you do," he said. "I believe this time he delivered the envelope himself. He was dressed like a maharaja, the ensemble completed with a saffron turban. I only know this, madam, because I happened to be glancing out the window at the moment the person in question slipped the envelope through the letter box. I suppose it is conceivable you have more than one acquaintance eccentric enough to adopt that manner of dress, but on the off chance it proved to be Mr. Capet, I sent two of our largest footmen after him. There was a bit of a struggle, but they emerged victorious and brought him back to the house. I then took the liberty of securing him in the drawing room."

"Securing him?" I asked.

"I've tied him to a chair."

"Well done, Davis, well done." I rose to my feet and shook his hand.

He winced. "It is not the sort of thing to which I would like to be accustomed, madam."

With that, he turned on his heel and retreated from the library. Knowing Davis did nothing by half measures, I didn't have to worry that Sebastian would escape. It would do him good to stew for a while. I poured myself a glass of port, drank it slowly, and then headed for the drawing room. There was Sebastian tied, as described, to a Louis XIV chair, two impressively tall footmen standing guard. I dismissed them. When they were gone, Sebastian glowered at me.

"This is not an acceptable way to treat a friend," he said. "I'm most put out."

"I don't believe my butler considers you a friend. He objects to random men leaving romantic notes for me, as does my husband."

"I'm hardly random and the venerable Mr. Hargreaves doesn't mind, I'm sure. He knows it's all in good fun. Unless you've had a change of heart, my dear, and have transferred your affections to me. If that's the case, you'd best let me know so I can spirit you off somewhere before he comes after me."

"I shall not dignify that with a response," I said. "What sort of trouble are you stirring up now, other than stealing Lady Harrington's tiara?"

"Do please untie me, won't you? This is no way to receive a caller." I did as he asked, knowing he would not flee when he had my undivided attention. He made a great show of inspecting his wrists, as if Davis had fastened him so tightly they'd been rubbed raw, which they had not.

"Tell me about the tiara."

"It's not something I would want in its current state, but the parts are what drew my notice," he said. "It was made from diamonds originally placed in a necklace that belonged to Madame de Pompadour."

"You've moved away from Marie Antoinette, then?" I asked, knowing he would never reveal how he acquired this information.

"Good heavens, no, but I've never limited myself only to her possessions. You know that well enough."

"And the rest of the parure?"

"Nothing interesting to be had. The tiara was made ten years earlier than the other pieces. Whoever was the current marquess at the time had the necklace, earrings, and brooch designed to match. They're fine, but not remarkable enough to entice me."

"It doesn't trouble you to see the set ripped apart?" I asked.

He flinched. "What troubles me is that someone was insensitive enough to remove the stones from their original setting. They need to be put back."

"The original setting is bound to be long gone."

"Yes, but there's a painting of Pompadour wearing it. I'll have it reconstructed."

I noticed a faint flush on his cheeks. "Is there someone in particular you plan to give it to? Your mistress, perhaps?"

"If that's what you've decided to become, I shall of course present it to you."

"Don't be absurd."

"You didn't like the Sappho?"

"We're not discussing the Sappho," I said. "What did you see in Harrington House the night you stole the tiara?"

"What is there to notice in any such house?" He flopped onto a silk-covered settee. "Tasteless people in tasteless surroundings."

"The Harringtons have a fine collection of Old Masters."

"Yes, I'm afraid I did notice that."

I walked toward him. "Do not even consider going back and—"

He waved me off. "No, no, that's not a project for now. I'll file it away for later."

"How did you get into Harrington House?" I asked. "From what the dowager marchioness told me, you must have come during the day."

"It's too easy to sneak about at night. Few households have anyone on watch, and I prefer a challenge." He brushed the arm of his jacket and sneered. "You might ask your butler to get in some rope that's less linty."

I ignored this. "How did you get into the house?"

"The truth is, it was remarkably disappointing. I dressed as a delivery-type person and carried an enormous vat of white roses. It was simple enough to ascertain they are the dowager's favorite. I was admitted through the servants' entrance and directed to the ballroom."

"And from there?"

"Look here, Kallista, I'm not going to give away all my trade secrets, even to you." His eyes, sapphire blue, danced.

My first husband had referred to me as *Kallista*, taken from the Greek word meaning *beautiful*, in the pages of his journal. How Sebastian had learned this, I did not want to know, but he used the moniker when he particularly wanted to annoy me.

"Am I being interrogated like one of the suspects in your investigations?" He was grinning.

"Sebastian, this is important. Stop messing about. You committed an illegal act in a home on the day a murder occurred. Do I need to explain how unlikely it is that the authorities will entertain the notion that there were two criminals in the marquess's property at the same time?"

"I was long gone from the house before the ball started."

"What time did you arrive and what time did you leave?"

"I entered the property at one seventeen in the afternoon, had the tiara in my possession a quarter of an hour later, and departed immediately thereafter."

"You're certain."

"I made a point of checking my watch in case something occurred that might lead you to question me about it. You know I never want to disappoint you."

"How did you get into the room?"

"Picking the lock took less than a minute. I've yet to find one that's given me any trouble. The entire experience was quite a let-down. I expected that I would at least have to go to some lengths to avoid the servants observing me, but there was no one in the corridor. In fact, I went down the main staircase instead of using the servants' in the hope I might be noticed. What fun is it if one doesn't have to trick anyone into believing you're someone you're not?"

"Is that the point of your current garments?" I asked. "No one is going to believe you're a maharaja."

"Quite right, Kallista, but you see I'm his most trusted adviser. His daughter is getting married tonight and I wanted to dress appropriately for the occasion."

I raised an eyebrow.

"And if you don't believe that—which you should, as it's true—you'll easily accept that I've been too long in the East and have gone native."

"You're appalling," I said. "Please, Sebastian, I need you to give this matter careful consideration. Given your criminal activities, you have to be more observant than the average flower deliveryman. You had to have been aware of what was going on in the house."

"I do like it when you use my Christian name." His eyes met mine. "I told you, nothing stood out as unusual. It was all just the chaos one would expect when the household staff is preparing for a ball. Why do you think I chose that day to take the tiara?"

I tilted my head. "Yes, why did you, given that you like a challenge? Wouldn't it have been more difficult to do it on a day when they're weren't so many distractions?"

"I hate to admit it, but you raise a valid point," he said. "I'm rather ashamed, if you must know. I understand that the dowager wanted her future daughter-in-law to wear the tiara for her wedding and not taking it before the ball would have meant running the risk of having to take it from the Goldsboroughs' house. A child could manage that."

"How did you know Lady Harrington planned to make a gift of the jewelry before the ball?"

"People talk, my dear, and everyone knew the dowager was going to present Miss Goldsborough with something to wear at the wedding. It's no secret what it was. There's nothing more to be said."

"A young lady is dead. Are you certain you can't tell me anything at all that might help me discover who ended her life?"

"Kallista, I do love your passion, even when it's only directed at your work." His countenance turned sullen and serious. "I wish I could help, truly I do, but I neither saw nor heard anything."

I believed him. "You do realize you must return the tiara?"

"That's already impossible. It's not currently in my possession, and, as I explained, it won't be a tiara for long. Now, I must beg your forgiveness. I hear someone in the corridor and it's likely your husband. I'd prefer not to encounter him." He leapt to his feet, grabbed my hand, raised it to his lips, then pulled open a window and climbed through it. Fewer than two minutes later, Colin entered the room.

"Where is he?" he asked. "Davis told me you were in here with Capet."

I motioned toward the open window. He growled and crossed over to close it. "He had nothing useful to tell me," I said.

"The man is maddening."

"I hope your pursuits were more fruitful," I said.

"Only in that they've narrowed our pool of suspects. Bradfield has been abroad for the past fortnight, so he's out. The earl's son was at the ball, but it doesn't appear he had any serious designs on Miss Goldsborough."

"Then why did he call on her so frequently?"

"He claims because he enjoyed her wit."

"You believe that?" I asked.

"Not as such. Rather, I'd say he knows his prospects are limited at best. His father wants him to take a commission in the army, but he has no taste for it. He thought if he could convince the earl he had a shot at the most celebrated debutante of the Season, he might be able to put off the inevitable."

"The earl would never believe Lady Goldsborough would let Victoria marry a second son. She's meant to secure a fortune and raise her sisters' hopes."

"Let's just say the son isn't the brightest star in the sky."

"What if he realized his father wasn't falling for it and decided if Victoria were dead, he could play on the man's sympathy for a while?" I asked. "That might buy him a certain amount of time."

"Theoretically possible, but a weak theory."

"I agree."

"What did Capet send you?" Colin asked. "Davis told me about the letter."

"Sappho. I've left it on my desk. You're welcome to read it if you'd like."

"I'll save the pleasure for another time. What about the diary?"

I summarized it. "So you see, it's rather strange," I said. "It reads as if Victoria wrote it hoping it would be discovered."

"Yes, but by whom? You might recognize the discrepancy in her character, but many others wouldn't."

"Her family might. They knew she wasn't vapid."

"Her sister made a point of saying she didn't think any of them should read it."

"Which makes me all the more suspicious," I said. "How do we know Victoria actually wrote it?"

"What are you suggesting?"

"We need to confirm it's her handwriting, but I also think we ought to take another look at the Goldsboroughs and their servants. Victoria could well have been poisoned at home."

12

Britannia

Ovid surprised me. I figured anything called *Amores* would be full of erotic drivel. Which it was, sort of, but not in the way I'd expected. To be fair, none of it was drivel. I only used the word to avoid sounding sentimental. It was rapturous, at least to me. The language, the meter, the emotion. The surprise came from the character of the narrator of the poems. Ovid, I guess, although probably not the actual man himself. At least I didn't think so, but then, I knew nothing about him.

At any rate, the poet as narrator was no worthy hero. He was a shameless womanizer, a rogue, a reprobate. Yet he was also witty and sly and irresistible to the reader. Maybe this was always the way with Latin poetry. I couldn't say. This was the first of it I'd read.

"What's that scroll, Vatta?" My neighbor Minura had ducked

into the house. "Every time I've seen you in the past two weeks you've been glued to it."

"Poetry," I said.

"Roman poetry, from what I hear. It's being talked about, mostly because Solinus joined their army."

"I didn't want him to."

"Of course not," she said, "and everyone knows poetry is more boring than dangerous, but you ought to be careful."

"Not to alienate myself more than I already have?"

"Is it so hard to fit in?"

"It shouldn't be, but I'm interested in things that most of the rest of the village thinks are worthless."

"You overdramatize everything. Most people don't care what you do with yourself—or what anyone else does—but they feel like you hold their disinterest against them."

"I've never even thought about whether they're interested."

"It would be nice if you gave them some thought instead of keeping yourself apart."

I hated when she said things like that. "I'm not sociable."

"You are in the right circumstances. Try harder."

I tried to take her words to heart. The fact is, I'd always struggled with this sort of thing. I was awkward, which people mistook for aloof. It hadn't mattered all that much before and I knew the real problem wasn't the Romans or poetry. It was that my parents needed me to marry and my father was having a difficult time finding anyone willing to take me on. As a result, my oddness was being talked about. By everyone.

There wasn't much I could do about it—nothing, really, unless I wanted to alter my very character, which didn't appeal—so I went for a ride. It would make me feel better, and that mattered, didn't it? It certainly did to me.

That ride was how I came to Boudica's attention, and that's how everything started to change. I had no idea what I'd set into motion.

13

London

The next morning, Colin returned to the Goldsboroughs' to further interrogate both the family and their servants. Afterward, he would lunch with Lionel Morgan. This left me to call on Frances Price, Victoria's dearest friend. Her family resided in Bayswater, not far from Paddington Station, on a stretch of Westbourne Terrace known as Radical Row.

"We didn't earn the moniker ourselves," Mr. Price said. He'd answered the door himself and guided me to a comfortable sitting room on the first floor. "It comes from the political positions of residents who lived here in the previous century. At the time, this house was occupied by Richard Cobden, who was instrumental in getting the Corn Laws repealed. Without his work, the lower class would find it nigh impossible to feed themselves."

"Don't bore the poor lady with politics." His wife entered the room. She was wearing a white dress with a sash that read *Deeds not Words: Votes for Women Now!* draped over her chest.

"Darling, this is Lady Emily Hargreaves," her husband said. "She's sympathetic with our beliefs."

"Oh, of course, what a delight! I'm surprised our paths haven't crossed before. We know your husband."

"She's come to speak with Frances about this dreadful business with Victoria."

Mrs. Price sank onto the sofa next to me and clutched my arm. "It's beyond awful. I don't know how anyone could've done it. She was—"

"Don't start rhapsodizing, Mother." The door opened again and a young lady who could only be Frances entered. "We all know how you felt about her. There's no need to be disingenuous."

Mrs. Price's eyes flashed. "As you wish. I'm late to a meeting, so you must all please forgive me for rushing off. You'll see me out?" The look she gave her husband ensured he would, and they left me alone with their daughter.

"I'm more sorry than I can say for the loss of your friend. This is such a difficult time, and I hate to compound it by—"

"By coming and asking awkward questions," Frances said. She was a tall girl, with a flawless figure and jet-black hair that glimmered almost blue, a similar shade to her eyes. "I received your note and understand you've been given charge of the investigation. I'll do anything I can to help. What do you want to know?"

"Everything you can tell me." It was often best to let people say what they would, without prompting them. I wanted to give Frances the space to speak about whatever she considered pertinent.

"Victoria and I have been friends forever, but you'll already know that. Portia will have told you. She's very thorough, Portia." Her voice was ever so slightly acerbic. "We were on the cusp of seeing our lives come together the way we'd always dreamed. Her marrying Peregrine was going to make it all possible."

"Was she very much in love with him?"

Her eyes widened, just for an instant. "He was everything she'd ever wanted. She couldn't have made a better match. He's the perfect English gentleman."

"And you? Had you also found a suitable match?"

"Nothing is official yet, and we can't announce anything now, of course. It wouldn't be appropriate so soon after my friend's death, but, yes, I have an understanding with a young man, Oscar Tenley. I didn't get to speak with Victoria at the ball and shall always regret that. I'd seen her that afternoon. She called on me to discuss what we both planned to wear." She closed her eyes. "What an awful, innocuous, trivial conversation to have as our last. A waste. An utter waste."

"Were you there when she collapsed?"

"I was in the garden, with Mr. Oscar Tenley. He's Peregrine's best friend. We heard the commotion and returned inside, but by then, Victoria was already gone."

"You knew her better than anyone, Miss Price. Did she have enemies?"

"Do call me Frances. Let's leave useless formality in the previous century, where it belongs. Victoria was the most celebrated debutante of the Season. Every other girl in town despised her."

"Enough to want her dead?"

"Poison is a woman's tool, is it not?"

"Whom do you suspect?"

"I wouldn't know where to start. That's the thing, isn't it? Scads of girls were jealous of her, yet how many of them could be bothered to actually do something about it? It pains me to say, but I don't think the average racketer is going to tear herself away from her social life to figure out how to kill someone."

"What about a young lady who thought she had a chance with the marquess and was in desperate need of his fortune?"

"The truth is, that's a perfect description of Victoria," Frances said. "I'd be more inclined to search for someone desperately in love with the man."

This suggested to me that Victoria was not herself desperately in love with her fiancé. "You don't have any suggestions?"

"Half of London would tell you Cressida Wright, but I'm not convinced."

"Why is that?"

"It would require too much effort and thought."

"You don't like her?"

"Not at all, so now when someone murders her, you'll know where to come." She laughed, so hard it brought tears to her eyes. "Forgive me, that's altogether inappropriate. I ought not find anything amusing at present."

"These situations are beyond difficult. Welcome anything that helps you through it."

"I appreciate your understanding."

"So if not Miss Wright, is there anyone else you could envision wanting to harm Victoria?"

"You knew her, did you not? She wasn't the sort to go around causing offense."

"Not so far as I could tell, but you were much closer to her. My mother and her grandmother are inseparable." Thinking about my mother brought the concerns I had about Victoria's diary to mind.

"I understand you do not share your parents' political views. Was Victoria of the same mind? Her grandmother certainly is."

"As is your mother," Frances said. "We both believe that the best way to happiness is found by following a traditional path."

Her words sounded carefully chosen, almost rehearsed. "You don't believe women would benefit from having the right to vote?"

"Lady Emily, my mother incessantly barrages me with questions related to this issue. Must you as well?"

She made a neat job of avoiding giving an answer to what I'd asked. I decided to let her get away with it, at least for now. "I had the impression that Victoria was rather enlightened when it came to such things."

"Enlightened? Yes, I suppose you could say that. It doesn't mean she was going to publicly campaign for suffrage."

"What did it mean?"

"She had deep concerns about the inadequacy of young ladies' education. Hardly the sort of thing that would make someone want to murder her."

"So what was the sort of thing that would make someone want to murder her?" I asked. Frances was being evasive, not candid in the least. "Given what occurred, it's essential that we start looking at individuals who disliked her or harbored a grudge."

"I don't mean to be unhelpful, Lady Emily. That's the last thing I want. The truth is, I'm overwhelmed. I suppose whenever someone is murdered, those who loved them can't fathom anyone doing such a thing. Victoria had her quirks and her foibles, but nothing that would incite violence."

"Yet clearly someone was incited to violence."

"Could it have been an accident?"

"I don't believe anyone accidentally puts poisonous yew in a beverage," I said.

"Even though her prospects were hopeless, Cressida could've been jealous of Victoria. Peregrine might've wished his fiancée was more madly in love with him, but only if he were a different sort of man."

"What about other suitors? You've admitted how popular she was."

"There were none, not serious ones, at any rate. Peregrine's courtship was a whirlwind. There was no time for anyone else to think he stood a chance with her." She scrunched her forehead. "I suppose it's Cressida you should be looking at, although I find it hard to believe."

"Not the marquess?" I asked.

"No. He was getting exactly what he wanted from her. She made sure of that."

14

Britannia

I mounted Aesu. Not the first Aesu, the one from my childhood; he was long dead, but I'd named his successor after him. We rode east from the village toward the marshes that stretched all the way to the sea. Heavy slate-colored clouds hung in the sky and the air was full of mist, but it wasn't raining. At least not yet. I brought Aesu to a gallop, then slowed down when the ground became soft. That's when I saw her. Boudica.

I recognized her from a distance. She was tall, even taller than me, and people were always goading me about my height. She must have been a decade older than I was, but there was no silver in the tawny hair that reached to her hips. She wore it in a single plait hanging down her back. Around her neck was a heavy torc that looked like it had been made from twisting multiple gold ropes together. The design complemented the enormous brooch clasping her cloak.

I'd seen her before, more times than I could count, but we'd never had a conversation. She was the wife of our king, Prasutagus; we didn't exactly move in the same circles. Not that there were many circles in our community. The truth is, I didn't move in any of them. Unless I was with Solinus, I'd preferred to keep to myself.

She waved her arms above her head. "Stop! Please!"

I did as ordered. She told me she'd been thrown from her horse and the beast had run off. "I've been trying to lure him back here," she said. "You can see how well it's going. Not that I ever thought it would work, I just wasn't thrilled with the idea of walking all the way home."

"You won't have to now. I can take you and then return to look for the horse." You could see forever on the flat marshes. The animal was long gone, but had left clear tracks in the ground.

"He's bound to make his way back to the village eventually."

"He wasn't headed in that direction."

"He knows there'll be food there."

Arguing with her probably wasn't the best idea. Plus, it was starting to rain. I helped her onto Aesu behind me and she held on, her arms around my waist. I'd never expected to find the queen in such a position.

"You're Vatta, aren't you?" she asked. "The one who reads Roman poetry."

"That's a singular way to describe me."

"I don't mean it as a criticism. I read it, too. The Romans aren't our enemies. My husband and I owe much of our prosperity to them."

"Then it seems we share an unusual way of looking at things."

"We both know what happened to the druids at Mona. I see no benefit to bringing that on the Iceni. Better that we keep the Romans as friends."

It's no secret that the Romans found the religious practices of native Britons barbaric. Rich, coming from them, at least so far as I can tell. The province had a new governor, Suetonius, who wanted to make a name for himself the old-fashioned way, through glory in battle. He headed for the faraway island of Mona, where his soldiers were shocked to see women ready to defend their land. They like things neat and orderly, the Romans. That's not what they found.

Some of the soldiers claimed the women were the Furies, their goddesses of vengeance, born from the gore left when their father was castrated by a son he despised. See what I mean about their religion? Anyway, the female Britons scared them, with their long unbound hair and loud wailing. Eventually, however, the army found their nerve and attacked. Killed everyone they could see, women included. Burned down a sacred grove of trees. All in all, a bad day for everyone.

Except the Romans, of course. Isn't that always the way?

"I suppose you're less happy with them now. They lured your brother away," she said.

"You know about that?" I asked.

"He came to see Prasutagus. I was there. He's a good man, Solinus. I understand why he went."

"I wish he'd stayed."

"And he wishes you'd get married. He told me as much. Do you let him plan the navigation for the path of your life?"

I figured this was a rhetorical question, so didn't reply. There wasn't much more to be said. When we reached Venta Icenorum, I left her at the palace. Not a palace by Roman standards, but glorious in its way. The shape was similar to the ordinary roundhouses the rest of us lived in, but instead of a single structure, four joined together, creating different rooms. The interior was decorated opulently, full of beautiful pottery—some of it Roman—and stunning examples of Iceni metalwork. Every cup was gold or silver. Smooth stones formed the floor instead of compressed dirt, and painted designs covered the walls.

That would've been the end of it if I hadn't turned straight around and gone back to the marshes. It took me nearly two days, but I tracked her horse and brought it to her. That's when she learned she could trust me. Depend on me. Until I became dangerous.

15

London

There was much to contemplate after I left Frances Price. I couldn't help feeling she'd tried to deliberately manipulate me. All that talk of suffragettes and politics and Victoria having given Lord Harrington exactly what he wanted. What did it mean?

I mulled over our conversation as I walked toward Cressida Wright's house in Mayfair. It was no short distance, but I welcomed the time it would take. I entered Kensington Gardens and followed the Long Water to the Serpentine. I never much liked taking a direct route through the park. Crossing the bridge, I continued on, past the Superintendent's Lodge and the site of the Reformers Tree, burnt down in 1866 during protests supporting the expansion of voters' rights. The following year, the requirement of owning property was dropped from the law. Now, renters, too, could vote, provided, of course, that they were over twenty-one and male. I exited through

Grosvenor Gate, not far from my own house, and soon was in Grosvenor Square.

The Wright family occupied the domicile at Number 26, which stood on the site of the once-famous Derby House designed by Robert Adam. Eventually, the Dowager Duchess of Cleveland leased it. After her death, the property was demolished and this new structure built in its place.

The butler took me to a drawing room crammed full of furniture, carpets, and enormous arrangements of pink roses. Hardly a surface was left uncovered. A curtain hung in the middle of the room, secured to a column, and wine-colored velvet wallpaper filled the spaces on the wall between plaster embellishments. I felt a headache coming on before I'd even sat down.

Tea arrived ahead of Miss Wright. I'd finished two cups and a cake in the time I waited for her. When at last she appeared, she greeted me brightly, despite the fact that we'd never before met. I explained who I was and why I had come. The gravity of the situation had no visible impact on her.

"It's awful, of course, that someone murdered her. People ought not do things like that." She sat on a settee across from the chair I occupied and picked up one of the remaining cakes, not bothering to take a plate. "It's most uncivilized, isn't it? And to do it in London during the Season makes it an offense even greater. What are we to do now? Cancel all the rest of the festivities? One hardly knows how to behave."

"That largely depends on how well one knew Miss Goldsborough," I said. "Those close to her are in mourning and will behave accordingly."

"And what about the rest of us?" She was halfway through the cake.

"You go on, unaffected."

"Laden with guilt," she said. "I don't like it when I have the impression I ought to feel differently than I do. Shouldn't I be devastated by her death? Terrified that someone of an age with me could be struck down in such a manner? Some girls would be afraid of attending balls after all this."

"Not you?"

"No, not me." She wrinkled her pert little nose and popped the last bite of cake into her mouth. "My most glaring flaw is my inability to lie, even for the sake of politeness. As I didn't know Miss Goldsborough well enough to feel a personal loss, I instead am consumed with a deep relief that she's gone. It leaves less competition for the rest of us."

"On the Marriage Market?" I asked.

"What else is there? It's what young ladies of means and rank are brought up for. I came out two Seasons ago and made a right mess of it. My mother reminds me daily that I did not cultivate the right acquaintances."

"I would think she'd have approved of the Marquess of Harrington."

"You know about that? Of course you do. There was so much gossip. Despite having the best of intentions, I made a spectacle of myself. Mama would've approved if I'd been successful. I was not. Hence, I'm her great disappointment." She leaned forward. "The phrase must be uttered with utmost severity."

"And now, with Miss Goldsborough gone, you have another chance."

"Not this year. Except for the funeral, Peregrine won't be seen in public again for ages."

"I obviously wasn't privy to the details of what occurred between the two of you in the past. Did he welcome your attentions?"

"I believe so," she said. "Shortly after my debut, he called on me. We had a riotously entertaining conversation and his subsequent behavior at balls and parties encouraged me. I thought we were on a path toward an understanding. As a result, I did not hold back when it came to him. I didn't play the coquette or disguise my feelings. I prefer honesty. I made a deliberate choice to let him know I cared."

"What was his response?"

"He never complained, certainly, and although he didn't single me out above other young ladies, he gave every appearance of enjoying the time he spent with me."

"Yet he did not propose?"

The corners of her mouth drooped. "Obviously, we wouldn't be sitting here now if he had. I wasn't wholly discouraged, however. Not every relationship is sealed in the course of a single Season. I saw him in the autumn at several shooting parties and attended his mother's New Year's ball at their estate in Kent."

"Did she approve of the connection?"

"One can never tell with the dowager," she said. "She's so perfectly correct in her behavior I'm convinced she would apologize for the inconvenience if you stabbed her to death."

My eyebrows rose.

"That was inappropriate in the context, but you take my meaning. Last Season, I decided I would not sit back and wait any longer. I was getting heaps of pressure from my parents and every other relation. Even my youngest brother began pestering me, and he's barely twelve years old. As a result, I came on perhaps a bit too strong. I can be something of a force of nature."

"I'm told the marquess has a temperament rather like his mother. He approves of the sort of behavior dictated by current social mores."

"Yes, he does, and I manage to like him nonetheless." She sighed. "Sometimes I wish I were American. A girl with my spirit does far better there, and here, for that matter. American heiresses can get away with things I'm brutally chastised for. When they do it, it's a breath of fresh air. We English girls are supposed to sit around talking about the weather."

"So what happened last Season?" I asked.

"I let Peregrine take certain liberties at another ball at Harrington House, thinking that would secure his affection."

This admission shocked me. "It did not?"

"Quite the contrary. He barely acknowledged me the next time we met."

"That must have infuriated you."

"Yes, I was irate." She sat up very straight. "Irate enough to poison him, were I clever enough to come up with such an idea, which, sadly, I'm not. You must not think I allowed things to go too far, Lady Emily. What occurred was nothing of extraordinary impropriety. I'm not a fool."

"Did your feelings for him change after he ignored you?"

"Much as I hoped they would, they did not," she said. "If anything, they intensified. And so, to anticipate your next question, I was all the more upset when he started openly courting Miss Goldsborough. Miss Goldsborough, of all people! She was boring as anything and made no effort whatsoever to enchant him. It's maddening. I did my best to move on and have become close to another gentleman, but now, however, she's dead and I might have another chance with Peregrine. Awkward, isn't it? I didn't kill her, but I acknowledge freely that I have every intention of benefiting from her death."

I hardly knew what to say after this and decided the only way forward was to mirror Miss Wright's honesty. "That's rather shocking. You're admitting to the person investigating Miss Goldsborough's death that you're profiting from it. This would suggest to most people that you had a strong motive for murder."

"I notice you say *most people,* which doesn't necessarily include yourself. That makes me think you're intelligent enough to know the actual murderer would never admit such a thing."

"Not necessarily," I said.

"The truth is, I might've done it, had I any reason to believe without doubt it would bring Peregrine back to me. And, obviously, that I wouldn't get caught. There's no certainty on either ground, however, so it wouldn't have been worth the risk."

"You were at the ball that night?"

"I was."

"Did you see or speak to Miss Goldsborough?"

"I was in the garden when she arrived."

"Alone?" I asked.

"I wasn't the only one there, if that's what you mean, but I was standing on my own, where no one could notice me."

"What were you doing?"

"Watching Frances Price make a fool of herself with Peregrine's best friend."

"Oscar Tenley?"

"Yes, the very man who'd been wooing me this year," she said. "Oscar is at least as traditional as Peregrine. He would never respect a girl who kisses him in the moonlight at a ball. It was a grievous error on her part."

"How did you come to be watching them?"

"It does me no credit. I was irritated that Miss Price seemed to be on the verge of making the second spectacular match of the Season, despite the fact that her family are absolutely appalling! Her mother is a suffragette and her father a radical of the worst sort."

"What sort is that?" I asked.

"I admit to being not entirely sure, but it's what everyone says, and who am I to argue? I noticed Oscar and Frances heading to the garden, the site of my own embarrassment the previous year, and followed them. I'd believed he was close to making an offer of marriage to me. I suspected in an attempt to ensnare him, she was about to do exactly what she did in the past and I hoped she would get as bad a reaction from the gentleman as I did from Peregrine."

"It appears she did not."

Miss Wright's candor was astonishing. Unlike Frances Price, she censored nothing she said. I was half appalled and half impressed.

"What made you think he was about to make an offer to you?" I asked.

"We've become close in the past few weeks," she said. "I was careful not to make the mistakes I have before and the strategy was working. It made him want me more. I've always liked him well enough and decided I might as well open my heart to him."

"You must've been upset to see him with Frances," I said.

She shrugged. "I was never going to feel so strongly about him as I had Peregrine. It didn't matter all that much."

"Other than yourself, who do you think despised Miss Goldsborough enough to want her dead?"

"That's the odd thing about it," she said. "I can't think of anyone. She was so perfect, living up to her all her family's hopes for her. I never saw her display anything but kindness and generosity to other girls, so I doubt you'll get anywhere with them. They might have been jealous of her, but no one could hold her success against her. She was always trying to lift up those around her, not push them down."

"You sound as if you admire her."

"I suppose I did. If it hadn't been for Peregrine, I might have even liked her." She paused for a moment, then shook her head. "No, I wouldn't have. She was too perfect and would've been an absolute bore as a friend. She probably never gossiped in her life."

16

Britannia

I'd gone back to my parents' house briefly before I set off in search of Boudica's horse. I knew I wouldn't find him quickly, so gathered some supplies and told my mother not to worry if I was gone for a few days. She didn't try to stop me, which you'd think she would've done. It can be dangerous, a woman heading out into the fens alone. She must've figured that doing a favor for the queen would raise interest in me among the unmarried men of the village. I could only hope the nature of the favor would put off many—if not all—of them. Who'd want someone like me, wild and reckless, running their household, let alone raising their children?

Personally, I shuddered at the thought.

I took greater care than you might have assumed. I wasn't going to harm my own horse, and marshy ground was perilous. I let Aesu set the pace; he went slowly, gingerly. It had started to rain, but not hard, so I was able to find Boudica's steed's tracks. We followed them until darkness fell. Stopping sooner would've been smart, but I managed to light a fire and put up a makeshift shelter nonetheless.

Despite the return of daylight, it was worse in the morning. The rain was falling harder and became relentless. A harsh wind blew it into my face. It was hard to see, but Aesu and I trudged on, following the general direction the other horse had taken. Beyond that, I paid attention to my instinct. To where I thought the animal would have gone.

We stopped again and made camp as the sun dipped low in the sky. The weather cleared and I lay on the ground, looking up at the stars, happy that I'd come. Yes, my bedroll was damp; yes, I was cold; yes, I would've had a better meal if I'd stayed home. None of that signified to me. I preferred being out here, alone, listening to nothing but silence and the occasional owl.

Sleep outside is sublime. I awoke with the sunrise, energized. The weather held so well it was nearly too warm. Although, no one who's been in Britannia would believe that, especially not the Romans. They're convinced the weather the whole world over is nothing compared to that in Rome. So why didn't they go back? Why did they need more land? More wealth? More slaves? More resources?

The questions answer themselves, don't they? I've seen it before, and not just from the Romans. It's all too human to want more. To not know when to stop. To have no concept of what it means to have enough. To keep taking and fighting and clinging until you've ruined it all.

That's why I preferred nature. Animals. Simplicity. Solitude.

But then, there was poetry, something that didn't seem to occur until the world was more civilized than I liked. That was the conundrum, the paradox. Was there any way to eschew one and embrace the other?

I was ruminating on that thought when I heard a horse whinny in the distance. We'd found him. He was grazing contentedly like nothing had happened. Aesu walked over to him while I looked around, wondering if I could remember where we were, if I knew how to get home.

Of course I did. The fens and the sky and the land all around never deserted me. Never disappointed me. Never kept me from where I needed to be.

I tied a rope gently around the other horse and led him back to Venta Icenorum, where a surprised and delighted Boudica received us.

"I had begun to fear for the worst," she said. "Not only for the horse, but for you. You took a great risk going off on your own like that. It's a testament to your bravery."

"We're all capable of more than we think," I said. "In this case, however, I deserve no credit for courage. I knew I could manage it."

"Your confidence is an inspiration, as is your ability to handle horses. Will you teach me to be better at it?"

No one in their right mind would say no to the queen.

17

London

When I returned home, I found Colin bent over a chessboard in the library, a worn copy of John Thursby's *Seventy-Five Chess Problems* in his hand. I gave him a quick kiss. He put down the book and pulled an envelope from his jacket.

"For you, from Capet. Slipped through the letter box as usual. Unfortunately, this time Davis didn't tie him up."

"You didn't open it?" I asked.

"I would never violate your privacy."

I picked up a letter opener from my desk and sliced through the envelope. Inside, as always, was a single sheet of heavy linen paper.

καὶ τῷ βραχυκαταλήκτῳ δὲ Ἀνακρέων ὅλα ᾄσματα συνέθηκεν·
μεγάλῳ δηὖτέ μ' Ἔρως ἔκοψεν ὥστε χαλκεὺς
πελέκει, χειμερίῃ δ' ἔλουσεν ἐν χαράδρῃ.

Once again Love has struck me with his mighty axe
like a smith, and doused me in the icy mountain stream.

"Anacreon?" Colin peered over my shoulder. "Can it be Capet is broadening his horizons to include the lyric poets? If it were anyone else, I'd applaud him."

"I've had a copy of the *Anacreontea* lying on my bedside table the night for weeks. You don't think—"

"That he slunk into the house, probably when we were asleep, to see what you're reading? It sounds perfectly in keeping with everything we know about him. At least he's not leaving you roses on your pillow anymore."

He'd done that more than once, before Colin and I were married. "He's lucky you're confident rather than jealous," I said.

"No one, Emily, could replace you for me or me for you. There's nothing I know so well." He held my gaze six beats longer than necessary. My entire body tingled, but I could not let myself be distracted.

I tossed the note aside. "Tell me about your day."

"I got nothing more from the Goldsboroughs and their servants beyond the address for Ida Davies's mother."

"Ida was Victoria's former maid?" I asked.

"Yes. Her mother will be able to tell us where to reach her in New South Wales."

"I'll write to ask her straightaway."

"I also obtained a sample of Miss Goldsborough's handwriting. So far as I can tell, it's a perfect match for the diary. I consulted with a graphologist at Scotland Yard who concurs."

"And Mr. Morgan?"

"I invited him to dinner tomorrow evening. I'm sorry to spring it on you with so little notice, but I want your opinion on him. Our luncheon left me with more questions than answers. He's an odd bloke. Extremely enthusiastic about his prospects, as gamblers tend to be, but tethered to nothing. The hundred pounds we know about isn't the only money he's borrowed from Harrington."

"However does Mr. Morgan manage it?"

"That, my dear, will become clear when you meet him. He can be charm itself when it suits him."

I debriefed him on my own conversations from the day, which astonished him nearly as much as Mr. Morgan's loans had me.

"Miss Price is hiding something, there's no doubt of that, but it's Miss Wright who stuns me," he said. "She all but admitted committing murder."

"She didn't do it," I said. "I'm sure of that."

"How can you be certain?" he asked. "She has a motive, she has the means. She claims not to have seen Miss Goldsborough at the ball, but we have no reason to believe her. If she was skulking about spying on people, she could just as easily have been lying in wait for Miss Goldsborough and offered her some refreshment."

"I've been thinking about the yew," I said. "It has a bitter taste, which would surprise no one who's smelled the leaves. The killer needed to mix it with something else to cover the flavor. That would've been simple at the ball. Anyone could have brought her a cup of punch and spiked it with the poison. The Goldsboroughs had tea. Normal tea. That wouldn't disguise a bitter brew."

"I did inquire as to whether Miss Goldsborough had anything to drink while she was dressing for the evening, but no one could recall with clarity." He frowned and ran a hand through his dark curls.

"Do you really suspect Miss Wright?" I asked.

"I think we must consider her very seriously. Given what you've told me about her personality, she's impetuous and a bit reckless.

Harrington humiliated her, yet she has no compunction for disguising the fact that this spurred her on to want him more, not less."

"If we didn't know that, it would've made more sense for her to have killed him than Victoria."

"But we do know it and, further, no one has killed Harrington. I wonder if Tenley and Miss Price had any idea she was watching them at the ball?"

"Surely they would've behaved differently if they did."

"They could've noticed after the kiss," he said. "It's important that we establish where Miss Wright was, be it in or out of the house. We ought not accept her claims without confirmation."

"Her candor made me believe her," I said. "You're right that we've no reason to trust her, but Frances did admit to being in the garden with Mr. Tenley when Victoria collapsed."

"Miss Price suspects Miss Wright. Miss Wright dislikes Miss Price. Somehow, we are going to have to separate their social enmity for each other from the essential truths in their observations."

"If there are any," I said.

I sent a footman with a letter inquiring after her daughter's whereabouts to Ida Davies's mother that evening. A reply came in the morning post.

I am loath to share my sad news, but have no choice given the nature of your inquiry. I don't understand why you believe my daughter to be in New South Wales. We buried her in the East London Cemetery after she took her own life by stepping in front of a train.

I am grieved to hear of Victoria Goldsborough's death, but am afraid I have no information that can shed light on it. My dear Ida was a kind, sensitive girl, quite devoted to her mistress. If she were alive, she would've done everything possible to assist your investigation, but, alas, she's gone, leaving us all heartbroken and wondering what caused her to do such a terrible thing to herself.

Speechless, I handed the letter to Colin. Half an hour later, we were back at the Goldsboroughs' house.

"I promise you, I had no idea this would crop up," Lady Goldsborough said when we confronted her. "It's nothing to do with Victoria. Ida's death was a terrible shock, but it happened weeks before the murder. One does not spread gossip about suicides. The poor girl ought to be left to rest in peace."

"Did she exhibit signs of melancholy?" Colin asked.

"None that I was aware of, but my interactions with her were extremely limited."

"I'm getting the distinct impression, Lady Goldsborough, that you are deliberately hiding things from us," Colin said. "Choosing to do so will delay, if not prevent, bringing your granddaughter's murderer to justice."

"The details of Ida's death aren't something I thought you needed to know."

"I'd prefer you allow us to make that decision," he said. "Every time you censor something, you hinder our investigation."

She looked to me. "You understand, Emily. We kept quiet about it at first because we didn't want word of the scandal to get out. I don't know why the poor girl did what she did, but making her fodder for gossip—"

"You didn't want Society connecting your household to a suicide," I said. "Let's not pretend this was about protecting Ida."

"Yes, you're right, but there's nothing wrong with what I did. My instincts to say nothing kept the news from Society."

"Please send Portia to us," I said. "We'll need to speak to her alone."

"I want to be here as well."

"You've already shown yourself unreliable," Colin said. "I cannot have you encouraging Portia to behave similarly."

Lady Goldsborough wrung her hands. "I do apologize for having made such a mess of things. One doesn't know how to behave in these situations. Of course I don't want to impede your investigation, it's only that . . . it's difficult to have it all so far out of my control. I'm used to knowing what's best for my granddaughters. Now, it seems, I've not only let them down, I'm making matters worse."

Colin's voice softened. "So long as you correct course now, we'll manage."

"I'll fetch Portia," she said and started to rise from her seat.

"Let's ring for someone else to do that," I said. "You need to take care of yourself as well. You've been through a terrible trauma. Perhaps you'd like some tea sent to your room?" I didn't want her to say anything to Portia out of our earshot.

Lady Goldsborough accepted my suggestion. We kept her in the sitting room until Portia appeared and asked no questions until her grandmother had retired upstairs.

"Yes, I knew what happened to Ida," Portia said. "We all did, all except Winnie and Seraphina, of course. They're far too young to be exposed to such things."

"I'm surprised your grandmother let any of you know about it," I said.

"She had no choice. All of the servants were talking about it. We heard the news from them."

"Have you any idea what led her to do it?" Colin asked.

"Not in the slightest," Portia said. "Ida had always been a bright light, cheerful and eager. She was an excellent listener. Victoria and I both spoke openly to her, but she never shared much about her own life."

"Was there any change in her behavior before her death?" I asked.

"She did seem a bit glum, but not in a way that caused any concern."

"You didn't ask her about it?"

"No. It wasn't any of my business. It's not as if it kept her from performing her duties. We all get into a funk on occasion. I certainly had no idea she was going to harm herself."

She had nothing more to say. Although I couldn't precisely blame her, it appalled me that she'd be unaware of the depth of Ida's despair. One likes to believe that such things can't be hidden altogether, but of course that's not true. Ida had disguised her pain too well. The result was heartbreaking.

18

Britannia

How quickly things change. In the span of a few weeks, I went from being little more than a nonentity in the village to seeing my popularity soar. Nothing was different about me, but now that Boudica was publicly observed to value my talent for working with horses, it was as if the rest of the tribe was seeing me for the first time. Amazing how the notice of a single important person alters one's standing.

There were two things about this. One positive, one, not so much. I found a friend in the queen. She was the only person besides my brother in the tribe who'd ever shown interest in spending time with me. It was unexpected and enriching. I now had someone to ride with. Moreover, I started to take on the role of training horses, a position that brought me further respect. I liked it.

But I didn't like the fact that now, all of a sudden, I was considered a desirable marriage prospect. Nearly every night another man came to our house, eager to spark up an acquaintance with me. The ones my parents liked were invited to dine. The ones they didn't took to hanging about outside hoping to catch a glimpse of me.

Just thinking about it makes me laugh so hard I can hardly hold my pen to write.

Not surprisingly, I didn't find any of them particularly compelling, a reflection of my general disinterest in crops and sheep and a distrust of anyone who found me suddenly fascinating when they'd never given me a second thought before.

"Even the girls love you now," Minura said to me one afternoon, when she'd shown up at my family's fields. "Half of them are pretending to share your affinity for horses. Most of them can barely ride."

"If they think befriending me takes them a step closer to Boudica, they're wrong. I'm not a conduit to her."

"It makes them hope, and there's nothing wrong with that. How long do you think your parents will give you before they insist that you choose a groom?"

"Choose a groom. I never thought I'd have a choice."

"Neither did I," she said. "This is good, though, Vatta. It's always better to have a voice in your fate. Do you like any of them? Even a little?"

"Not really. Duro seems less stupid than the rest." He was a friend of my brother's, which made me inclined to give him a bit more of a chance. He was an inch shorter than I was, but he had a thick head of sandy-colored hair and eyes with a hint of wildness in them. The latter intrigued me.

Which is not to say I wanted to marry him.

"That's unfair. They're good men, kind and strong and capable. You can't expect everyone to read poetry."

"Believe me, I don't," I said. "I might not even like a husband who shares my passion for it. The truth is, I'd rather be alone."

"Alone has never been an option."

"No, I suppose not."

A voice called my name. Gaius Marius. I hadn't seen him for weeks. I can't say I'd missed him.

"How are you finding Ovid?" he asked.

"Delightful," I said. He smiled and looked like he was waiting for me to elaborate. The fact I responded at all was only because I felt obligated since he'd given me the book. I wasn't going to reveal more. Unfortunately, Minura had more of a flair for social graces than I did.

"Who is this Ovid?" she asked. "I've seen Vatta with the scroll, but she's told me nothing about it."

"He was one of the finest Roman poets," Gaius Marius said. "*Amores* is composed in elegiac couplets, where the first line is written in dactylic hexameter and the next in dactylic pentameter."

"I haven't the slightest idea what any of that means," Minura said. I didn't either; I hoped he would explain.

"The technical details don't matter, I suppose."

What a disappointment.

He continued. "The poems recount the history of a love affair told by a man enamored of an upper-class woman."

"Does he win her heart?" Minura asked.

"You'll have to read if you want to find out."

"Will you read it to me, Vatta? And translate from Latin?"

"Neither of us has time for that," I said. "We should be getting home."

"I'm burning. In my vacant breast love reigns. / So in six beats my verse must rise today, / And settle back in five. / Farewell, you strains / Of steely war! Farewell to you, / And to your epic meter too!"

Minura's eyes widened. "He writes about love?"

"Yes, but also about poetry, hence the mention of beats and meter."

"I'm more interested in love."

"Then you should study Latin and have access to the whole story."

I wanted to roll my eyes. If he was trying to make me jealous by getting my neighbor interested in poetry, it wasn't working. What was, however, was the suggestion that he understood the technical parts of a poem. I knew nothing about meter or couplets or any of the rest, but I wanted to. I shouldn't have said anything, but I did.

"What's *elegiac*?" I asked.

"A type of poetry," he said. "There's epic, of course—we've already talked about Homer, but I think you would like Virgil, too. Then you have lyric, which is shorter and something like a song in terms of rhythm. There's also iambic, but that's often obscene."

"Is it only the meter that makes something elegiac?" I asked.

"The meter defines the form," he said. "Do you want to know more?"

I couldn't help myself. "I do."

How easy it is to bring doom crashing down upon oneself. I'd like to say I should've known better, but how could that be? I knew nothing. Nothing at all. It would be the end of me.

19

London

Speaking with Portia about Ida Davies had not proved illuminating, but the same could not be said for the conversations Colin and I had with the ill-fated maid's colleagues. While they had been reserved when we asked them about Victoria and the murder, they spoke much more freely on this new topic. One of the parlormaids told us that Ida had suffered some sort of trauma. She'd seen bruises on the girl's wrist, but had no idea who or what had caused them. Further, the housekeeper revealed that Ida had disappeared for two days several months before her death.

"It wasn't like her to behave so irresponsibly," she said. "If it had been, I'd have let her go without hesitation, but, other than that single time, Ida was reliable and steady. She worked hard and never complained. She had her afternoon on Wednesdays. When she didn't return to the house that evening, I assumed something was wrong. I heard nothing from her until that Saturday morning. She came straight to my room and apologized, explaining that her mother had fallen ill. Ida hadn't been in a position to send word to me and hoped I would not hold it against her. Her contrition was genuine, and I had no reason to doubt her, so, after giving her a bit of a dressing-down and ensuring she understood she was never to do such a thing again, I let her return to work."

"Did you hear anything further about her mother's health?" Colin asked.

"She never mentioned it again."

"Did the quality of her work change after that?" I asked.

"She seemed more worried than she had been before, but did not shirk her duties."

After learning this, we questioned again the other maids who'd been close to Ida. So much time had passed that none of them could remember what Ida had planned to do on that particular afternoon off, nor did they have any further information regarding her mother's illness.

Confident there was nothing more to be learned on the subject at the Goldsboroughs', Colin and I set off for the East End, to speak to Ida's mother. We found her at home, in a squalid little flat above a butcher shop not far from St. Mary-le-Bow church. Mrs. Davies had the appearance of someone who hadn't been healthy in years, the result of chronic malnutrition and too much physical labor. The grief caused by the loss of her daughter had made her condition even worse.

"No, no, I promise you I never asked her to come here and take care of me," she said, when we asked her about the days Ida had missed work. "I wouldn't dream of doing such a thing. She needed that position. It was a good one, far better than anything I've ever had for myself. Service is much preferable to factory work, which is all I've known. The Goldsboroughs are a good family with good values. They treated her well and Ida knew and appreciated it. She wouldn't have done anything to risk losing that job."

"Did you ordinarily see her on her afternoons off?" Colin asked.

"No, not on Wednesdays. We often went to church together on Sundays, but weren't able to spend much time together beyond that. I'm still working, you know, and I'm not free Wednesdays. Once in a while she'd wait for me outside the factory and bring me a bit to eat on her Wednesdays. That was a nice surprise. She was a kind girl, my Ida."

"Did she have a young man?" I asked. "By all accounts she was a lovely girl with a pleasant temper. I imagine she was quite popular."

"No, no, I'd warned her not to get entangled in anything like that. That's a prime way to lose a position, isn't it? She knew better. Men might say they love you, they might even marry you, but you'll never be able to rely on them all the way. She had lots of friends among the other maids and the kitchen staff, but she gave the lads a wide berth."

"What did she do on her afternoons off?" Colin asked.

"She liked to go to the Victoria and Albert Museum to view all those exotic things from faraway lands. She especially admired the Persian carpets and porcelain from Turkey, I think it was. Not that I'm suggesting she was trying to get above her station or putting on airs. It's just that she loved beautiful things. Always did, from the time she was a tiny girl."

"Did anyone go with her?" I asked. "Any friends?"

"No, she liked to have the time on her own. You don't get much of that when you're in service, do you? She shared a room with three other girls and spent lots of time in the servants' hall, of course. There was always someone about."

"Did she have friends outside of the Goldsboroughs' staff?" Colin asked.

"Only Fenella, who lives in the flat across the hall with her mother. We both raised our girls here. It's not the finest accommodation, but it suited us well enough."

"We'll speak to her," Colin said. "Thank you."

"I don't understand why any of this matters," she said. "It's not going to bring back my Ida."

"No, unfortunately it can't do that," I said, "but it may help us discover what happened to Miss Goldsborough."

Mrs. Davies nodded solemnly. "Ida would like that. She'd have wanted to help."

I squeezed her hand. "It's also possible that we may discover what prompted your daughter to do what she did."

"I would like to know that, Lady Emily. It's awfully hard having no answers to all these questions. They keep me up at night, they do. I can't understand what would drive such a bright, cheerful girl to . . ." Her voice trailed and a tear rolled down her cheek. "It's a lot to bear."

"We'll do everything we can to try to bring you some measure of comfort."

We left her and crossed the hall, where we found Fenella cleaning the windows in the small room she shared with her mother. It was as poky and dark as Mrs. Davies's, but far tidier. Colin and I introduced ourselves and asked her about Ida's afternoon off.

"It seems likely that something happened to her that particular day," I said. "She didn't go to work for two days thereafter, and she told the housekeeper she'd been home assisting her mother, who was ill."

"It wasn't true," Fenella said. "I remember the day in question. She couldn't face returning to her job."

"Why was that?" Colin asked.

"You're right that something happened that afternoon. She'd gone to meet a friend in the park." She stopped and studied our faces, as if she were deciding whether to tell us more. "I suppose it doesn't matter anymore, keeping her secret."

"You can trust us to keep any information you share as private as possible," I said.

"I don't want her mother to know."

I felt a sinking sensation in my abdomen, suspecting the worst. "We don't have to tell her."

"She's convinced she wants answers, to understand why Ida did what she did, but she'll get no comfort from the truth. Sometimes it's better not to know."

"Was there a man?" I asked.

"Isn't there always?" Tears shone in Fenella's eyes. "He was good to her for a long, long time. Long enough to make her confident she could trust him. To believe—" She stopped and looked at her hands. Her lips trembled and I feared she would say no more.

"To believe what?" I asked. "That he would whisk her away to a better world? Marry her?"

Fenella snorted. "Ida was far too smart to believe anything like that, but she did believe he cared about her and that she was safe with him. Safe enough that she didn't protest when, after their walk along the Serpentine, he offered to bring her somewhere more private."

Colin's countenance darkened. "I believe I understand your meaning. I'm sorry if sharing the details makes you uncomfortable."

"It's all right, sir," Fenella said. "I'm telling you all of this in the hope that you'll stop him from doing this to anyone else."

"What's his name?" Colin asked.

Her shoulders drooped. "I don't know. If there were young men living in the house where she worked, I'd guess he was one of them, but there weren't."

"One of the other servants?" I asked.

"No. He's a gentleman, I know that for a fact. She was smitten with him. He'd taken his time with her, in order to gain her trust, never giving any sign he'd eventually take advantage of her."

"Do you know if she met him in the Goldsboroughs' house?" Colin asked.

"That I do not, sir. She was very discreet. Never wanted to cause anyone embarrassment."

"What do you know about him?" I asked.

"He wasn't married. He was catastrophically handsome. He plays cricket." She counted each point on a finger. "His family is ever so important. Very high class. He's quick to help others. Now, these are all things Ida told me. She believed them, but I've no proof they're true."

"Did they meet frequently?" Colin asked.

"Every Wednesday afternoon when he was in town."

"Always in the park?" I asked.

"Yes," Fenella said.

"Her mother believes she went to the Victoria and Albert Museum every week," Colin said. "Did she ever go there?"

"She used to, before they met. Then, it was the park and only the park."

"He wasn't afraid anyone would recognize him?" Colin asked.

"He knew they would, but he told her he had nothing to be ashamed of," Fenella said. "If they encountered one of his friends or acquaintances, he promised he'd introduce Ida and speak to them. So far as I know, that never happened."

My husband and I exchanged a look. "I can see you think that's odd," she continued, "but it's part of the reason Ida trusted him. He never gave any sign of wanting more than friendship from her. She wasn't naïve, you know. She knew what most young men are after. After some time, she came to be rather . . . interested romantically, I suppose you could say, in him, but she didn't believe the feeling was mutual."

"Did things change after she started to develop feelings for him?" I asked.

"I don't believe he ever noticed."

"What did she like about him?" I asked. "The more you can tell us, the more likely it will be that we can identify him."

"He likes being outdoors. That's why they always kept to the park. She suggested going to the museum more than once, but he always declined. Their conversation was generally about things happening in the world. Politics and that sort of thing."

"Was Ida interested in that before meeting this individual?" Colin asked.

"Would it be so shocking?" Fenella glared at him.

"Not in the least," he replied. "However, if it was an interest that she came to only after making his acquaintance, then we can assume it's something he's passionate about."

"I understand," she said. "She was always interested in the broader world. The housekeeper at the Goldsboroughs' let her have the newspaper every day when the family was finished with it."

"Do you know where, exactly, he took her the day of the incident?" Colin asked.

"Somewhere near Buckingham Palace. I don't know more than that. She was very upset when she told me what happened."

"Of course she was," Colin said. "I'm so very sorry she was forced to suffer through this."

"Did she tell you immediately after it happened?" I asked.

"She did," Fenella said. "He'd ripped her dress and had . . . had . . . used her so ill she had bruises on her wrists and on her neck. My mother was out, as she usually is, so Ida came to me. I cleaned her up and put her in one of my gowns so that her mother wouldn't notice anything was amiss. She was awful upset and stayed home the next day, at least, if I remember."

"And when things took a turn for the worse, some months later, was that because she realized she was with child?" I asked.

"Yes, Lady Emily, it was. What else could she do? She'd lose her position, her income, and break her mother's heart."

I didn't want to point out that what she had done broke her mother's heart. It was all so tragic.

"She couldn't raise a child on her own, that's obvious," Fenella said, "but she made it all sound hopeful. Well, maybe not quite hopeful, just not altogether hopeless. I thought she'd arranged with him to send her off to one of those places in the countryside where girls in trouble go to have their babies. I never thought she'd kill herself."

"Was she still in contact with the man who did this to her?" Colin asked.

"I didn't believe so at first, no. She hated him more than anything. She didn't want to see or speak to him ever again. She said she had no choice, though, that he was the only person who could offer her any assistance. I never should've believed it. He wouldn't have helped her if she had got in touch with him, and she knew that. I should've known that, too."

"This was not your fault," I said.

"No, but if I'd been thinking more clearly, I might have been able to stop her. I'll always regret not having done anything. I suppose I wanted to believe her."

"We are going to find this man," Colin said. "He'll never touch another girl again."

20

Britannia

Two weeks later, I was sitting next to the River Wensum with Gaius Marius, eating bad Roman sausages and talking about poetry. This is when you're supposed to think I was falling in love with him. I wasn't. That was never going to happen. I didn't even like the man, but I'd recognized the futility of turning him away. He knew about poetry and was willing to teach me. There was no one among the Iceni who could do that.

For that matter, there probably wasn't anyone else among the Romans who could, at least not in the vicinity of Venta Icenorum. It was a real backwater of the empire. The soldiers stationed nearby complained incessantly, but there was always something in their voices that made me wonder if they'd been sent here as a punishment. Someday, I'd ask Gaius, but not today. Today was for Ovid.

"Who would want their husband and their lover at the same

dinner?" I asked. "The lover asks his mistress to arrive before her spouse, but what's the point? They'll have no time alone."

"The poet admits as much. *Not that I can / See quite what good arriving first will do.* He gives her instructions after admonishing her to come early. He wants her to sit beside her husband and give every appearance of being the perfect wife. It's a game they're playing, a game that titillates them both."

I unrolled the scroll and read out loud. "*When you recall our games of love together, / Your finger on rosy cheeks must trace a line.* He thinks it's all a game, but we have no idea what she's thinking. Maybe she can't stand him."

"She wouldn't be his mistress if that were the case," Gaius said.

"Wouldn't it be more interesting if we knew her thoughts as well?"

"That's not how poetry works."

"Why not?"

He shrugged. "I don't know, it just doesn't."

"I understand the need for rules about meter and form and all that, but why limit a poet's scope? His point of view?"

"Sometimes the limitations of rules force a writer into expanding his creativity," he said. "Suppose Ovid weren't concerned with meter. Would the poem sound as beautiful? It would not; it would be ordinary prose. Pleasing, perhaps, but not rhapsodic. By being required to choose words that fit the meter, he is obligated to search for the perfect word, one that not only communicates the right image, but has the correct rhythm."

"You're very good at ignoring my questions and saying whatever it is you want to," I said. "All of those things could still remain true if we saw the woman's point of view."

"Yes, but who would want to read it?"

"I, for one."

"A poet needs an audience larger than one."

I pulled a piece of bread off the loaf that was on the blanket between us and threw it, hitting him directly in the center of his forehead.

"You've excellent aim," he said. "Perhaps you should join the army."

I scowled but let the jab pass without comment. I still missed Solinus; that would never change. I still blamed Gaius for his departure; that, too, would never change. However, I'd started to come around to the idea that I gained no pleasure by fixating on grievances. It was much more fun to argue about poetry.

"I want to better understand the forms of poetry," I said. "The rules. To learn how to choose the right word for the right image."

"Then I'm not your man. I prefer reading to writing. I've never claimed to be a scholar. My knowledge doesn't go beyond the basics."

"Are all Roman officers like you?" I asked. "Smart enough to feign greater intelligence than they possess? No need to answer. I can draw my own conclusions."

He rose from the blanket on which he'd been sprawled and brushed crumbs from his tunic. "I've enjoyed this, Vatta. Talking with you makes me miss Rome less. I think you'd like it there."

21

London

After taking our leave of Fenella, Colin and I walked past the church of St. Mary-le-Bow, whose bells are said to have prompted Dick Whittington's return to London, where he became lord mayor. Being born within their sound makes a person a true Cockney. The church was rebuilt by Christopher Wren after the Great Fire in the seventeenth century. We continued along Cheapside until we reached St. Paul's churchyard.

"Lots of Wren to be seen today," I said. Colin, still visibly upset by what Ida had suffered, hadn't spoken two words together since Fenella closed the door behind us. He was walking so quickly I could hardly keep up with him. "Let's go inside for a spell. We have much to ponder."

He nodded but remained silent. We entered the cathedral and sat on chairs in the back.

"It troubles me greatly when men use their physical strength to take advantage of women," he said, after some minutes had passed.

"As it should. Ida was used abominably."

"When I find out the identity of the bloody entitled bastard—" He stopped. "Forgive me."

"Your use of language is perfectly appropriate in context," I said. "No one could object. Did you notice the book in Mrs. Davies's flat? There was only one: *Dreams,* by Olive Schreiner. It's popular with the suffragettes. Ida must have supported them."

"Every thinking woman ought to. When you consider what she suffered, she knew better than most what happens when men are given too much unchecked power." He gave himself a little shake. "Better to focus on the work at hand than to give in to emotion. Do you think Ida's attack is connected to Victoria's death?"

"Two violent crimes in the same household make for an odd coincidence, but they happened months apart and, so far as we can tell, neither any of the other servants nor the family knew what prompted Ida's suicide."

"Miss Goldsborough might have," Colin said. "We know Ida's attacker to be a gentleman. Miss Goldsborough could have been acquainted with him."

"Or engaged to him," I said. "I believe Lord Harrington played cricket at school and he frequents Lord's. Victoria mentioned his love of the sport in her diary."

"Nearly everyone plays cricket at school, so that doesn't narrow the field much. Even so, if he is guilty and Miss Goldsborough learned of it, she might have threatened to go public with it."

"That would certainly give him motive to want her dead, but

would she have done such a thing?" I asked. "She would've had a moral obligation to, of course, but not many young ladies of her class would have the stomach for it. They're trained from birth to avoid scandal."

"Surely she wouldn't have let her engagement to Harrington continue if she knew him to be capable of such vile actions. What if she threw him over at the ball and he killed her?"

"With a flask of a poisoned beverage he keeps in his jacket pocket?"

"There are yews in the garden at Harrington House," Colin said.

"Yes, but the marquess wouldn't have had the means to brew them during the ball after his fiancée arrived. If she'd already thrown him over or threatened to, I can't believe she would've gone to the party."

"I agree. He wouldn't have known in advance, if it happened at all."

"Even so, we must consider him a viable suspect for both crimes," I said. "He doesn't give the appearance of the sort of person who would—"

"You can't ever tell by appearance alone what sort of person a man is. The most well-bred, handsome gentleman may be capable of the worst atrocities."

"I couldn't agree more. Any of the gentlemen who called on Victoria might have run into Ida at the house."

"Let's not forget Lionel Morgan either," he said. "His morals are questionable at best and he operates from a position of desperation more often than he ought."

"Yes, but Ida's attacker spent months cultivating her trust. Would Mr. Morgan bother to play such a long game?"

"I'm not sure. Let's see what you think after he comes to dinner tonight."

I'd not before met Mr. Morgan and knew very little about him, beyond the fact that he was a friend of Lord Harrington's and had a gambling habit that kept him in a near-constant state of financial difficulties. When he presented himself at Park Lane, I observed him to be of average height, sturdy build, and in possession of pleasing, symmetrical features. His voice was a clear tenor, but when he laughed, it dropped several octaves. He laughed frequently, often at himself.

"So you see, Lady Emily, I'm a hopeless cad, despite my best efforts," he said, after regaling us with tales of his escapades as an undergraduate at Oxford. "It's only by some sort of miracle that I managed to earn a degree at all." His smile was winning and lit up his whole face.

"You shouldn't admit these things to me, Mr. Morgan. It will negatively influence my picture of you."

"I've never cared for subterfuge." We were sitting at the dining table, waiting for Davis to bring port and cigars. "I'd rather those around me understand who I am, the good and the bad."

"So far as you've led me to believe, there's very little good to be found." I couldn't help teasing him.

"Your observation tells me you've paid attention to my wretched stories," he said. "How very kind of you. I'm so pleased your amiable husband invited me to dine tonight. It's a tragedy that we were not before acquainted."

"That's remedied now," Colin said. Davis appeared and deposited a decanter of port and three glasses on the table. He then opened a wooden cigar box and offered it to my husband and our guest. He pretended not to notice my presence.

"There's no avoiding me, Davis. You'd might as well accept the inevitable."

"As you wish, madam." He opened the box for me and I took a cigar.

After our butler left, Mr. Morgan burst out laughing. "I've always been rather proud of the fact that my behavior is a scandal, but I've nothing on you. A lady who drinks port and smokes cigars? Are you sure you're English?"

"I'm more English than the king, but then, most of his ancestry is German. I've never understood why any woman would voluntarily retire to the drawing room for coffee and sherry when all the interesting conversation takes place while the gentlemen stay behind in the dining room."

"You're a delightful surprise."

"You make a great show of telling us, Mr. Morgan, that you're scandalous, but to this point, you've not shared anything all that shocking," I said. "Undergraduate pranks hardly make the measure. You'll have to try harder if you want to impress me. I've a number of degenerate friends whose antics far exceed yours."

"I don't like to horrify new acquaintances, only to give them a taste of what's to come."

"I've heard you're well-known in Monte Carlo," I said. I'd debated the wisdom of openly addressing his gambling issues, but in light of the things he'd already told me, I felt comfortable going ahead.

"You're nearly as blunt as I," he said.

"I do love roulette." This was a lie; I've always considered gambling a waste of time and money, but it was the only casino game I felt reasonably confident I understood.

"There's nothing quite like its thrill."

"One never wins, though, not in the long run," I said. "I'm not convinced it's entirely fair."

He laughed again. "I don't think it's meant to be."

"You're quite right there, Morgan," Colin said. "It's a fool's game."

"Yet a diverting one. Losing is the cost of entertainment. That's how I've always thought of it. I can never bear to think about the long run. The present has always been enough for me. Why plague oneself with worry about what comes next?"

"Do you often come out ahead?" I asked.

"Blackjack is my preferred game," he said. "I'm a master at it. Which is not to suggest that I don't lose to the house more often than I'd like."

"Do you indulge in any pursuits more likely to scandalize the ladies in your life?" I tapped ash from the tip of my cigar. "I'm a society matron, which means it's my duty to see you well married. You can't expect me to ignore the matter all evening."

"I shan't discuss it over port, Lady Emily. It will spoil the occasion. I confess I'm not eager to wed. I shan't have much say in the matter, you see." He reached for the decanter and refilled his glass. "My father has distinct opinions that he feels worthy of more consideration than my own on the subject. That's the way it often is for us second sons."

I considered pointing out that less time spent gambling might lead to improved prospects, but recognized the futility of such action. In some ways, he reminded me of my friend Jeremy, Duke of Bainbridge, whose oft-stated purpose in life was to earn the moniker of Most Useless Man in England. Mr. Morgan shared with him a certain ease of manner and affability. Enjoying his company took little effort. However, there was a hint of darkness behind his shining eyes entirely absent in Jeremy. I couldn't quite figure out from whence it stemmed. Was it a result of Mr. Morgan's financial difficulties? Was it resistance to taking a bride of his father's choice? Or was it something far more sinister?

He stayed until well after midnight. After he'd gone, we retired to our bedroom and, rather than call for my maid at such a late hour, I'd asked Colin to undo my corset. He was standing behind me, gently tugging on the laces.

"Do you see what I mean about him being a bit odd?" he asked. "He's almost too sociable, too good-natured."

"You're quite right. I can't quite identify what it is about him that troubles me, but I'm not convinced he's the sort to spend months cultivating a pseudo-friendship with a maid only to take advantage of her."

"He's more likely to take what he wants the instant he decides he wants it. I doubt he has a great deal of patience."

"I couldn't agree more. But what about him as Victoria's murderer? If she was aware of the loans her fiancé gave him, she might have pressured Lord Harrington to stop offering them."

"And Morgan, not wanting to lose his most reliable source of income, killed her?" He tossed my corset onto a chair and started to remove the studs from his evening shirt.

"It's possible," I said, "but would've been an awfully risky course of action. After all, he couldn't have expected his friend to fund him indefinitely. Murder is a capital crime. If he did it, he'd face hanging if he were caught. Would it be worth it?"

"I'd say it wouldn't be, especially given what he said about his father, who wants to marry him off, undoubtedly to some dowdy girl with a modest fortune. He's the sort to prefer someone of striking beauty."

"A girl like that would never consider him. Even if she were poor, beauty would ensure she'd have more enticing prospects," I said.

"Yes, unless she found him particularly charming," Colin said, "which is not entirely impossible."

"Especially if the hypothetical lady in question were the type to embrace Wilde's observation that *in matters of great importance, style, not sincerity, is the vital thing.*"

"Many a debutante would agree with the sentiment. So where does that leave us?"

"Wondering if the Marquess of Harrington has something to hide," I said. "At the moment, his motive is particularly strong."

"Only if he is guilty of the attack on Ida," Colin said, "and for now, his potential involvement in that is pure speculation."

"You always say murders are most often committed by the people closest to the victims. Lord Harrington certainly qualifies."

"Indeed he does, but—and I hesitate to say this—something is preventing me from liking him for either crime. I can't explain it."

"Heaven forfend! Can it be you're listening to your intuition?"

"Don't get carried away, my dear, it's only that we have no solid evidence to condemn any of our suspects, Harrington included."

I stepped out of my petticoats and pulled a dressing gown over my filmy cotton batiste chemise. "You're becoming more aware of your intuition, and I find it most appealing."

"I shall do everything possible to distract you enough that you have no memory of this conversation in the morning." He slipped the dressing gown off my shoulders, let it fall to the floor, and set about doing exactly what he intended.

22

Britannia

For some months, I fell into a routine more satisfying than I'd ever had before. *Amores* made tending my family's sheep less tedious. There were five scrolls in total. When I'd finished the first, Gaius brought me the second. I saw him frequently now, usually once a week. There was nothing intimate between us, only poetry.

It's obvious to say *Amores* is erotic by definition. There's a clue in the title and all that. Yes, it was about love, but I found more humor in it than anything else. A poet explaining how to seduce women isn't exactly going to get us ladies excited, but it might make us laugh. Best of all were the tantalizing references to poetry that I couldn't begin to understand. Not yet, anyway. This was only my introduction and I already wanted more.

When I wasn't reading and tending sheep, I was with Boudica. We spent much time riding, but I also taught her to drive a chariot, a skill she took to in a flash. When night fell, we'd sit near the fire in her house and tell stories. Sometimes, her daughters hovered nearby, listening. They weren't all that much younger than I was, but they were still girls. It would be a while before they started being pressured to marry.

Unlike me.

One morning, my mother stopped me when I was leaving the house. "Sit," she said. "It's time you made a decision."

"The sheep—"

She didn't let me continue. "You know you must marry, and you're fortunate that the queen's attention has expanded your pool of potential grooms."

"I don't like any of them."

"Then choose whoever offends you the least."

I snorted. "What lofty standards."

"Vatta, your father and I have indulged you since you were a child. Maybe that was a mistake. Maybe it's left you with the impression you can do whatever you'd like. If so, you couldn't be more wrong. You need to set up your own home. Have your own children. Make your own life."

"Why does that require marriage?"

"Because it does," she said. In the annals of uninspiring explanations, this had to be at the top. She sat next to me and took my hands. "Does your indecision come because you're hoping for an offer from your Roman friend?"

I pulled my hands away. "No!"

"Good. I was worried that might be what was holding you back. Roman soldiers don't take provincial wives back to Italy. They abandon them and leave them helpless and unprotected."

"Maybe the Britons don't like the idea of living in Rome," I said. "I'd rather stay here."

She narrowed her eyes. "I'm not sure I believe you, but I hope your words are true. So, which of the men do you prefer?"

I felt panic welling in me. I'd known this day would come eventually. I should've been ready. I wasn't. "Can I have another week to decide?"

"A week and not a day longer. Use the time wisely, Vatta. This decision will shape the rest of your life."

I hated that she was right and stormed out of the house. Halfway to the pasture where our sheep were contentedly grazing, I slammed into Duro. That's what happens when you don't look where you're going. All of a sudden, your future knocks you in the face.

23

London

I woke in a glorious mood the next day, not only as an aftereffect of my husband's delicious attentions, but because the weather had turned. Summer was finally upon us. Colin cynically suggested that we should enjoy it, as it was the shortest season of the year. If we were fortunate, it might last three days together. My view was that it was preferable to what they get in Scotland. So far as I could tell, summer there was unpredictable, but often came on a Tuesday afternoon and stayed all the way until nightfall.

Wanting to speak to Frances Price again, I sent her a message asking her to meet me in the park. It was too beautiful a day to squander indoors. She was waiting for me in front of the statue of Achilles when I arrived.

"An appalling thing," she said, nodding at it.

"The man himself or the statue?" I asked.

"An interesting question, Lady Emily, and one I shall have

to ponder before answering. The truth is, I said it only because it seemed less obvious than owning I find it desperately appealing. What a fine figure!"

I laughed. "I've always preferred Hector."

"I don't think I'd enjoy anything about the *Iliad*. A terrible thing to admit, I know."

"You might find it surprises you."

"War bores me," she said. "I despise violence."

"There's a lot of that, to be sure, but it's not the only thing to be found in its pages. *There is the heat of Love, the pulsing rush of Longing, the lover's whisper, irresistible—magic to make the sanest man go mad.*"

Her eyes widened. "I see how wrong I must be. Once again, I'm made to face the shortcomings of the education of young ladies. I promise, someday, to give it a chance."

"I like little better than discussing Homer, but it's not why I wanted to see you. Can you tell me more about the time you spent in the garden during the Harringtons' ball?"

"Not without being lurid." She blushed.

"I didn't mean that," I said. "Who else did you see there?"

"Oscar and I were tucked away in a quiet corner."

"Yes, but surely you passed other people on the way there?"

"Could we walk?" She started down the path and we strolled in the direction of the Serpentine. "I'd be better able to respond if I know what you're trying to discover."

"I wouldn't want to shape your answer in any way."

"You're brave to come out in this sun without a parasol," she said, once again neatly diverting from my question.

"Your attempts to change the subject will prove ineffective. I welcome the sun on my face, partly because I like the way it feels and partly because every bit of ensuing color horrifies my mother."

"You surprise me." She closed her own parasol. "I shall follow your example despite the fact that it won't horrify my own mother in the least."

"Who else was in the garden that night?"

"You are relentless, aren't you?"

"A good investigator can't let herself be distracted," I said. "Your evasion makes me wonder what you're trying to hide."

"Nothing, I assure you. It's painful recalling that awful day. There was a gaggle of extremely foolish young ladies in the garden giggling over something or other. None of them could claim a particular acquaintance with me or with Victoria. I presume you're interested in their relationship with her."

"Possibly," I said. "Did you see Cressida Wright?"

"Cressida? No, I did not."

"Are you certain?"

"Why wouldn't I be?"

"I believe your claim of certainty, but not that you are truthful."

She stopped walking and faced me, her eyes wide. "I don't much like being accused of lying."

"And I don't much like being lied to, especially by someone who claims to want justice for her murdered friend."

"Yes, I saw Cressida. Why does it matter?"

"She saw you and was entirely candid about what she witnessed. Naturally, she has less cause to be discreet than you in this particular circumstance, but I use her as an example of someone who is not holding back my investigation. Do you want to see Victoria's killer brought to justice?"

"How can you ask such a question? Of course I do."

"Then make me believe the veracity of your words. I know you are withholding things from me. That must stop now."

She frowned. "I'm sorry. I didn't mean to—"

"I've no interest in your intentions." I looped my arm through hers and pulled her toward a bench shaded by a towering plane tree. We sat down.

"I promise to tell you the truth," she said.

"What do you know about Victoria's maid, Ida?"

"Ida? The poor girl who killed herself?"

"Yes."

She gulped. "I know everything. So did Victoria. Ida confided in her."

"Everything?"

"Enough to be horrified," she said. "Victoria shared the story with me. She wanted to do something to help, but didn't know how."

"What options did she consider?"

"Ida didn't want to go to the police and refused to tell us the name of the man." She hesitated. "As a result, there weren't any options to consider. He got clean away with it."

"Did you ever speak to Ida yourself?"

"No. Victoria didn't want her to know she'd broken her confidence by telling me what had happened. She only did it because the entire situation was so upsetting and she needed to talk to someone about it. She'd hoped that my parents, with their radical views, might be able to help."

"She told them, too?"

"No, she asked me to consult with them on the matter."

"Were they helpful?" I asked.

"They were full of useless ideas like campaigning to change laws. My mother quoted some long-dead judge who said a rape accusation was, if I remember correctly, *easily . . . made and hard to be proved, and harder to be defended by the party accused.*"

"That was Lord Chief Justice Sir Matthew Hale in the seventeenth century. The laws should be changed, so that they're less vicious to the victims."

"It couldn't be changed fast enough to have helped Ida."

"No, it couldn't."

"This is why I object to their political lives," she said. "They don't try to force change."

"I don't agree with that at all. The suffragettes—"

"The suffragettes are losing their way. Their calls for violence, for deeds not words, will not help the plight of women in the long run. It will only alienate people who might have been their allies."

"You sound as if you support the fight for equality."

"I don't want to be treated badly, if that's what you mean, and don't think anyone else should be either."

"Do you want the right to vote?" I asked.

"I thought we were talking about Ida and Victoria?"

"Quite right. So your parents were no help. What happened next?"

"I'm ashamed to say nothing happened." She tapped her parasol against the ground and shook her head, looking deflated. "What could we do? Victoria tried her best to console Ida, and I do believe she succeeded to some extent. That's why Ida's death came as such a shock. So much time had gone by—it had been months—we couldn't understand why she succumbed to despair."

She clearly didn't comprehend that it would take more than a few months to get over the trauma Ida had suffered. Furthermore, either Frances was avoiding discussing the girl's delicate condition or she was proving the stance she took on the inadequacies of the education of young ladies.

"You truly don't know what catalyzed Ida's suicide?" I asked.

"No. Do you?"

I believed she was telling the truth. "She was with child and saw no viable way to contend with the situation."

"I didn't know that detail. An unmarried woman in that condition would lose her job and have no way to support the baby."

"Precisely."

"And she would bring shame to her family." Frances's face had gone white. She bit her bottom lip. "It's appalling. What is wrong with a world in which a woman feels she has no choice but death as a result of violent actions taken against her?"

"There are many things wrong," I said. "Prejudice and fear and a tendency to judge others are all rife."

"Did Victoria know about the baby?"

"I hoped you could tell me."

"I don't believe she did. If she had, she would've confided in me. We would have done something, anything, to help. The poor girl."

"Did either of you suspect any man in particular of attacking Ida?"

"No," she said. "Victoria told me he was a gentleman. That's all. We both considered every man of our acquaintance who had called at the Goldsboroughs' house. They might have seen Ida and followed her or lured her out or . . . I don't know the methods of these sorts of men."

"What did you conclude from pondering these various individuals?"

"Primarily that no one we know behaves in a fashion that would draw suspicion, which we found utterly unsatisfactory. Presumably, a successful criminal—which I define as one who gets away with his crime—doesn't let his twisted predilections show."

"Did you have a secondary conclusion?"

"Yes, that only one gentleman of our acquaintance struck us as having some degree of antisocial tendencies: Mr. Lionel Morgan. I do not mean to accuse him. He's never behaved outside the bounds of propriety and treats everyone with kindness. However, some of his pursuits might lead him into dark corners of London, places where he might encounter others with fewer scruples. If he was with one of these individuals and encountered Ida in a public place of some sort, he might have inadvertently drawn attention to her."

Although this was theoretically possible, it did not seem probable. Ida's assault was not a crime of opportunity. "If the man who did this discovered Victoria knew of his crime, he's likely the murderer."

"That only confirms to me that it's definitely not Mr. Morgan. He wouldn't have harmed Victoria. He's a dear friend of Peregrine's and adored her. He couldn't have been happier about their marriage."

"Portia claims not to have known about Ida," I said. "Is that true?"

"Absolutely. There was nothing Portia could do to help, so Victoria saw no benefit to upsetting her."

"Yet she had no such compunctions when it came to you?"

"As I already told you, she thought I—or my parents—might be able to help. Further, she's aware of my strength. I can deal with troubling situations without falling apart."

"And Portia can't?"

"She's far more emotional. It's not a criticism, but it did keep Victoria from fully confiding in her."

"Only about Ida, or about other things as well?"

"There are some things, Lady Emily, that no one wants to share with family members. That's what best friends are for."

24

Britannia

Duro had never struck me as the sort of man who would inspire passion and adoration. He was good-looking enough, even if he wasn't all that tall. To be fair, it was only my own height that made him seem short. Conventional wisdom would tell you he was fine, I was the aberration. He had broad shoulders, could handle a sword well, and seemed generally reliable in all ways. No one in the village disliked him, which is quite a compliment in a tribe full of competitive warriors. He was always at the center of activity, mates with all the other men.

He'd distinguished himself in battle on more than one occasion, but he wasn't showy about it. Never presented himself as a hero. Never used it to get attention. At least it didn't look that way. The end result, not surprisingly, was that he was showered with compliments about his skill and his humility.

I didn't have the impression he was particularly humble, more like he wasn't all that concerned about what anyone else thought about him. That isn't to say that he had boorish manners or was antisocial. Quite the contrary. To me, it read that he had enough confidence in himself not to have to flaunt any good qualities he might possess.

That should be appealing, right?

I apologized when I slammed into him. He laughed.

"I've been wondering when this would happen," he said. "Half the time your face is buried in a scroll and you show no sign of having any idea of what's going on around you. Now I know it's not only the scroll distracting you, because you're not holding it now."

I couldn't think of anything to say in reply. Luckily, he liked talking enough to do it for both of us.

"I've been watching you. Not because of Boudica—my interest goes back further than that. The parade of fellows going into your father's house tells me I shouldn't have waited so long."

"Waited so long?" I asked. "For what?"

"To ask you to marry me. You're of the right age and I think we would get on well enough."

"What an exciting prospect. How could I resist?"

He laughed again. "The truth is, I've always found you engaging. You speak your mind. You don't do what's expected of you. It's enticing."

"We barely know each other."

"We're from the same tribe. We share the same culture. We've both reached the age when we'll have to marry soon. Our families are of the same rank. There's no reason to believe we wouldn't get along. What more do you want? Love that sweeps you off your feet? That's a myth for little girls."

"I'm not that naïve." I crossed my arms and stared into his eyes.

"You know, Duro, I'm not sure what exactly it is, but I don't doubt that there is more, and that I would need it to be happy."

"Then I will make it my mission to figure it out. When I do, I expect a positive answer to my proposal."

"You sure know how to tempt a woman, don't you?"

"I do." He pulled me close to him and kissed me in a way I hadn't known was possible. It stunned me. I pushed him away, but with a grin. I almost liked it.

25

London

When I returned home, my mother was waiting for me in the sitting room. Davis warned me; I steeled myself as I opened the door. She'd been there for more than an hour and would not be best pleased, despite the fact I'd had no indication she was coming. The remains of tea and biscuits sat on a table next to her. Her eyes narrowed when she saw me.

"There is so much to cover I shan't have time to express my displeasure at having been kept waiting. Other matters are more pressing. I am deeply concerned about what you've got yourself into, Emily," she said and held up a hand to stop me from approaching a chair. "Don't sit down. You'll pay better attention if you're standing. And do attend to your posture. Slouching is unbecoming. Are you wearing a corset?"

I was not, but had no intention of sharing that with her. I'd recently acquired several gowns from the Frenchman Paul Poiret, made in a new design he'd been playing with, inspired by those worn in ancient Greece. That, naturally, appealed to my intellectual interests, but more exciting was that their empire waists eliminated the need for a corset. Constructed from beautifully draped soft fabrics, they were undeniably elegant without binding the body.

"Have you come here to discuss undergarments, Mother?" I asked. "That strikes me as terribly inappropriate. What if Colin were to stumble upon us in the midst of such a conversation?"

"I'd prefer never to speak of such things, but if you will insist on gallivanting around town dressed in such a manner, you can hardly expect me to refrain from comment."

"You expressed concern about what I've got myself into, and, as you have so keenly observed, that isn't a corset. So what is it that's worrying you?"

She raised her hand to her forehead and pulled a face. "My despair consumes me. I need a moment."

I stepped out of the room, went to the library, and returned with a book.

"Your manners are incomprehensible," she said. "To abandon me—"

"You said you needed a moment. I wanted to give you one and thought occupying myself with a book would be the best way to ensure I didn't disturb you."

"What book is it? No, don't tell me. The problem of your sordid habits will have to be saved for another day. I've come on most urgent business. As you are well aware, I constantly apply myself to activities benefiting myself and others, particularly you. Currently, I've been using my connections to understand all that happened at Harrington House the night of poor Victoria's death."

"Is that so?" The very thought terrified me.

"Ordinarily, I would never be so crass as to discuss a murder, or any kind of violent death, but your husband always says small details matter greatly in these cases. I've spoken to everyone important who was at the ball. Important due to rank, but also as a result of their ability to observe what is going on around them."

"Gossips?" I asked.

"Precisely. They ought to be of use occasionally, don't you think? Most of what I've learned was tedious, but one thing cropped up that may figure in your investigation. I'd hoped to speak to Mr. Hargreaves, but your butler informed me he is not home."

It would've been too much to hope she'd planned to tell me. Instead, she was no doubt taking pleasure in at least being able to make it clear that, in her opinion, I was far less significant than my spouse. "Indeed he is not."

"Then I have no choice but to share my discovery with you. I assume I can rely on you to pass it along to him?" She did not pause for me to answer. "There is a new underground movement threatening decent society. Formed by a cohort of young ladies who ought to know better, they are suffragettes of the worst sort."

"What sort is that?" I asked.

"I understand your meaning full well and appreciate it. You're quite right that suffragettes of all sorts are undesirable. The petty differences between them are insignificant. This group call themselves Boudica's Sisters. Can you imagine? Using that name and, hence, tarnishing the reputation of one of Britain's finest heroines in the service of such rot?"

"Boudica was a warrior queen who led her tribe to victory against the Romans. I'm confident she would have approved of the suffragettes."

She waved her hand. "I should've known it was too much to

hope you'd started to accept what it takes to make a civilized society function. The suffragettes want to destroy the social structure that keeps order. We women have our rightful and important place within that structure, but it is not the same as that occupied by men. The material point is that these girls are bent on corrupting their fellow debutantes."

"By what means?"

"Convincing them to support women's rights, of course."

"How is this any different from what Mrs. Pankhurst and the others are striving for?"

"Their goals may not be unique, but their very persons make their efforts more dangerous," she said. "There are some young ladies—many, I'd say—who are put off by the efforts of old crones like Mrs. Pankhurst. It's the only consolation I have at present. Yet when a vibrant, popular girl of their own age approaches them, they may prove vulnerable. They may listen. They may get ideas. Ideas that are nothing but dangerous."

I'd long been a member of the Women's Liberal Federation. We fought not only to reform the voting laws to include women and disenfranchised men but also to instigate social change that would benefit our society at large. Mrs. Pankhurst had formed the Women's Social and Political Union nearly four years ago. Their approach was more militant than ours, but I was beginning to wonder if their strategy might be what the situation required. So far, peaceful protest and earnest speech had failed to accomplish our goals.

"Mrs. Pankhurst is not even a dozen years older than I. She's hardly an old crone," I said.

"She behaves like one. It's ghastly."

"I should think most old crones are resistant to new ideas," I said. "Fascinating though this all is, I don't see how it pertains to Victoria's murder."

"Apparently, she had received an invitation to join Boudica's Sisters."

"How do you know?"

"A young lady told me after I cornered her in the Royal Academy. She had spent a shocking amount of time standing in front of a painting I found most inappropriate for a girl her age. The subject matter was scandalous, but the less said about that, the better. I feared for her moral center, confronted her, and warned her off looking at such things. One thing led to another, and soon I had to point out the insidious damage the suffragettes are doing to this country. That's when she mentioned Boudica's Sisters and said that they claim to be helping the country, but that she wasn't convinced—praise heaven—because they'd asked Miss Goldsborough to join and look what happened to her."

"How did she know they'd approached Victoria?"

"It's apparently the talk of town among her set at the moment, which doesn't guarantee there's any truth to it, but I thought it's the sort of thing Mr. Hargreaves would want to look into. This girl will be of no use. She's a silly little thing who has not been nominated for potential membership. Evidently, their scheme is to make their little club exclusive, no doubt because it creates the false impression that it's an honor to be associated with it. Only a few are given invitations, which are delivered anonymously in the middle of the night, with no one in the household disturbed. The girls are sworn to secrecy and are never to speak about any of it."

"Then how has it become the talk of the town?" I asked.

"My dear child, the more one tells people not to speak about something, the more they will. Isn't that obvious?" She rose from her seat. "I've no more time to waste here today. I'm off to see Lady Goldsborough. I hope you're grateful for the information and that it proves helpful to Mr. Hargreaves. Do tell him if he requires anything further from me, I'm at his disposal."

With that, she departed. I rang for Davis and asked him to call for the carriage. Despite my involvement in the fight for women's rights, I'd never heard of Boudica's Sisters. This suggested to me their presence was not known to the Women's Liberal Federation. Mrs. Price, who was aligned with Mrs. Pankhurst, might have more details.

I'd hoped the carriage would get me to Bayswater faster than walking, but the traffic in town had grown so much over the past few years, I didn't save all that much time. Mrs. Price opened the door herself, greeted me with enthusiasm, and took me into the same sitting room where I'd been received on my previous visit. I accepted her offer of tea, wanting our conversation to have a congenial feel.

"I'm afraid Frances isn't here," she said. "She's gone to stay with friends in Kew and won't be back until tomorrow. I thought the two of you spoke this morning in the park? Did you need something more from her?"

"No, it's you I wanted to see. I've recently learned about a group of suffragettes I'd not before heard of: Boudica's Sisters. Are you familiar with them?"

"I've heard rumblings, but don't quite know if there's truth to any of them. It's said they're young ladies of high rank who meet regularly to discuss the right to vote. So far as I can tell, they've not taken any specific actions nor have they attempted to engage with the public in any way."

"What is their aim?" I asked.

She shrugged. "That is unclear. Mrs. Pankhurst hasn't had any interaction with their members, but believes they must be thinking it's a way to recruit unmarried ladies from their class who might otherwise resist the movement. Perhaps the idea is to open their minds to the topic before gently moving them toward greater participation."

"Why unmarried?"

"I haven't the slightest idea," she said.

"Do you have an inkling as to who their leaders might be?"

"No, nor does Mrs. Pankhurst. It gives every appearance of being an odd little group. No doubt you've heard about the way in which they ask people to join?"

"Invitations delivered in the middle of the night."

"Strange indeed, but just the sort of thing a bunch of pampered debutantes would find exciting."

"If so, it's a good method, likely to entice them."

"You're quite right," she said. "I don't mean to criticize them, it's only that at this time, we ought to be far beyond the point of earnest conversations that lead to nothing. There's a time for talk, but women's groups have been talking for decades. We need more."

"I agree, but at the same time see value in expanding our numbers. If these young ladies can persuade others to join, surely that's a welcome step. Not everyone can be instantly ready for direct action."

"You raise a valid point. What I would like to see, however, is a plan to bring them further along once they've decided to support the cause. Perhaps there is one, but given the way they shroud themselves in secrecy, I can't help think it's less serious than I'd like it to be. Often, young ladies lend their support to a cause in order to make themselves feel they're part of something. It's more about giving the appearance of virtue than doing anything that actually matters. I'd like to be wrong, but unless something further happens, I doubt Boudica's Sisters will have any impact on our fight."

I spent a pleasant hour with Mrs. Price, discussing our approaches to suffrage. We didn't agree on all lines, but there is always benefit to listening to those whose opinions differ from our own. No one can be right all the time, and we ought to welcome new ideas. When I left her, I felt buoyed, hopeful about our chances for winning the vote. Multiple groups with multiple approaches gave us broad coverage throughout the nation. Eventually, the government would have to take notice.

Now, though, I needed to learn more about Boudica's Sisters. Victoria did not support the suffragettes, but the group may have thought her persuadable. She did, after all, have a picture of Boudica on her bedroom wall, and her maid had a copy of *Dreams* in her flat. Could these ladies be more militant than Mrs. Pankhurst? Were they willing to murder those who didn't subscribe to their cause? There was one person who might be able to shed light on the organization, the only man I knew who liked to surreptitiously deliver things in the middle of the night without disturbing a soul: Sebastian.

26

Britannia

In private, only to myself, I admitted that I almost liked Duro. Which is not to say I wanted to marry him. However, in the circumstances, with my parents expecting a decision by the end of the week, I could hold him up as a possibility. Maybe that would gain me a little more time.

I met with Gaius the next day, to continue our discussion of poetry. We'd gone to our usual spot near the river, but the weather turned and rain drenched us.

"You can see why I'm not fond of this place," he said, after gathering up the blanket we'd been sitting on and picking up our basket of food. "In Rome, a person can enjoy the outdoors."

"When you're in Rome, or anywhere else in Italy, do you complain about the heat? About the relentless burning of the sun?"

"I don't ordinarily complain about the weather here. Today is an exception."

"Why?"

"Because I was looking forward to seeing you. To continuing our conversation."

"And a little rain is enough to put you off?" To be fair, it was falling so hard it half hid the expression on his face. "There's a spot with shelter not far from here. Nothing glamorous, but it will keep us from getting even wetter."

I led him to it, a place built for shepherds. There was enough wood inside for a fire, and soon we were warmish.

He'd removed his toga, that bizarre garment Romans of rank liked to wear when not in military uniform, and was wringing the water from it.

"You must trust me, bringing me to a secluded place like this," he said.

"Trust you?" I considered it. "I suppose I do, to a degree. Do you believe you're strong enough to overpower me? I'm a fierce tribeswoman. Only think how the druid women terrified your soldiers at Mona."

"Are you a druid?"

"I'm terrifying, isn't that enough?" He didn't need to know anything about my beliefs.

"It's quite enough. I'm not the sort of man who thinks about overpowering women. To do so would be uncivilized."

"Except in war."

"Even in war."

I looked at him, skeptical. "*Noli irritare leones*, I suppose." Don't poke the lions.

He laughed. "*So I'm to face fresh charges every day! / I win, but all those battles are a bore.*"

"I, too, prefer not to fight."

"I'm glad to hear it. Women can be formidable opponents. I prefer to keep them as friends."

"Do you find it difficult to do that?" I asked.

"No, not so far, although I'm never quite sure with you."

"Why not?"

"You're a puzzle to me. You don't seem to fit here."

"What's that got to do with keeping me as a friend?"

"That's the other thing about you, Vatta, you don't stand for any nonsense. You'd do well around politicians in Rome. They'd never be able to trick you."

"You didn't answer my question."

"You're like no one I've ever known. I value our conversations. And you're beautiful. *All perfect in my sight,* to quote our favorite poet. Combined, this all makes me nervous. Keeps me unsteady. I'm afraid of losing you."

Now I laughed. "Losing me? Are friends in Rome so unreliable?"

He shook his head. "Not as such. Between the two of us, though, things could become more complicated." He reached up and touched my cheek. He stared into my eyes. And then he looked away. "I must resist, lest I scare you away."

"Resist, then. It makes no difference to me." This was a lie. My heart pounded. Sweat beaded on my forehead. My stomach burned. His approach was different from Duro's. I couldn't decide which I preferred.

"I don't want to believe that, but shall take you at your word," he said. "If you change your mind, inform me without delay."

27

London

One of the numerous difficulties in dealing with Sebastian was the rigmarole required to contact him. I had not the slightest idea where he stayed while in London, and he certainly was not the sort to belong to a club that might receive his post or an urgent message. Even if he did, he'd be using an alias rather than his proper name. Thinking on it, I doubted Sebastian Capet was his proper name.

In the past, I'd posted notices for him in *The Times* classifieds and would have to wait for him to reply. Granted, he'd always done so promptly, but I was growing weary of his games. Maintaining an acquaintance of any sort with a person involved in criminal activities was endlessly frustrating. Accepting the inevitable, I asked my driver to take me to Fleet Street.

When he deposited me back in Park Lane, Sebastian was waiting for me outside the house. He was no longer dressed as a maharaja. This time, he looked the picture of an English gentleman, in an exquisitely tailored riding jacket and jodhpurs. He removed the cap from his head when he saw me and bowed low.

"A delight as always, Kallista."

"Don't irritate me. How did you know I was looking for you?"

"I have my ways."

"Are you following me?"

"Heavens, no. I wouldn't violate your privacy in such inelegant fashion. I've been riding on Rotten Row. Why else would I be dressed like this? An associate alerted me to your desire to see me."

"What associate? No, don't tell me," I said. "I've no interest in your methods."

"Shall we go inside and have a spot of tea?"

"We'll go in, but you'll get no refreshment."

"I don't like to agree with your mother, but your manners are diabolical."

I walked in front of him and didn't speak again until we were in the library. "What do you know about Boudica's Sisters?" I asked, after ordering him to sit on a chair across from mine.

He pulled a face. "I believe she famously had daughters, didn't she, but can't say I recall sisters. I'm no student of history—"

"Don't play games with me, Sebastian. I'm in no mood to humor—"

"My dearest girl, don't get so upset. I'm only teasing. They're a group of young suffragettes. You'd like them, I think. Frankly, they could use your guidance. Their motives are pure and their intentions good, but I've little hope that they'll accomplish much of anything. They'd be most interested in certain aspects of my current pursuits, but I'm not ready to reveal details yet."

"Who are their members?"

"That I cannot tell you."

"Cannot or won't?"

"Won't." He slumped in his chair. "Will you at least let me have a whisky if there's no tea to be had?"

"What are their names?"

"I gave my word as a gentleman that I would never expose the identities of any of their members."

"I know precisely the value of your word as a gentleman."

"That's unfair, Kallista."

"Don't call me that. How did you become involved with them?"

"It was a matter of sublime coincidence. I was at work one evening, well past midnight, when I noticed a badly disguised young lady attempting to enter a house through a back window."

"What were you doing there?"

"Preparing to liberate an item that shouldn't belong to the homeowners."

"Will you ever cease vexing me?"

"I don't know why you ask questions whose answers are certain to irritate you," he said. "I had just scaled the back wall. She was in the garden and struggling with the window."

"So you opened it for her?"

"Heavens, no. I've no interest in corrupting youth. Look how badly that ended for old Socrates. I asked her purpose and she burst into tears. It was rather off-putting, if you must know. I've never liked weeping young ladies. What is one meant to do with them? She confessed at once. Evidently, she hadn't seen me coming over the wall and drew the erroneous conclusion I lived in the house."

"This doesn't ring true," I said. "She admitted what she was doing when she believed you were—what?—the father of the young lady she was trying to reach?"

"I'm wounded at the suggestion I look old enough to be the father of a debutante." He shuddered. "I don't know whom she thought I was. She was frightened and not thinking clearly. I explained that I, too, was on a private errand. This piqued her interest and calmed her down. I told her that if she gave me the whole truth, I would help her."

"And she did?"

"Yes. I confirmed what she said by reading the invitation she'd planned to deliver to the young lady asleep inside."

"She gave you details about Boudica's Sisters?" I asked.

"Enough that I felt comfortable offering my services to them, yes. I admire the enthusiastic idealism of youth and feel strongly it's a scandal you ladies are not given the full rights you ought to possess. One ought to help if one can. Imagine my delight in finding they required services that I'm particularly good at. Further, it ties in rather neatly with another project I'm currently pursuing."

I wasn't about to humor him by asking about the other project. "So you deliver their invitations?"

"I do. That is the limit of my involvement."

"How many times have you done it?"

"Three this Season."

"How many last?"

"None. They've only recently formed."

"Did you bring one to Victoria Goldsborough?"

"No, I did not," he said. "I'm not sure how that bit of gossip got started."

"Was she involved in the group?"

"I never spoke to her, so how would I know?"

"Is it possible Miss Goldsborough was killed because she threatened to expose Boudica's Sisters?" I asked.

"If they can't even manage to successfully deliver their invitations themselves, I hardly think they're capable of murder."

"Will you carry a message to them from me?"

"That might be interesting, but I'll have to pass. They would be furious to learn I'd told anyone of my connection to them, even you."

"I need you to do it, Sebastian."

"Not a chance, Emily. Trying placing an ad in *The Times*."

Colin returned home a quarter of an hour after Sebastian left. He'd been to Scotland Yard. "It was an utter waste," he said, shrugging off his jacket and tossing it across a chair. The day had grown quite warm, and despite my having flung open all the windows in the library, it was stuffy inside. "I expected nothing else. The official attitude to crimes of a sexual nature is a disgrace. There has been nothing reported similar to the attack on Ida."

"Not much of a surprise," I said. "Ida didn't notify the authorities either."

"Women would be more likely to do so if they were treated better when they did. It's a systemic problem, and one I don't know how to begin to fix."

"Not through earnest speech, if you're to learn anything from the suffragettes." I told him about Boudica's Sisters and reminded him of the picture on Victoria's wall and the book I'd seen in Mrs. Davies's flat.

"I noticed that as well." He'd removed his waistcoat and was rolling up the sleeves of his shirt.

"The books in Victoria's room raised questions for me as well.

Nearly all of them were ordinary, aside from Thackeray's *The Rose and the Ring*."

"That stands out only if one understands its satire. I suspect that passes most readers by."

"Not Victoria. She was a bright girl. I'd like to go back to her room and search it again. Portia said she found nothing else with the diary, but what if there's a second hiding place? One not meant to be discovered?"

"You think she wanted the diary to be read?"

"Something about it doesn't sit right with me. The voice doesn't sound like her and the views she expresses in it certainly don't mesh with the girl I knew."

"You hadn't spent a great deal of time with her in recent years. Young ladies do change as they approach womanhood."

"Yes, but I cannot accept she became a wholly different person, one obsessed with nothing more than making a good marriage."

"Given her grandmother's values, it wouldn't be surprising," he said. "Not everyone shares your rebellious streak."

"It's entirely possible Sebastian is lying about Victoria not getting nominated by Boudica's Sisters. If she refused them and threatened to go public . . ."

He considered my words. "I still can't see a group of idealistic young ladies murdering her. However, I can't deny it's possible, particularly given the method employed."

"It's also conceivable that Sebastian isn't the only one who delivered their invitations. We're accepting the idea that the group is made up solely of debutantes, but suffragettes don't separate themselves based on class. They welcome women from all backgrounds. That's part of what makes the establishment so uneasy when it comes to them. Ida could've broached the subject with Victoria."

"And risked the possibility of losing her position?" He shook his head. "Given that she and Miss Goldsborough confided in each other, it's likely Ida knew her mistress's feelings on the subject. Further, she'd absolutely be aware of Lady Goldsborough's opinions on suffrage."

"What if Ida had persuaded Victoria to change her point of view?" I asked. "Perhaps she did join the group. Perhaps she was involved in planning some sort of action and wrote her diary specifically to make it appear she held a different set of beliefs."

"Your imagination is running away with you, partly, I think, because you want to believe Miss Goldsborough was more enlightened than evidence shows."

"No, that's not it. Something isn't right. I'm sure of it."

"Then let's return to the East End and question Mrs. Davies again."

I adored the man. Even when he didn't agree with me, he respected my opinions and my intellect enough to support my ideas. The same could not be said about his views of my intuition, but one cannot have everything.

Our conversation with Ida's mother was brief. She knew very little about her daughter's involvement with the suffragettes.

"I told her to keep away from them," she said. "Being associated with that kind only brings trouble, and we neither of us needed any of that. She went to hear that Mrs. Pankhurst give a speech and came home all fired up. I explained to her how her reputation would suffer if word got out. She was mighty displeased at first, she was, and went across the hall to complain to Fenella, but her friend told her I was right."

"May I look at the book she had?" I asked.

"I don't see why not."

I picked it up off the table and opened it. The endpaper was inscribed:

To Ida Davies, a fellow soldier in the fight. We shall never surrender.

Your friend,
Frances Price

28

Britannia

After a lifetime of being ignored by most people around me, it was an interesting study to compare the methods Gaius and Duro employed to woo me. Don't think I'm ignorant enough not to see what Gaius was doing. Where Duro was direct, the Roman was subtle. He wanted to lure me to him. Wanted me to come of my own accord.

Would it be my own accord if he'd manipulated me into wanting him? But then, isn't all courtship a form of persuasion? Where do you draw the line between manipulation and persuasion? Is there a difference?

Frankly, I found the whole situation entertaining.

On the surface, I had greater respect for Duro's bluntness. He told me what he wanted; he showed me he could take it. He made sure I would like it, and I knew I could always step away. That last was important.

Relatively speaking, that is.

I wandered toward the meadow where Aesu was grazing, alongside Boudica's horses. The queen was there, standing next to her husband. I walked more quickly, eager to see them both, until I heard raised voices and realized they were arguing.

I hung back and stepped behind a tree. They were shouting at each other now.

"It matters. Of course it matters," Boudica bellowed. "How could it not? You're excluding me."

"Only for our daughters' sake." Prasutagus had balled his hands into fists.

"You do it to curry favor with an emperor who doesn't even know who you are. Do you think he cares? That leaving him half your kingdom will make the slightest difference to him? He's in charge of most of the world. One small bit of a province his people can barely tolerate isn't going to matter."

"You're wrong about that. The resources found in Britannia matter greatly to Rome," he said. "That's why they're here. You agreed with me that it was better to accept peace than to wage war. We've befriended those who might have been our enemies and the entire tribe has benefited as a result."

"That was the right decision," she said. "This isn't."

"It guarantees our line will continue to rule the Iceni. If I left half of my estate to you instead of the girls, they would eventually be at risk. The emperor could easily take everything from them."

"Because they're not men? Not warriors." She spat on the ground. "You disappoint me."

"I'm being realistic and practical. It's the only way to protect their futures."

Boudica turned her back to him and, in a single fluid motion, mounted one of the horses. She urged it forward and soon was ought of sight. I'd been watching her so intently I hadn't notice Prasutagus approaching me.

"Did you hear all of that?" he asked.

"Only the loud bits," I said. "I didn't mean to."

"You should've announced your presence."

"I don't like to get in the middle of domestic squabbles. They're none of my business."

"You must understand, what I'm doing will—"

"Stop there. I didn't hear enough to know what you're doing, so no explanations are required. You might think about going after her, though."

"I've other work I've already neglected too long." He started to walk away, but then came back to me. "You won't tell anyone what you've seen, will you?" It wasn't really a question.

"I've never liked gossip and don't plan on starting now."

"You've been a good friend to her. We both appreciate that."

Now, this was true enough, but he was saying it in an attempt to buy my silence. If I were the sort of person amenable to bribes, I'd want more than idle flattery. As I wasn't, I made a vague noise he could take as assent. Then, without another word, I leapt onto Aesu's back and went in search of my friend.

29

London

Knowing we wouldn't be able to confront Frances until the following day when she returned from Kew, we went across the hall, where Fenella confirmed what Mrs. Davies had told us. Ida had shown interest in the suffragette movement, but pulled back from it after her mother's warning.

"You can't blame her, can you?" Fenella asked us. "Of course we deserve the same rights as men and of course we should have the vote. We're human beings, aren't we? Citizens of Britain. I don't like being paid less simply because of my gender, but reality doesn't allow people like us to take risks like you lot. You've got enough money to keep yourselves safe and cozy, no matter what others know about your opinions. Ida and me, we didn't have that luxury."

"Are you at all acquainted with Miss Frances Price?" Colin asked. She shook her head. "Never heard the name."

"Were you aware Ida had this book?" I held up *Dreams*. "Miss Price gave it to her."

"Yes, I knew Ida had it because I saw it in her flat, but she never talked about it and I never asked. I'm not one for reading."

We thanked her and headed straight to see Lady Goldsborough. She was as mortified as one would expect to learn that her granddaughter's maid was a suffragette.

"Unless . . . is it possible we're overreacting to this entirely?" she asked. "Frances Price is no supporter of Mrs. Pankhurst. I can state that with absolute confidence. Could the book have been a little joke?"

"That seem unlikely," Colin said. "No doubt you've heard gossip about Boudica's Sisters."

"We all have, Mr. Hargreaves, but I don't see how that matters. Victoria would never have involved herself with such a group."

"Might she have been nominated as a candidate for membership?" I asked. "If, as rumor has it, they strive to persuade young ladies to come around to their cause, surely getting her on their side would've been a coup. She was the most celebrated debutante of the Season."

"I can assure you that if she had received such an offensive invitation, she would've told me straightaway. Further, there is no possibility that anyone could gain entrance into this household in the middle of the night without an alarm being raised."

"Everyone believes that about their homes, Lady Goldsborough, but the truth is a skilled burglar is far more capable than you'd think," Colin said.

"I would never be so derelict in my duties as to allow for the possibility that any of my granddaughters would be subjected to such a thing. I have two servants whose only job is to guard the corridor outside their bedrooms overnight."

Sebastian would've loved working around that. In general, he preferred avoiding corridors altogether, but there was no sense in sharing that with Lady Goldsborough.

"You don't think—" She knitted her brows. "It's too dreadful to consider, really, but could these ridiculous girls be responsible for Victoria's death? No, no, it can't be. Even if they've been corrupted by the likes of Mrs. Pankhurst, they all have too much breeding to stoop to murder."

"Unlikely though it seems, we shall nevertheless have to investigate the group," Colin said.

"I shouldn't pay them any attention," Lady Goldsborough said. "No doubt that's what they're after. It's all too much to bear. Of course you must investigate them, but I hate giving them anything they want."

"Given their efforts at secrecy, I doubt they're looking for publicity," I said.

Tears poured down her cheeks. "I don't care what they're looking for or what they get. Nothing can bring Victoria back. Our hopes are all ruined. Forgive me, I—" She gulped and blotted her face with a black-trimmed handkerchief.

"I apologize for our having distressed you," Colin said. "You need some peace now. There's only one thing further we need today, and that is to take another look at Miss Goldsborough's room. Would that be all right? You need not accompany us, we know the way and have already asked too much of you."

"Of course," she said. "Do whatever you must."

We went upstairs, but only after summoning Portia to sit with her grandmother and calling for tea. I felt a momentary pang of guilt opening the bedroom door, as if our work was intensifying the family's grief.

Inside, we went over every square inch of the space. Colin checked each floorboard and looked for false backs in the furniture. I flipped through the books and then sat down and read all of Victoria's correspondence. We removed the watercolor of Boudica in her chariot from the wall. Nothing was hidden in the frame or between the painting and its backing.

"I can't help but thinking this picture is significant," I said. "Frances Price painted it and it depicts Boudica. Surely that's no coincidence?"

"I agree. Let's hope Miss Price can enlighten us."

"We must be missing something," I said, sitting on the bed and feeling deflated. "I can't accept there's not more to find."

"Perhaps if Miss Goldsborough had another hiding place, she picked somewhere other than her own room, where no one would think to look."

"We can't ransack the entire house."

"We can do whatever is necessary," he said. "This is not like you, to hold back. Is it because of Lady Goldsborough's friendship with your mother?"

"I admit that has given me a certain amount of pause. Not enough that I would impede the investigation, but sufficient to make me feel awful some of the time." I hesitated and considered what to do next. "I have a strange idea."

"Go on," he said.

"Follow me."

We went back downstairs, to the piano in the music room. Victoria played often, but her sisters didn't share her talent. Portia sang, and the younger girls both played the harp. I lifted the lid of the bench.

At the bottom of the storage area, beneath scores of sheet music, was a single book: the second volume of William James Hickie's *The Comedies of Aristophanes*.

"Now things are getting interesting," I said. I flipped to the table of contents, found what I expected, and turned to a specific page before handing the book to Colin.

"*Lysistrata?*"

"Hardly a favorite of young ladies looking for a traditional marriage."

"You're correct, there," he said. "Lady Goldsborough would never approve."

That was quite an understatement. Lady Goldsborough would be shocked beyond measure at the thought of her granddaughter reading a play in which the women of Greece withhold conjugal pleasures from their husbands in an attempt to bring an end to the Peloponnesian War.

"We shall have to speak to Miss Price as soon as she's back from Kew tomorrow—I sent a note to her father asking for her train information," Colin said. "Until then, let's try and give our minds a rest. We'll spend the evening at home. You've run all over town today and must be exhausted."

"We're supposed to attend a ball."

"It can go on without us."

"I was looking forward to waltzing with you." I uttered the words without thinking and now almost shuddered. Waltzing had been Victoria's last action on earth.

"I know what you're thinking," Colin said. "Don't let a criminal's actions take pleasure away from something you love. It won't help. We'll go and we'll dance."

He was right. Going to the ball would also afford us the chance to speak to numerous people who'd been at Harrington House the night of the murder. I willed away the gloom beginning to consume me. If only emotions would bow to our wishes.

The party that evening was far too crowded. Our hostess, Mrs. Trumble, had a ballroom nearly as large as that at Devonshire House, but the heat of the day hadn't dissipated as the sun went down, and the crush of people combined with the heat of dancing made it almost unbearable.

I was wearing another of M. Poiret's Hellenistic creations, this one fashioned from the finest shell pink silk and trimmed with silver embroidery. Instead of my usual pompadour, I'd had Meg put my hair in a simple bun against the nape of my neck and tie a silver ribbon around my forehead as a nod to the styles favored by the ancient Greeks. Much to my surprise, I garnered a great deal of attention from the young ladies. They approached to compliment my gown, but that proved a ruse. They wanted to ask questions about Victoria's death.

All of them had been at Harrington House that night. Most claimed to have seen her collapse. None could offer any useful information. Hot and frustrated, I decided to retreat to the garden.

"Lady Emily, I did not realize you would be here tonight." If Lord Harrington was surprised, I was dumbfounded to see him. "I shouldn't have come, not so soon after . . . but I was starting to go mad locked away in the house."

"Locked away?" I asked, raising an eyebrow.

"Not literally, of course, but my mother makes it feel so. Mourning is dreadful." The only visual cue of his grief was a black armband.

"It's far easier for gentlemen than ladies. We don't have the option of escape. A husband can marry again as soon after his wife's death as he likes. Can you imagine a widow being allowed to do the same?"

"Ladies are in possession of wholly different temperaments to men," he said. "My understanding has always been that the rules are constructed to allow adequate time and space for comfort and consolation as is needed. The variation in standards is a nod to those different temperaments."

"I'm afraid there are some deep errors in judgment when it comes to assumptions about the temperament of ladies. I can assure you no one asked them what they'd prefer." He looked rather stricken as I spoke. "Please understand, I don't mean to scold you. I only wish we all shared the same freedom to act in a manner that best suits us."

"Sometimes we don't know what best suits us. Rules set by Society can help ladies when this occurs."

It wasn't the time to argue with him over the inanity of this statement, so I changed the subject. "I'm glad to see you," I said. "I wanted to ask you if you've heard these rumors swirling around about a group of suffragettes called Boudica's Sisters."

"The name is familiar, but I'm afraid I've not much interest in the suffragettes."

"Did Victoria?"

"Good heavens, no," he said. "We'd have been wholly incompatible if that were the case. Victoria and I both shared the belief that the social construct holding our world together is a delicate balance, one that's been perfected over the centuries. Men and women are not the same and, as such, ought to have separate spheres and expectations."

"You make it sound as if we ladies ought to be locked away in a harem."

"Not at all, I assure you! What a scandalous thing to say. You must be joking."

"Not entirely," I said. "Would it not be preferable for all individuals to be allowed to live in a manner that suits them? Why should one gender be kept separate from another?"

"It's always been that way, and it's working beautifully. There are things men are good at and things that we must leave to you ladies if we want them done well."

"Yet our society certainly doesn't value both equally."

He tugged at his collar. "This is an awfully serious subject for a ball."

I smiled. "Forgive me. It's this investigation. We've begun to suspect the suffragette movement may be connected in some way."

"Were they the ones—surely you don't think—I've never supported them, but I shouldn't have thought they'd turn to this kind of violence?"

"Did Victoria ever speak to you about them?"

"Not in any significant way. It's a topic that rears its head on occasion, but she always said she didn't comprehend it. She thought ladies who support it felt compelled to because they were being let down by their own husbands or fathers or brothers. When the system works properly, those individuals ensure the women in their lives are well taken care of."

"As you would have done for Victoria."

"Of course," he said. "I never gave her any cause to doubt that."

"Do you know Frances Price well?"

"She's Victoria's dearest friend, so, yes, to a degree. We all spent time together, but given the speed of our courtship, not enough that I could say we're close."

"Her mother is a prominent suffragette."

"Yes, we all had a good laugh about that. Frances escaped the affliction. She once suggested organizing an anti-suffrage march, but we all agreed it would only result in giving the dreadful women yet another opportunity to complain. They don't tolerate those who disagree with them, you know, so it's not as if one can have a reasonable discussion and hope to bring them round to what's right."

His every word irritated me, but I was careful not to let it show. "I apologize for bringing up the topic," I said. "It's bad form to discuss politics."

"A murder investigation requires we all accept that ordinary social intercourse may suffer until it's through. I do appreciate what you're doing. Dare I ask if you have a suspect in your sights?"

"Not yet, but as we continue to gather—" I stopped speaking because Cressida Wright was walking toward me, swaying and in danger of losing her balance.

"Lady Emily, could we please talk," she said, slurring her words. "Something has happened and I'm not sure—"

She collapsed, her body trembling, and then lay still on the ground, too still.

All the color drained from Lord Harrington's face. He dropped to his knees next to her. "It's just like Victoria. Exactly the same. She's dead."

30

Britannia

Boudica's skills as a horsewoman had improved with our acquaintance. As a result, it took me longer to catch up with her after she fled from her husband than it would've when we first met. She didn't notice me approaching from behind, so I shouted at her. She turned, saw me, and stopped. We both dismounted and tied the horses to a tree, not saying a word until we sat down on a moss-covered fallen log.

It was damp, of course, but that's what you get in Britannia. We were used to it.

"How did you find me?" she asked.

"I saw you and Prasutagus. When you raced off, I decided to follow."

"Did you hear his plan? He's leaving half of our kingdom to the girls and the other half to the Roman emperor."

"What about you?"

"My daughters will provide for me. That's not the issue."

"Why should Rome get a piece of our kingdom?" I asked.

"I knew you would understand. Giving them so much, or, for that matter, anything, will only make them want more. He's abandoning our chance of remaining independent."

I thought about this for a while before replying. "How independent are we, really? Don't think I'm being deliberately obtuse. Yes, we have our own king and queen, but if either of you wanted to adopt a policy the Romans found objectionable, do you think they'd stand by idly and say *Oh, our friends the Iceni are free to rule themselves?*"

"No, I've never thought that," she said. "When they first invaded, Prasutagus and I agreed no good would come of making them our enemies. We didn't want our people killed and our villages razed. Our land is too marshy for their mines, so we hoped we could generally escape their notice so long as we didn't trouble them."

"Yes, but we did rebel when they threatened to take our swords away from us."

"We did. That showed them we weren't submissive fools. They needed to see our strength to understand we wouldn't tolerate being denied our rights."

"We held our own well enough," I said.

"And afterward, they recognized Prasutagus as an ally."

"Or a client king."

"Yes, I suppose that's how they see it."

"It's the reality," I said. "We're a sovereign people in theory, so long as we don't test the bounds. If your husband hands them half of his kingdom, does sovereign in theory lose what little meaning it has?"

"I'm afraid it will. If I were the emperor, I'd take it as a sign of weakness, an indication that the Iceni can't stand up to Rome. Why settle for half when I could demand the rest?"

I wondered if we could stand up to Rome. The realist in me doubted so, but I also knew how fierce our warriors were. "What is Prasutagus's view?"

"That if he leaves half to me and half to our daughters, the Romans will attack straightaway. It will be viewed as an insult."

"They probably think a kingdom ruled by a woman, with only daughters as heirs, would be easily defeated. They're wrong there."

"That they are."

"Prasutagus isn't unhealthy. Maybe you don't need to worry about this for a while," I said.

"He's not young and we never know how long we have on this earth. It's always a mistake to assume we have time. He needs to settle this matter."

"I didn't hear all that much of your conversation, but it sounded to me like he thinks it is settled."

"He will come to see the error of his ways."

31

London

"She's dead." Lord Harrington kept repeating the words, over and over. I knelt next to him and felt for Cressida's pulse; she had none. The others who'd retreated to the garden for quiet conversation or a bit of clandestine privacy heard the commotion and started to gather around us.

"Go find my husband, now," I ordered the marquess. "There's nothing more you can do here." He was reliving the trauma of losing his fiancée; giving him a simple task might keep him from immediately sinking into despair. A man stepped forward, saying he was a physician. I moved aside so he could examine Cressida, but I knew there was no hope. He confirmed what I'd already ascertained. She was gone.

Colin reached me quickly. Lord Harrington was with him, but he hung back, looking ill. I sent the doctor to him.

"This time there will be no assumption of a natural death," I said to my husband.

"I've already ensured that no one will be allowed to leave the house," Colin said. "Tell me exactly what happened."

"I was talking to Lord Harrington and Cressida staggered toward us. It was evident there was something desperately wrong with her. She wanted to speak to me. She said my name, but before she could get much else out, she fell to the ground and was dead almost instantly."

The news of the tragedy made its way through the guests in a flash. Colin removed his jacket and placed it gently over Cressida's body, so the gathering crowd could not gawk at her. A man pushed forward and grabbed my husband by the arm.

"What has happened to my little girl?" He pulled the jacket away from her face, only for a moment, then replaced it and took the body in his arms. "Get these people away from her. This is no spectacle to watch. Where is my wife? I must speak to my wife."

"Harrington!" Colin called. The marquess had declined the physician's services and was standing apart from us looking lost. "Send someone to fetch Mrs. Wright. Then, I need you to ensure that no gawkers come within thirty feet of this spot. Can you assist me with both of those things?" He, too, thought the man was in need of occupation.

This prompted the marquess to snap to attention, and soon he had the onlookers held well at bay. There were far too many people in the house for us to deal with them all on our own. My husband notified Scotland Yard, and soon the place was teeming with officers.

I spoke to Cressida's distraught parents in Mr. Trumble's study, a small, comfortable room decorated in the manner of a gentleman's club. After offering my condolences, pouring them both brandies, and giving the usual apology for having to question them in the midst of such a terrible tragedy, I asked what time they and their daughter arrived at the ball.

"We were here by half eight," Mr. Wright said. It was barely nine thirty now. If, like Victoria, Cressida had died from yew poisoning, it was likely she'd ingested it before having left home.

"Did anything unusual happen before you set off to come here?"

"Not at all. The entire day was perfectly ordinary. Cressida rode on Rotten Row in the morning. I lunched at my club. We had tea before dressing for the ball."

"And you, Mrs. Wright?" I asked.

"I helped Cressida decide which gown to wear this evening and directed her as to what jewelry would be most appropriate for the occasion. She had a tendency to be rather too flashy."

The woman might rival my mother when it came to criticizing daughters. "Did Cressida leave the house after she came back from riding?" I asked.

"I couldn't say for sure. I was gone for much of the afternoon," her father said. "She was home when I returned."

"She did not leave again." Her mother scowled. "I forbade it. I wanted her well rested for the ball. This is her second Season. She needs to catch a husband."

She was a difficult woman, but her use of the present tense broke my heart. "Did she have any callers?"

"Several people called, but I ordered our butler to send them away," she said. "As I've already told you, I wanted her to be at her best tonight."

"Your daughter's death was strikingly similar to Miss Goldsborough's. Lord Harrington witnessed both events and confirmed that they transpired in the same way."

"Then isn't it obvious he's behind both murders?" Mrs. Wright said.

"Not necessarily. According to the coroner, yew is a poison that doesn't act instantly. It can take an hour or longer for symptoms to develop depending on the amount given to the victim."

"If it's even remotely possible he did it, he should be arrested at once," Mr. Wright said. "The man has the resources to flee and disappear."

"Mr. Hargreaves and I shan't allow that to happen. Do you believe Lord Harrington had a motive to want your daughter dead?"

Mr. Wright stared at the floor and rotated the brandy glass in his hand. He ground his teeth. "It pains me to admit, but Cressida gave him a rather tough time. He could well have been irritated with her."

"Irritated?" His wife glared at him. "If her behavior had been more civilized, we might not be sitting here now."

"Are you suggesting she brought this on herself?" I asked.

"In a manner of speaking, yes." She turned to me. "None of this would have happened if her father hadn't indulged her so recklessly. But he did, and her outrageous forwardness put off Lord Harrington. If she'd acted in the manner a well-bred young lady ought to, perhaps she wouldn't have driven him away. In that case, she would already be a respectable married woman and not a target for random murderers."

"What, specifically, did she do?" I asked.

"I refuse to go into details. You know as well as the rest of Society she's been throwing herself at him since she came out."

"That's hardly grounds for murder. Is there anyone else who disliked her or felt threatened by her?"

"She wasn't in the position to threaten anyone," her father said. "She's—she was—a typical young lady. What could she do? Steal someone's dance partner? Insult their fashion choices? Either of those things could wound a person with a fragile ego, but prompt them to commit murder? I think not. Cressida may have been silly on occasion, but she was never vicious."

"Did she have opinions on the suffragette movement?"

Mrs. Wright snorted. "She had no interest in anything political."

"Do you know if she was invited to join Boudica's Sisters?"

"She certainly never mentioned it to me. If she had, I would've absolutely forbidden it."

"Cressida was not connected to any suffragette group," her father said. "My wife may scold me for indulging her, but my intent was to give her control over significant decisions in her own life. This led to my discussing suffrage with her. She simply wasn't interested in it."

"You discussed this with her?" Mrs. Wright had turned bright red. "It's a wonder calamity didn't befall her sooner. That her own father would encourage such outrageous—"

"For the moment, let's concern ourselves with what must be done immediately, given the tragic circumstances," I said. "If neither of you objects, I would like to speak to your servants and look through your daughter's room. There may be a clue in her correspondence or possessions that points us toward whoever did this to her."

"Whatever you need," Mr. Wright said. "I'll send word to my butler immediately and tell him you're to have full access to the house and staff. We shan't go home until Cressida is . . ." His voice trailed off.

THE SISTERHOOD

Murder is a crime with far too many victims, both the living and the dead. Colin and I had to stop the perpetrator from striking again.

My husband continued his interviews of the Trumbles' guests while I went to the Wrights' house. Searching Cressida's room yielded gold: a note asking her to come to the center of Grosvenor Square an hour before she arrived at the Trumbles' ball. It stated that the sender had information about Lord Harrington that would bring her deep happiness and was signed *A friend who cares*. Her maid confirmed that she left the house, was gone for less than a quarter of an hour, and returned in high spirits.

"That must be when she was given the poison," I said to Colin the next morning as we waited at Paddington Station for Frances Price to arrive on the train from Kew. I'd fallen asleep before he returned home.

"There's no chance Harrington sent for her," my husband said. "He didn't want anything to do with her."

"Perhaps the strain of Victoria's death left him unhinged. He may have felt that, with his fiancée gone, Cressida would start vying for his attention again, something he couldn't bear to face. So he summoned her and eliminated the problem."

"If he killed Cressida, are we to believe he killed Victoria as well? If not, we'd be looking for two separate murderers. I don't think that's likely."

"Once again you're relying on intuition rather than evidence," I said. "Perhaps my influence is finally starting to rub off on you. I'm inclined to agree with you, however, primarily because I don't believe he had any reason to want Victoria dead. He was besotted with her."

"Yet he is the only thread we've found between the two girls. I don't know what to make of that."

"What if both of them were killed in an attempt to punish him?"

"For that theory to hold water, Harrington would've had to feel more warmly toward Miss Wright."

The train from Kew came to a stop along the platform. Frances descended from a second-class carriage, carrying a small case, just the size for an overnight stay. Colin called to her. She looked startled when she saw us.

"Do please tell me nothing else terrible has happened," she said. Interesting her thoughts went there. It made me wonder if she'd really been in Kew, or if it had been a conveniently staged alibi. My imagination was getting the better of me. We didn't believe there were two killers, and there was nothing to suggest she wanted her best friend dead.

"Cressida Wright has been murdered." I watched her as she listened to my words. A ripple of surprise crossed her face. Was it sincere?

"Good heavens, that's awful. What happened?"

Colin gave her a terse account of what had transpired at the Trumbles' ball. "It's evident you've not been straight with us," he said once he'd finished. "Now a second young lady is dead. Unless you'd like to see a third succumb to the same fate, it's time you start telling the truth."

I held Ida's copy of *Dreams* and Victoria's Aristophanes up to her face. "Do you recognize these?" I asked.

"Oh dear." She looked utterly deflated. "I think perhaps we'd better find somewhere to sit. What I have to say may complicate things."

We took the first unoccupied bench we could find in the station. It was another hot day, and an oppressive mixture of smoke and steam coming from the locomotives filled the air.

"I apologize for not having been entirely honest with you," Frances said. "Sometimes, it's hard to know what to do in these situations. I'm well aware of Boudica's Sisters. Victoria and I founded the organization."

32

Britannia

Boudica wanted to stay away from Venta Icenorum overnight. She thought it would send a message to Prasutagus. I agreed it would, but told her I wasn't keen on the idea of sleeping in the open with no food or supplies. She saw the wisdom in this. We rode back, but instead of going to the palace, she came to my house.

This sent my mother into a flurry. It also started the neighbors talking. Before long, Duro showed up, acting like he'd been planning to dine with us. My father went along with his scheme. I half expected them to pull my friend into a discussion of our possible marriage. Fortunately, her mind was on other things.

"Duro, do you think we could defeat the Romans?" she asked.

"Of course, Majesty. There are no finer warriors than the Iceni."

"I'm not looking for pretty answers that mean nothing," she said. "Could we defeat them?"

He considered the question. "In the right circumstances, yes."

"What would those be?" she asked.

"We'd have to strike first and catch them by surprise. The enterprise would have to be planned so as to take advantage of natural geography, otherwise their superior numbers could crush us. That's the primary problem. They've far more resources than we do."

"Would we stand a chance if they attacked us?" she asked.

"A chance, yes, but not much more than that," he said. "Letting them choose the time and place of battle would be a mistake. Do you expect them to attack? I had no idea Prasutagus was having problems with them. Have we done something to provoke them?"

"We most certainly have not, but I'm not convinced that means we're safe." She folded her arms.

"I've seen no sign to suggest they're displeased with their relationship with us," Duro said.

"Why would they be?" my father asked. "We trade with them and give them no trouble. So far as they're concerned, we learned our lesson after our little rebellion. There's been no hostility since Prasutagus made peace with them."

"What do you think would happen if he died?" I asked. "That's what we need to be asking ourselves. Boudica is right to be looking to the future. Their alliance is with Prasutagus, not the tribe."

"Do you plan on poisoning your husband, Your Majesty?" Duro asked and then laughed. "I'm teasing, of course."

"It's no joking matter," she said. "We are all aware of how fragile life can be. If something were to happen to him, I want to be prepared."

"I can't imagine there will be any problem so long as you swear your allegiance to Rome as our queen," my mother said.

"You're most likely right," she said. Obviously, she didn't want to tell them about her husband's will. "Even so, it pays to know our strength. Duro, will you consider the best strategy we could employ should it become necessary? Speak to no one else about it but me. I ask all of you here to keep my secret."

"Even from Prasutagus?" Duro asked.

"There's no need to cause him distress," she said. "As you've suggested, these plans won't ever come into play during his lifetime. He has enough burden to carry without worrying about what will happen when he's gone."

With that, she got up and left, not saying another word. As she moved across the house to the door, she stood taller than I'd seen her before, with her shoulders flung back and her expression cold. She was the picture of a warrior, a woman unafraid to take on the might of Rome.

33

London

"You and Victoria founded Boudica's Sisters?" I asked Frances. I looked at my husband. Anger burned in his dark eyes.

"This goes beyond being not entirely honest, Miss Price," he said, "and, contrary to your statement, one does know what to do in these situations. You've stood in the way of our finding your friend's killer and may have paved the way for Miss Wright to be murdered. You have a great deal to answer for."

"I didn't dare tell you about our work. It would've been a betrayal of Victoria and everything we've strived to achieve. I promise you, it's nothing to do with her death. Cressida being the second victim proves that."

"How so?" I asked.

"She wasn't involved with us. She's never shown the slightest interest in suffrage. We didn't consider nominating her for membership. Anything she knew about us can only be what she heard from dodgy rumors."

"Am I correct to surmise that *Lysistrata* provides the inspiration for your group?" I asked. "You seek Society marriages and, once in them, plan to work on your husbands to see the error of their ways when it comes to women's rights?"

"You see straight to the point," she said. "That's why Victoria had to marry Peregrine. To convert a man of that rank and influence to our point of view would be an enormous coup. Mrs. Pankhurst and her lot are bent on becoming increasingly militant, but Victoria and I have long believed a more subtle, subversive tactic would prove superior. Social change comes slowly, and it's only when those in the highest positions begin to support it that there's hope for a wholesale shift in the way people think."

"Hence your own interest in Oscar Tenley?" Colin asked.

"Yes."

"Who else is in your group and what husbands are they vying for?" I asked.

"No one else was yet set to make a match this Season," she said. "We've only just begun recruiting members. Our idea was not to present ourselves as radical suffragettes. Rather, we told a select group of young ladies we would help them improve their prospects on the marriage market. The first step in convincing them was to make spectacular matches ourselves. We thought a secret club would appeal to them and that once they'd joined, we'd slowly begin to educate them about women's rights. The goal was to have a stable of young ladies poised to make brilliant marriages and influence their hapless husbands from the inside. We never thought this alone would win us the right to vote, but alongside what other groups are doing, it could make an enormous difference. We chose the name Boudica's

Sisters because if Mrs. Pankhurst and the Women's Social and Political Union are warriors akin to Boudica, we are like that ancient queen's more peaceful siblings."

It was a fascinating scheme. I quite admired it. The opinions of those closest to us often have the strongest influence. That, coupled with a willingness to demand their husbands' support, taking inspiration from *Lysistrata* if necessary, could well work. Men are, after all, susceptible to the charms of ladies. It was, of course, manipulative and underhanded as well, and I could never support the idea of marrying someone under false pretenses. However, many—if not most—Society matches were based on shakier ground.

"Very clever in theory," I said, "but it appears your membership is not so discreet as you'd like. All of London knows Boudica's Sisters are suffragettes."

"Yes, that's been rather disappointing, but it won't negatively impact us in the long run. After all, we are all committed to giving every appearance of being dedicated to the Establishment. Our husbands won't have the slightest clue as to our true beliefs until it's too late. Men are shockingly easy to manipulate if one knows how to do it."

"Oscar Tenley wasn't a sure bet for you, was he?" I asked. "He'd been wooing Cressida Wright as well. Convenient that she's now dead, isn't it?"

Frances shot to her feet. "I had nothing to do with that. If Oscar chose her, I would've moved on to someone else. There are plenty of influential bachelors in England. It's not as if I'd be hurt if he rejected me."

"Not hurt, no, but thwarted in pursuit of a cause about which you feel strongly," Colin said. "That's a position I find a far more viable motive for murder than romantic disappointment."

She looked genuinely scared, but only for a moment. "I didn't kill Cressida. Further, obviously whoever murdered her did the same to Victoria and no one could possibly believe I would ever have harmed her." She sounded almost smug.

"Cressida was in love with Lord Harrington," I said. "Perhaps she eliminated her rival, and when you realized this, you decided to take revenge."

"I've been in Kew!"

"Yes, convenient, isn't it?" Now that she had vacated her seat, Colin, who'd been standing in front of the bench sat down next to me, leaned back, and crossed his legs. "We shall confirm that. It's only a short distance from town. You could easily have made a brief return."

"I didn't, I swear."

"Was Portia involved?" I asked.

"No. Victoria was adamant that none of her sisters should know anything about it."

"What about your parents?" Colin asked. "Are they aware?"

"No," she said. "Because we anticipated that some information was bound to leak out about the group, we had to be careful no one could tie us to it. If even our families believed we objected to suffrage, that would put us in a stronger position."

"If you expected breaches in confidence, surely you knew your identities might be exposed," Colin said.

"No." Her voice was clipped, confident. "Being well aware of young ladies' propensity for gossip, we made it clear that if even a single name of any of our members came out, we would ruin the entire group socially. Fear of rumor is a powerful thing. We all know how fragile a girl's reputation is."

What a chilling thought. No doubt such a threat would keep

their members in check. "That's out the window now," I said. "We'll need all the names, immediately."

"Lady Emily, please, don't ask me to commit such wholesale betrayal. Anything but that. I've guaranteed them confidentiality."

"Confidentiality is wholly incompatible with murder investigations," Colin said. "The names. Now."

Frances identified her compatriots; she had no other viable choice. Then, before we started to make our way down the list, we escorted her to her parents' house, a short walk from the station, and enlightened them as to their daughter's activities. They reacted with pride. That emotion shifted when we told them she was also a suspect in Cressida Wright's murder.

"I need your word, Price, that you won't let her leave town," Colin said. "I shan't send for the police so long as you guarantee me that."

Needless to say, he agreed.

We didn't have enough evidence to have her arrested, but they weren't to know that. They were afraid and would keep Frances in line.

It didn't take us long to interview the remaining members of Boudica's Sisters. There were only three; Sebastian had been honest about the number of invitations he'd delivered. Each of them was from a family of good reputation and decent wealth and each was a stunning beauty. Victoria and Frances had determined the latter was the easiest way to ensure they could catch a gentleman's attention. Once he expressed interest, they could deploy the tactics they'd taught their girls to secure their targets' affections.

We'd decided to preserve the anonymity of the members. At the moment, there was no reason not to, and doing so encouraged them to be open with us. We had called on them each one after another, and they all adored Colin on sight. The instant he vowed to protect their privacy, they would've done anything for him. Anyone who claims only we ladies are judged by our physical appearance isn't paying attention.

"I'd hoped they would prove more interesting than they did," Colin said after we'd finished and were making our way along Piccadilly. "I'm not convinced any of them could be turned into dedicated suffragettes. They're after spectacular matches, nothing more."

"It's early days, my dear. Given time and adequate indoctrination, anything is possible. Remember, they've been propagandized to believe the Establishment has their best interests at heart."

Most of what the three girls had to say was insignificant. They each confirmed what Frances had told us about the promise of assisting them in securing a good match. None was yet aware of the longer-term strategy of the group, but they all showed an openness to the concept of women's suffrage. The conversations didn't reveal anything pertinent to our investigations until our final interviewee mentioned that Lionel Morgan had made an unsuccessful bid for Cressida Wright's hand.

"Cressida never mentioned Mr. Morgan to me," I said. We were now skirting Green Park. "It's likely she never gave him the slightest consideration. She was still in love with Lord Harrington."

"Although, before Miss Goldsborough's death, she was prepared to move on with Tenley."

"Mr. Morgan would have never stood a chance next to his fortune."

"Unless she liked him," Colin said. "She wouldn't have needed his money."

"But he needed hers. Maybe her refusal put him in a murderous rage."

"My dear, a murderous rage must be acted upon immediately. It results in a crime of passion, not brewing yew leaves to bring to a clandestine rendezvous in Grosvenor Square."

"I didn't mean it literally," I said. "Her rejection gives him motive. His proposal could've been a last chance for financial rescue. When his hopes were dashed, and he realized Victoria might convince Lord Harrington to stop loaning him money, he became desperate. He could think of no way forward but to kill her."

"It makes for a nice fiction, but why, then, would he go back so much later and kill Miss Wright?" Colin asked.

"I haven't figured that out yet. Give me time." I stopped and turned to face my husband. "What if Cressida had loaned him money, perhaps because she felt bad turning down his offer? He could've come back for more, she refused his request, and he killed her."

"It's plausible."

"Let's see what Mr. Wright knows," I said.

Instead of continuing on toward Park Lane, we crossed the road, turned in to Half Moon Street, and, walking quickly, were in Grosvenor Square in almost no time. The butler admitted us and took us to the drawing room where I'd met with Cressida. Gone now were the mountainous arrangements of pink roses. Lilies had replaced them, and in such quantity that their perfume overwhelmed the space despite its large size. The curtains were closed; the clock was stopped; and every piece of furniture had been draped in black crêpe.

Mr. Wright looked almost hopeful when he entered the room and walked toward us. He apologized on behalf of his wife, who was in no state to accept visitors. "Dare I conclude you've already identified the beast who took my darling Cressida from me?"

"Not yet," Colin said, "but we are pursuing several leads. I understand Lionel Morgan proposed to your daughter."

"Yes, some weeks back, I can't remember exactly," Mr. Wright said. "I didn't think he'd actually go through with it. He came to me at my club and asked permission. I'm afraid I couldn't help but laugh. I gave him my blessing, only because I knew she'd never accept him, but I told him it was futile. The man had no chance with a girl like her."

"Why was that?" I asked.

"Cressida was made for better," Mr. Wright said. "I had already irrevocably settled upon her a sizable fortune, one that she would have control of apart from her husband, once she was married. There was more to come, of course, when she wed, but I wanted her to know she would always be financially independent."

"That would've made it possible for her to choose a spouse others wouldn't consider," Colin said.

"I wanted her to find happiness, whatever form it took. I didn't view this as taking an unreasonable risk. Cressida was a sensible girl. She never would've chosen someone like Morgan. He's an utter wastrel, despite his superficial charm. He's handsome enough, I suppose, but anyone close to him who isn't a fool couldn't avoid noticing he's got a gambling problem. My daughter was no fool."

"No, she certainly was not," I said. "She was, however, kind and generous. Might she have softened the blow of her rejection by offering him a loan?"

"I cannot conceive of her doing something so stupid."

"Is it impossible?" Colin asked.

Mr. Wright scowled. "No, it's not. If you'd like, I shall check her banking records and see what I can find."

"Did the two of you discuss Mr. Morgan's proposal?" I asked.

"We did. She found it shockingly hilarious," he said. "She admitted she laughed when he asked her to do him the honor of becoming his wife. That couldn't have been good for his ego. Might it have driven him to kill her?"

"It gives him motive," I said. "Do let us know what you discover at the bank as soon as possible. In the meantime, we'll speak to Mr. Morgan."

34

Britannia

For a few days, I buzzed with unexpected energy, brought on from having watched Boudica take action to gain control over her future. Then, like most things, its impact began to fade and life returned to normal. I read Ovid. I took walks with Duro. I even started to like him, a little, but I had come no closer to accepting his offer of marriage. My mother agreed to remove her spurious deadline of deciding in a week. I had some breathing room.

I also had Gaius, and our relationship was becoming more complicated.

He was building a villa not far from the Roman fort where he served. It was almost done. Structurally, it was complete. All that remained were decorative elements. A mosaic here, a wall painting there.

"It's not as if I live in a mud hut, but this is like nothing I've ever seen." We'd ridden there together so he could show off the place.

The entrance was deceptively simple. A small room with a plain cement floor opened onto the street. It was the perfect place to shed wet garments or boots. Beyond stood a wide corridor skirting an enormous courtyard and containing doors leading to all the other rooms.

"There will be paintings all along the corridor wall," he said. "Forest scenes, so it will be as if you're outside when you're in. Each room will have a mosaic floor." He led me into the first one. A man was crouched down, carefully placing tiny pieces of black and white stones in an intricate pattern.

"There's a hypocaust beneath the entire structure so I'll have underfloor heating throughout. Some consider that excessive, but I've been in Britannia long enough to understand the necessity of it."

"Does this mean you plan to stay here permanently?" I asked.

"I'll stay as long as the emperor requires me to."

"You prefer Rome."

"If you'd been there, you wouldn't ask the question."

We moved into the largest room in the villa. Here, the wall paintings were already finished. The background was bloodred on the top two-thirds and black beneath. Painted columns formed sections in the walls, and a golden band rimmed the room just below the ceiling.

The room had no window and was lit only by oil lamps. It reminded me a bit of a cave. A nice cave, obviously, but still. A cave.

"You're beautiful in this light," Gaius said. He moved closer to me and touched my hand. "Your skin is like cream."

I took a step back. "Let's not forget your friend laying mosaic in the other room."

"Is that your only objection?" he asked.

"The only one I need to call on right now."

"Could you see yourself in a house like this?"

"With you, or in general?" The air was heavy with possibility. Until he spoke.

"In general." He turned away from me and inspected some detail of the paint. "I imagine everyone in Britannia will adopt our style of building before long. It's far more comfortable than what you're used to."

"Heating isn't everything," I said.

"I'm sorry." He came back. "You act on me like nothing I've ever experienced. It's no secret I admire you, your quick wit and your intellect. I can no longer deny it's more than just that. Your beauty intoxicates me."

What could any reasonable person do in response to this other than laugh? Loudly. And for a long, long time. Tears came to my eyes. I doubled over. My gut ached.

"Not the reaction I'd hoped for," he said.

"Sorry." I wasn't. What did he expect? "Ovid wouldn't give you high marks for your technique. My beauty intoxicates you?" I started to laugh again. This time, he joined me.

"Ridiculous, yes," he said, gasping for breath.

"If that sort of thing works with the ladies in Rome, I'd say you're better off here. No one should be satisfied with a person who'd fall for that kind of drivel."

Our eyes met and we held each other's gaze for long enough that I started to feel uncomfortable. Well, maybe not quite uncomfortable. More like anxious. But not in a bad way. A way that intrigued me. Excited me. Tempted me.

35

London

Colin and I called on Mr. Morgan in his Knightsbridge house. It was dated and rather drab, but clean and serviceable, more spacious than it might have been, and located only a short stroll from Hyde Park. Empty spaces on the walls of the drawing room were a clue to where his money came from. There was a time, before I was born, when the Morgans were known for their collection of Old Master paintings. Whatever art they'd put in this house, even if it was destined for a younger son, would not have been inconsequential.

"I choose to spend my money on things other than creature comforts," he said, as he invited us to sit. I suspected the maid who answered the door was one of a very small household staff. She was young and doubtless inexperienced and, hence, wouldn't command much of a wage. "When I marry, I shall have to do otherwise. A wife requires a higher standard of living. I'm surprised to see you here. I presume this is not a social call."

"You're right on that count," Colin said. "Surely you've heard what happened to Cressida Wright?"

"An awful business," he said. "I always liked her. She had a capital sense of humor and was always game for a laugh. There aren't enough girls in England like that these days. It's a terrible shame what happened to her."

"You weren't at the ball," I said. "Why not?"

"I had a spot of trouble on the way there." There was a small bruise visible on his left cheek. "I'm afraid some of my associates are less than thrilled with me. They ambushed me en route and after they were through sending their pointed message, I came home. I wish I hadn't. If I'd been there, then perhaps . . ."

"Perhaps what?" I asked.

"If I'd been there with Cressida, maybe this wouldn't have happened."

"Had you gone, is there any reason to think she would've spent any time in proximity to you?" Colin asked. "I understand she refused a proposal of marriage from you, and not in a particularly kind fashion."

Mr. Morgan flung his arms into the air. "I can see why one might read the situation in such a way, but it wasn't like that between us at all. I never really believed she'd agree to marry me, but figured it was worth a try. We got on well and I amused her. She was aware of my financial difficulties, but never held them against me."

"Did she offer any assistance?" I asked.

"No, and if she had, I would've refused. What kind of gentleman would I be if I took money from well-bred young ladies?"

"Wright told us she laughed at your offer," Colin said. "That must have angered you."

"I won't claim it made me feel good, but I'd be lying if I said it took me by surprise. There had always been a frisson between us. We liked to flirt and to tease each other. She didn't exhibit a serious side with me. Why shouldn't she laugh at something she found ridiculous?"

"When you dined with us, you mentioned that you and your father have opposing views when it comes to potential brides," I said. "Did he approve of Miss Wright?"

"He bloody well would've if she'd said yes. Forgive me, Lady Emily. The man never fails to draw out the worst from me. I didn't let on to him my plan to propose. He would've laughed ten times harder than she did, and his ridicule is always meant to wound."

"Miss Wright's wasn't?" Colin asked.

"Sink me, no! We understood each other too well for that."

"I'm not convinced you understood her well at all if you didn't anticipate how misguided proposing was," I said.

"It wasn't misguided in the least. I asked, she refused. We went on as before. I wasn't wounded to the quick or anything so dramatic."

"We know Lord Harrington has provided loans for you in the past," Colin said. "What's the status of your repayment?"

"Look here, Hargreaves, that's nobody's business but my own."

"Surely Lord Harrington's as well," I said.

"Yes, yes," he said, agitated.

"Are you hoping for more assistance from him in the future?" I asked. "I can't help but wonder if his fiancée's death opens the door for just that."

He tugged at his collar and fidgeted in his seat. "If you're implying Miss Goldsborough stood in the way of that, you're wrong. Harrington would never discuss business with a lady."

"Even his wife?" Colin asked.

"Especially his wife. Or fiancée. To do so would be shockingly inappropriate. A lady knows her husband will take care of her. Beyond that, the details must be of no consequence to her."

"Perhaps Miss Goldsborough felt differently on the subject," Colin said.

"I assure you, if she did, Harrington wouldn't have remained engaged to her. He's as traditional as they come. He'd never tolerate nonsense from his intended bride."

"Speaking of Miss Goldsborough reminds me of something," I said. "Did you ever meet her maid, Ida Davies?"

"Her maid?" He pulled a face. "I can't fathom how that would ever have come to pass. Are you suggesting I was skulking about Miss Goldsborough's bedchamber?"

"Absolutely not," I said, hoping I was giving the appearance of abject horror. "It's only that I've heard it said Ida was something of a suffragette. I wondered if Miss Goldsborough knew?"

"It hardly matters now, does it?" Mr. Morgan asked. "Sadly, the question is moot."

When we returned to Park Lane, a wooden crate approximately three feet square was waiting for me on the center of my desk in the library. I rang for Davis and asked him who had delivered it. He blanched.

"Madam, I was not aware this had arrived," he said. "I can assure you, it was not received through any normal channel."

Colin inspected it. "It's not fastened on top. Capet must have brought it and wanted to ensure you could open it with ease."

"I am most distressed that this person—for he is no gentleman—continues to bother you, madam," Davis said. "Is there any action you would like me to take to prevent his attentions?"

"He's a pest, but a harmless one," I said. "Don't trouble yourself over it, Davis." He gave a neat bow before retreating from the room, but I could see he wasn't happy with my answer.

I looked into the now-open crate. A folded note card sat on top of a heap of cotton wool. On it was written two lines from the Greek elegiac poet Theognis:

ῥήιον ἐξ ἀγαθοῦ θεῖναι κακὸν ἢ 'κ κακοῦ
ἐσθλόν.
—μή με δίδασκ'· οὔτοι τηλίκος εἰμὶ μαθεῖν.

It is easier to make bad from good than good from bad.
—Don't try to teach me; I'm too old to learn.

Beneath this was a single line: *Forgive me.*

"Forgive him?" Colin asked. "For what first? Him being a thief? Lying to you? Hiding the truth about Boudica's Sisters?"

I tossed the note aside. "Does it matter? Help me get whatever it is out."

He did. Unwrapping the cotton wool revealed an ancient amphora, approximately a foot and a half high, covered in a charming octopus design. It was Minoan, probably from around 1500 BC, and would've been made in Crete.

"You can't keep it," Colin said.

I sighed. "No, I can't, not unless Sebastian tells us where it came from."

"Even if he did, you couldn't believe him."

"What a pity." I positioned the vase on a table between two chairs near the fireplace. It was as if the potter who'd created it had this very space in mind. I might not be able to accept the gift, but that wouldn't stop me from appreciating it for the brief time it was in my possession. I flung myself onto one of the chairs. "What are your thoughts about Mr. Morgan?"

"I don't accept his claim that Miss Wright's rejection didn't sting and I don't believe he would've refused financial help from her."

"And the bruise on his face?"

"If thugs sent by a creditor attacked him, they would've done a more thorough job, not left him with a single, smallish mark."

"What connects Victoria and Cressida?" I asked.

"They both wanted to marry Harrington. One, to forward her political agenda, the other for love."

"If Lord Harrington learned of Victoria's social views, he would've ended the engagement, but would it make him want her dead?"

"That seems unlikely, but not impossible."

"Mr. Morgan has stronger motives for both crimes," I said. "We need to know if Victoria asked her fiancé to sever financial ties with him. It's time we speak to the marquess again."

I was glad Curzon Street was a short distance from our house. One expects to be run ragged during the Season, but usually for more pleasant reasons. Exhaustion from excessive waltzing is preferable to that caused by one's inability to identify a murderer. Cressida's death pressed hard on me. Every day that passed gave the murderer opportunity to strike again.

Lord Harrington was home, seated at a small, round, iron table in the garden, with a cup of tea and a copy of a French book whose author, Maurice Leblanc, I had encountered years ago in Normandy in the midst of a case that involved Sebastian. Leblanc, who'd found his exploits charming, promised to immortalize him in fiction. Now, I saw the result: *Arsène Lupin, gentleman-cambrioleur.* Gentleman thief, indeed.

"Where did you get that?" I asked, after he'd received us and sent for more tea. "Is it new?"

"It was only just published," Lord Harrington said. "Oddly enough, it was pushed through my mail slot this morning. It's a most entertaining read, short stories about an unbeatable thief and master of disguise."

There could be no doubt as to the identity of the person who had delivered it. "I'm glad you've found distraction in the midst of so much sorrow." My tone was more harsh than I'd intended.

He put the book down and stared at me. "I cannot make out whether you mean that sincerely or if it's a barb."

"It is sincere," I said. "If you've picked up on my irritation, you should know it's due to my knowledge of who must've given you the book, not anything to do with you."

"How can you possibly know who gave it to me?" he asked.

"It's from the same person who stole your mother's tiara," Colin said. "The character is based on him."

"No, is it? I say, that's rather splendid. Almost makes me forgive him for the theft. You're sure?"

"Absolutely sure," I said.

"I've heard nothing from the police about all that, the tiara, that is. I don't suppose they'll ever recover it. But if you know the bloke's identity, perhaps you could persuade him to do the right thing and return it."

"If only that were possible," I said. Colin and I had, of course, shared everything we knew with the police. The detective in charge of investigating the theft had dismissed it all out of hand, saying it might make for sensational fiction, but that there are no thieves of that sort in real life. Further, he was convinced the murderer and the thief were the same person, and, as the murder investigation was ours, he had little interest in the rest.

"I don't care much about the tiara. Mother has plenty of other jewels. What matters is Victoria. What is the status of your investigation into her death?"

"We're continuing to gather evidence," I said. "Was she aware that you had loaned Lionel Morgan a great deal of money?"

"Of course not. Why would she be?"

"It's a substantial sum."

"Yes, but that's my business. She would never have needed to concern herself with such things."

"So she never told you to stop offering Morgan assistance?" Colin asked.

"No. She knew nothing about what I'd done."

That sank Mr. Morgan's motive for wanting her dead.

"The coroner has confirmed Cressida Wright was killed by a brew of yew leaves, just like Victoria," I said. "The two weren't friends, were they?"

"You know the answer to that question, Lady Emily. Cressida liked to think of them as rivals. Victoria never thought of Cressida at all."

"What was your view of the situation?" Colin asked.

"I know my own feelings well enough to state unequivocally that they weren't rivals. Cressida is . . . well . . . I suppose there's no polite way to put it. She was beyond persistent. I found it extremely off-putting."

"You didn't encourage her?" I asked.

"Never." He looked away from me.

"The impression I had was that you enjoyed her attentions enough to take certain liberties with her," I said.

"Look here, I am not going to discuss anything of the sort. To do so would be a grotesque breach of confidence."

"Not in the current context," Colin said. "We're not after details, but we do know you didn't reject all of her advances."

"Did she tell you that?" he asked.

"She did," I said.

"Well, then, I suppose there's no point denying it. We shared a marginally pleasant interlude, but it did not lead to a deeper emotional connection. Afterward, when I realized I could not summon the sort of feelings she longed for me to have, I severed ties with her. There was no understanding or anything serious between us, but I felt it necessary to make it clear nothing further would happen."

"Did you have a conversation to that effect?" Colin asked.

"No. I was a coward. I avoided her thereafter."

"Did she continue to seek your attention?" I asked.

"Everyone knows she did. It was often talked about."

"That must have caused you significant embarrassment," Colin said.

"I see what you're getting at, Hargreaves, but you're wrong. Yes, she irritated me, but that's hardly a capital offense. None of it matters now, regardless. I feel terrible she's dead."

"As do we all," I said. "I agree that unwanted flirtation isn't grounds for murder. Can you think of anyone who would have wanted her dead?"

"Only one man," Lord Harrington said. "Lionel Morgan."

36

Britannia

I didn't feel great when I left Gaius's villa. After all that buildup, nothing happened. I thought things were going so well, what with my intoxicating beauty and our shared laughter. It was as if he'd set my body afire and then walked away. You'd think he'd at least have kissed me. Did he want me or not?

"I hear you were with that Roman again today," Minura said, when I ran into her in the village. "How do you think Duro will feel when he hears about it?"

"I don't see why he'd ever hear about it."

"He'll hear about it because normal people talk. They have friends. They're part of the community."

"As am I," I said. "I don't appreciate people spreading gossip."

"Then you should give more thought to the company you keep. This Roman isn't going to marry you, so what's the point?" She studied my face. "Duro doesn't have a chance, does he?"

"I promised Boudica I'd give her more chariot training, so I'd better go."

"Avoiding the question won't make it go away," she said. "It's lucky you've become so close to the queen, but her support can be pulled away as quickly as it was given. You're more interested in Gaius and all things Roman than in your own people. I hate to say it, but your brother was the same. Why do you stay in this community if you despise it?"

"That's not fair," I said. "I don't despise it. The Romans aren't our enemy and there's nothing wrong with expanding cultural horizons. We Iceni have been less open to doing that than other Britons, which suggests that our neighbors are benefiting from their advances more than we are. Is that a good thing? Or is it holding us back?"

"Does Boudica know how you feel about that? It might change her opinion of you."

"That's an awful thing to say."

She shrugged. "I feel like I don't even know you anymore. Maybe I never did. You keep people at arm's length, Vatta. That doesn't work forever."

"I'm sorry. I—"

"Don't bother with a meaningless apology," she said. "Your behavior shows the truth. You might consider telling Duro he's got no hope with you. It's wrong to string him along. He wants a wife and a family. If you're unwilling to give that to him, walk away and leave space for someone else."

I started to reply, but she turned around and started down the path to the village. I called after her, but she didn't look back. Anger bubbled in my gut. Maybe that wasn't fair, but I couldn't control how I felt. Minura and I had grown up together, but we'd never quite been friends. She was the only person in the village other than Solinus who didn't dismiss me as awkward and strange. To the rest, I was more outsider than tribesman. I'd never belonged here and wondered if I ever would.

37

London

"What makes you think Lionel Morgan wanted Cressida dead?" I asked. Lord Harrington didn't reply at once. Instead, he rose from the table and walked toward the stairs that led to the lower garden, full of box hedges. He paused, took a deep breath, and returned to his seat.

"I don't make the accusation lightly," he said. "It pains me. I like Morgan, despite his many faults. I consider him a friend. Given what's happened, however, it would be wrong to hide from you that I know Cressida threatened him."

"How so?" Colin asked. His tone was more than a little skeptical.

"I'm not aware of the precise details. It had something to do with a secret, obviously, one so sensitive he kept it hidden from me. Cressida found out about it and made it clear she planned to expose him."

"What exactly did he tell you?" I asked.

"That's all," Lord Harrington said. "There was nothing further. He was terrified, that much was clear. Perhaps he'll be more forthcoming with you now that she's gone."

That seemed unlikely, but we returned to Knightsbridge nonetheless.

"I haven't the slightest idea what Harrington is talking about," Mr. Morgan said. "I never told him anything of the sort. My dirty little secrets have already been exposed. Even my mother's all too aware of my gambling issues. There's nothing left for me to hide."

"Why would the marquess invent something like this?" I asked.

"Perhaps to cover up something in his own life. He didn't want to marry Cressida, but that doesn't mean he wasn't open to another sort of relationship with her."

"What are you suggesting?" Colin asked.

"Harrington takes what he wants on his own terms. If his fiancée knew that—"

"Victoria was killed before Cressida," I said.

"If Cressida confessed something bad enough to Victoria, he might have needed them both dead in order to save his reputation. Killing his fiancée first would make his motive harder to discover."

"I thought the two of you were friends," Colin said. "These accusations are surprising."

"I thought we were, too. One can't rely on anyone these days."

The next morning, I returned to Grosvenor Square to comb through Cressida's belongings. In an ideal world, I would've immediately found a journal detailing every bit of her life. In the real world, I found a drawerful of dance cards, an enormous quantity of jewelry, and a total absence of correspondence.

The dance cards proved that, despite his protests to the contrary, Lord Harrington continued to socialize with Miss Wright even after his engagement. His name was on every card she'd saved, including those from this current Season. The only other gentleman she danced with as frequently was Oscar Tenley.

The jewelry, all of it of the highest quality, ought to have been secured somewhere safe. The Tower of London sprang to mind as an appropriate location. I'd never seen so many diamonds in one place, strewn across the surfaces of her furniture, none of it in boxes. A pearl and diamond tiara hung jauntily from one of the posts on her canopy bed. A heavy gold and ruby bracelet looked like it had been tossed onto the bedside table.

The lack of correspondence struck me as highly significant. Dance cards weren't the only thing Cressida saved. There were also theater and opera programs, invitations, train tickets, and hotel receipts from a journey through the Continent. This was a girl who collected memorabilia. Surely, she would not have discarded all of her letters?

"My housekeeper shouldn't have allowed you in here." Mrs. Wright was standing in the open doorway. "I'm most put out."

"I spoke to your husband," I said. "He told me I could do whatever I deemed necessary."

"Prying into my daughter's life is not necessary. I won't stand for it."

She'd frustrated me from the moment I met her. I'd tried to rein in my natural reaction to the way she treated me—and how she'd treated her daughter—but struggled. She reminded me too much of my own mother.

"If you want the person who murdered Cressida brought to justice, you'll let me do what I must. The more I know about her life, the more likely it is that I discover something that will lead us to her killer."

"Will doing so bring her back?"

"No, but surely—"

"It will do no one even the slightest good to stir things up. I've seen what happens in these situations. Yes, a criminal is caught, but at great expense to his victim's family and their reputation. Must they suffer all the more?"

"Mrs. Wright, I promise not to do anything that might jeopardize your family."

"Obviously he's the same person who ended Victoria Goldsborough's life. There can't be two murderers running through Society. You can find him through digging into her life. The Goldsboroughs have far less to lose than we. This entire situation is intolerable. I insist that you leave at once."

Confident that I'd found everything I could in Cressida's room, I didn't argue with Mrs. Wright. I did, however, hope to talk to her husband again before I left the house, but this was not to be. She took me firmly by the arm and escorted me all the way to the door. She ordered a footman to open it, but slammed it shut behind me herself.

Undaunted, I went around back, through the mews, and to the servants' entrance. Once inside, I asked a startled kitchen maid to fetch her master for me.

"Of course, madam, I'll send someone for him right away," she said, bobbing a curtsy. "You'll be more comfortable upstairs, though, so we'll take you—"

"No, thank you, I'd prefer to remain here."

I followed her to the servants' hall, where the cook brought me a cup of tea. In short order, Mr. Wright, looking extremely confused, came to me there.

"Lady Emily, I thought you were in Cressida's room. Of course, you're more than welcome to interview the servants, but if you require my services, you can find me in my study."

"Your wife removed me from the house," I said. "She objects to all investigation of your daughter's life. She's concerned about the family's reputation."

"That's absurd. You have free rein over this house, as I told you before. I shall speak to her and make that perfectly clear. Nothing is more important than catching the man who did this. On that note, the bank has confirmed to me that Cressida gave Mr. Morgan a check for fifty pounds three weeks before Miss Goldsborough's death."

"Thank you for letting me know." That was a blow to Mr. Morgan's motive.

"I apologize for the inconvenience caused by my wife," Mr. Wright said. "You shall not be disturbed again."

He offered to bring me back upstairs, but I refused, asking instead to interview the lady's maid who tended to Cressida.

"That would be Hazel," he said. "She dressed both my wife and my daughter. Mrs. Wright is occasionally fond of economizing. I'll send her to you at once."

Hazel was considerably older than I expected her to be. She had a stern, pinched face, better suited to an unpopular governess than the person responsible for enhancing a young lady's beauty. Yet, she was the one who'd ensured Cressida was always on the cutting edge of fashion. Her hair, in particular, had always been meticulously styled.

"Mrs. Wright will not want me to speak to you," she said. "Mr. Wright can order me around however he likes, but it's her I must answer to."

"I can assure you of my discretion."

"That won't stop Mrs. Wright from learning what I do, but I suppose I've little choice in the matter. He told me you want to know about Miss Wright."

"Yes." I waited for her to continue. She didn't. "Did she confide in you?"

"Never. She suspected that I was spying on her for her mother."

"Were you?"

"Yes."

"Surely, she occasionally chatted with you? Mentioned Lord Harrington, for example?" I asked.

"I have heard his name."

"Did she ever tell you about her love for him?"

"No."

She wasn't making this easy. "Your mistress is concerned for her family's reputation. Your master wants the man who murdered his daughter brought to justice. Do you find the two positions incompatible?"

"I don't, madam."

"Why not?"

"So far as I could tell, Miss Wright wasn't doing anything all that bad. I don't know this from her, of course, but servants do talk. Gossip. It's appalling, but, given my extensive personal experience, it can't be avoided, even in the best of houses. Footmen are the worst. You'd think it was the parlormaids, but you'd be wrong. They're wretched little things, but more interested in their own sordid lives than those of their betters."

"If only one could staff a household solely with people who share your moral fortitude," I said, careful that no hint of sarcasm slipped into my voice.

"It would be a magnificent project, would it not? Only imagine the results. Utopia itself!" She looked almost wistful.

"So it's the footmen one must watch out for?"

"Quite. They're always around, aren't they? Lurking in the background. The family doesn't even notice them, of course, and they shouldn't. A good servant should never make his presence known unless it's been requested."

"They eavesdrop?" I asked.

"Yes, and then broadcast what they've learned belowstairs."

"What did they say about Miss Wright?"

"That she was very free with her affection," Hazel said. "That she was too enthusiastic. That she did not seem much interested in discretion."

"I cannot believe she would've done anything untoward in the presence of a servant."

"No, nor can I. Their judgment was formed by observation not of inappropriate activity, but of her conversations with gentlemen. To put it succinctly, she was a flirt."

"Did Lord Harrington call on her in the past few months?"

"Yes," she said. "That's why the footmen increased their chatter. We all knew he'd thrown her over for Miss Goldsborough."

"Thrown her over?" I asked. "I didn't realize there had been an understanding between them."

"There wasn't, Lady Emily." Disapproval oozed from her pores. "For a long while, they had been shockingly free and easy with each other. Then, he decided it must stop. He changed his mind again a month or so before his fiancée was killed."

"What did your mistress make of all this?"

"The truth is, the staff hid it from her. Her invective is like nothing else, and none of us wants to lose our position."

"And Mr. Wright? Was he concerned?"

"He has always made the grave error of mistaking his daughter's behavior for some sort of charming eccentricity. It's almost as if he wanted her to be one of those dreadful New Women." She shuddered. "I blame him for it all. If he'd taken a firmer hand with her, she'd still be alive."

"Who do you think killed her?"

"Lord Harrington, of course," she said. "She proved too great a temptation for him."

38

Britannia

Boudica and I never got so far as hitching our horses to their chariots that day. When I arrived at the pasture, she could see I was upset. I told her about Minura. About how I'd never fit in with the tribe. I even confessed my confusing feelings for Gaius.

"Minura shouldn't criticize you," she said. "You know what kind of life you want. You know what drives your passions. We're living in a world that is undergoing tremendous transformation. Since the Romans arrived, the way people live has started to change. As you rightly pointed out to Minura, the Iceni have been slower to adapt. Given you are drawn to many things about their culture, it's not surprising you feel a pull away from the tribe."

"I don't want to be Roman, but I would like to read the work of an Iceni poet."

"If only we had some."

"We do," I said. "They just don't write down their words."

"You're being pulled between the culture you grew up in and new developments. I'm caught trying to reconcile understanding the benefit of having the Romans as allies with my anger over my husband adopting their template for his will."

"Your situation is different. It affects all of us. It's consequential on a large scale. Mine is not."

"Yours is a microcosm of mine. That doesn't make it less important. We've come to a critical time in our history. Are we content being a client state? Is it possible to gain more independence? What does it mean to be sovereign when your allies can smite you at will?"

"Has Duro given you a battle plan?" I asked.

"Not yet. I suspect he's afraid doing so would anger Prasutagus. A year ago, I would've discussed all of this with my husband. He would've understood the value of having a ready strategy, in case the Romans turned on us."

"What changed?"

"Maybe he started to feel his mortality. Maybe he's sensing a change in Roman policy. I don't know."

"Have you asked him?"

"I wouldn't know about his will if I hadn't. It's possible he hasn't changed at all. Perhaps it took me this long to realize he's more Roman than Iceni. I don't like it."

"That tells me you've already decided you don't want to become Roman, regardless of their capabilities when it comes to central heating."

"That goes without saying. It's the details that matter, Vatta. How much of Roman culture can we adopt without losing our identity? And at what point does our identity cease to matter? If we would all be better off in Roman houses, reading poetry, and visiting public baths, should we refuse those comforts simply to preserve a less-comfortable way of life?"

"There's more to it than just comfort," I said. I thought back to that conversation I'd had with Gaius so long ago, when he'd dined with my family. "Our culture is different, but that does not make it inferior."

"I agree with you."

"There's an enormous gap between incorporating progress and abandoning the familiar. We can build houses with central heating, but that doesn't mean we're obligated to pray to Roman gods. We don't have to become them."

"What if they insist that we do?"

39

London

Colin and I had declined all the invitations we'd received for that evening. We wanted a quiet night at home so that we might discuss the progress of our investigation. After a few warm, sunny days in a row, it had started to rain again. Not hard this time, but a soft, cool drizzle. I welcomed it. There's something cozy about curling up comfortably in a favorite space, sheltered from the elements.

"I don't believe for a second that Harrington was involved with Miss Wright," Colin said, pouring me a glass of port. "A man like him might not be faithful to his wife, but he would be very careful in his choice of a mistress."

"He wasn't even married yet." I took a sip of the port. We'd retired to the library after dinner. The Minoan amphora was still there; I'd not yet seen Sebastian to return it. I can't say I was in much of a rush to part with it.

"A pedantic detail, my dear. No one can convince me he would be carrying on with an unmarried young lady from his own social sphere who has made it clear she was desperately in love with him. To do so would be courting catastrophe."

"What if he couldn't resist the temptation?" I asked.

"He's not an animal. He has control over his behavior."

Ailouros, our cat, hissed. Evidently he objected to being included in a group accused of possessing so little dignity. I stroked his back as he walked past my chair. He ignored me. I was guilty by association.

"You're probably right," I said. "Mr. Morgan is a more likely suspect."

"I confronted him about the money he received from Miss Wright after you spoke to her father," Colin said. "He admitted to having lied about it and explained that he did so out of embarrassment. He's in a great deal of debt."

There was a knock on the door. After a momentary pause, Davis opened it and announced Lady Goldsborough.

"Forgive me for interrupting you like this," she said, accepting a seat. "I came across two things I knew I must bring to you without delay." She placed her reticule on her lap but did not open it.

"After Victoria's death, I'd ordered the servants not to disturb anything in her room. I couldn't bear to have it changed from the way it was when she'd last been in it. Today, just before dinner, I realized how morbid that was and decided it was time to at least tidy things up. I was considering what to do with her clothing. A debutante's wardrobe does not come cheap. Given my financial situation, I had to buy Portia and Victoria fewer gowns than I would've liked. With a few alterations, Portia will fit in what her sister has left behind. The styles might not be au courant next Season, but they will have to suffice. When I was considering how to broach the subject with her, I remembered Victoria's gabardine coat was hanging in a cupboard near our front door. I flew downstairs and pulled it out. As soon as I touched it, I recalled seeing her in it the day she died, before we sat down for tea."

"Before you dressed for the ball at Harrington House?" I asked.

"Yes," she said. "I hadn't remembered her being out that afternoon, but the image was so strong, I'm certain she must have gone somewhere. I searched the pockets and found these." Now she opened the reticule and removed a handkerchief and a note card. She held them out in front of her, one in each hand.

Colin took them. He read the note and then passed it to me.

Please meet me in in the center of Berkeley Square at 6:00 this evening. I am in possession of shocking news concerning your fiancé. Only you can protect him.
   —A Friend Who Cares

I looked up at Colin. So far as I could remember, the paper and handwriting were scarily similar to the note we'd found summoning Cressida Wright to Grosvenor Square the day of her death.

"I can't say for certain that Victoria went into the square that day," Lady Goldsborough said, "but I do remember she left the tea table around six o'clock. I queried all of the servants. None of them can recall whether she went straight upstairs to dress or if she stepped out. I've no idea at all when she received the note. It might have been in her pocket for weeks."

"In the circumstances, it's reasonable to suspect she received it the day of her death," Colin said. He turned his attention to the handkerchief. "It's monogrammed *LM* and has a stain on it."

"I'm convinced it's from the poisoned beverage that killed her,"

Lady Goldsborough said. She looked as if she might faint. "To think that this man, this evil man who cut her life short, was just outside our home, dispensing his awful poison to her. I don't know how much longer I can tolerate any of this. It's all too horrid."

"We will have it tested," I said. "It is unbearable, what you're going through, but it won't last forever. We will catch the murderer."

"It's obvious now who it is, isn't it? Lionel Morgan. I can't think of a single other person of Victoria's acquaintance with the same initials."

"I'm afraid she had some friends you may not have known about," Colin said, and proceeded to tell her what we'd learned about her granddaughter's involvement in Boudica's Sisters.

"No, that cannot be true," she said. "I categorically refuse to believe it. Victoria was no supporter of suffrage. To claim otherwise is an outrageous slander."

"We have it on good authority," I said.

"From whom? I demand to know."

"We've promised to protect the identities of the other young ladies in the group," Colin said. "It's the only way we could get them to open up to us."

"They're probably lying about it all, trying to use Victoria's reputation to enhance their own."

"I appreciate that it's hard to accept her role, but I assure you she was one of the leaders of the group," I said. "She orchestrated her engagement to Lord Harrington in order to be in a position to influence his own opinions and positions."

"More slander! What an appalling accusation." The veins in her neck pulsed. "Victoria would never have behaved in such an underhanded way."

"She believed she was staying true to her principles and ideals,"

I said. "She wanted to find a way to improve the condition of women's lives that didn't require violence."

"I don't want to hear any such nonsense." She paused for a beat. "Portia is not involved, is she?"

I wondered if this meant she allowed for the possibility.

"No," Colin said. "Victoria wanted her sisters all kept well clear of the group."

"I don't know what to think. This is impossible to believe."

"I know it's difficult, but having a clear, honest picture of her life will make it easier for us to find her murderer," I said.

"This is not information that need be circulated through Society, is it?"

"We will be as discreet as possible."

She sighed. "That, at least, is a relief. Whatever happens, I don't want her sisters to know anything about it. You will look into Mr. Morgan, won't you? I cannot imagine someone of his character could've harmed Victoria, but having found the handkerchief..." A small sob escaped from her lips. "One hardly knows what to think. Of course, she could've got that from him anytime, and the stain is probably innocuous. He wouldn't be so stupid to wipe up poison with something and then leave it with her. Particularly given the monogram."

"Also, if she met someone at six o'clock that evening, and didn't collapse until after ten, it would've been too early for her to have drunk the poison," Colin said.

"So you're certain someone at the ball gave it to her?"

"She might have been given it at home, but closer to the time of her death."

"I cannot bear the thought of her being poisoned in her own house," Lady Goldsborough said.

"We haven't yet found evidence suggesting she was," I said. "It's merely a possibility."

Colin gave her a reassuring smile. "I'm glad you brought these items to our attention. We'll keep you apprised of what we learn from them."

"Thank you, Mr. Hargreaves. You're a dear, truly."

She hardly acknowledged me again before she left. This came as no surprise; she was my mother's dearest friend. She, too, disapproved of my work.

Once she had departed, I picked up the handkerchief. "She's right that Mr. Morgan wouldn't have handed over a cup of poison along with a monogrammed handkerchief."

"I agree. We'll have the stain tested, but I doubt it's poison. The note, however..." I'd put the message I'd found in Cressida's bedroom on my desk. He walked over, picked it up, and held the two side by side. "The handwriting is identical. It looks rather unnatural, as if the author was deliberately disguising his natural hand."

"We can compare it to Mr. Morgan's easily enough," I said. "He wrote to thank me after we had him round for dinner." The note was still on my desk. I found it, removed it from the envelope, and we stood there, studying the samples in silence.

Eventually, Colin tilted his head, and squinted. "They're quite similar."

"Let's copy the text of the message to Victoria onto another sheet and then tomorrow ask him to write it out for us," I said.

"We'll have Harrington do the same."

"You don't suspect him, do you?"

"It will help eliminate him, if nothing else."

"What about Boudica's Sisters?" I asked. "Could we be missing something there? Victoria must have written the diary deliberately to be found, so that no one would suspect her involvement with the suffragettes. Was it specifically to mislead Portia?"

"Portia saw where she hid it, so that seems likely. Perhaps it was her way of protecting her sister."

"From what, though? If Victoria was a true believer in suffrage, which I can accept, wouldn't she have wanted her sister to see things from her point of view? Why exclude her?"

"Portia being aware of her sister's activities would've made it more likely their grandmother would find out as well. They'd be bound to talk about it and, even if they did their best to keep it quiet, it's likely a servant would overhear, or Lady Goldsborough."

"She did admit to keeping footmen stationed in the corridor outside the girls' bedrooms," I said. "Victoria would've known she had no meaningful privacy. Even so, if they were careful never to speak about it except outside of the house—"

"That's dangerous," Colin said. "Eventually, one of them might've slipped. Given how important this all was to Miss Goldsborough, she wouldn't have considered that an acceptable risk. It's also possible she knew Portia's views on the subject and they weren't compatible with her own."

"It's time for another tête-à-tête with Portia," I said. "I'll invite her here, so she'll be able speak freely, away from her grandmother."

Another knock sounded on the door. Once again, it was Davis announcing a visitor.

"Mr. Capet has appeared on the doorstep requesting entrance to the house. I have left him there as he's covered with mud and looks something like a drowned rat. What would you like me to do with him?"

Colin's eyebrows shot up and the look on his face made it clear I wouldn't want to hear his suggestion.

"Bring him to us, Davis," I said.

It was some time before the door opened again. When it did, Davis followed Sebastian into the room.

"Please do not sit, sir, until I've finished," he said. He then unfolded a tarpaulin, draped it over the sofa, and motioned to our guest. "There you are."

"Bring him some tea, please, Davis," I said. Sebastian did look dreadful, soaked to the bone. "What on earth have you been up to?"

"I've made a rather exciting discovery," he said. "Unfortunately, my presence at the location of it was not appreciated by the local bobby making his rounds. It was an amateur mistake on my part. I ought to have been more careful, but my enthusiasm carried me away. I see you received my gift." He nodded toward the amphora.

"You can take it with you when you go. I can't accept it."

"Anticipating your objections, I bought it through legitimate sources and have a fully documented record of provenance for you."

"That's only half of the problem," I said. "We can discuss it later. What is this discovery?"

"Only the greatest archaeological find of the century!"

"In London?" Colin asked.

"We have a rich history, do we not?" Sebastian asked.

"Yes, of course, but the competition is rather fierce. The amphora you so inappropriately gave my wife is from Knossos, is it not? Arthur Evans started his excavations there early this century and discovered the Minoans."

"Technically, that was the previous century. He started digging in 1900. Perhaps you, like so many, don't realize the new century started in 1901. There was no year zero."

"Don't be so condescending," I said.

"My mistake," Colin said. "I didn't realize the dig went back that far. There's also Hugo Winckler's work in Turkey. It looks like his excavations that began last year will prove the Hittites were an actual historical people, not just a biblical legend."

"That doesn't interest me in the least." Sebastian draped his arms over the back of the sofa. Rivulets of water dripped from them. I was glad for Davis's tarpaulin.

"I'm not surprised," Colin said. "So what is it that you've found?"

"The tomb every archaeologist dreams of finding."

"Alexander the Great was not buried in London," I said. "Nor was Cleopatra."

"No, of course not," Sebastian said. "But Boudica was."

40

Britannia

Tension is a funny thing. It can start small and isolated before it spreads like a plague. I was one of the few people in the village who knew of the trouble between Boudica and Prasutagus. The details of it, anyway. But that didn't stop bad feelings from seeping into nearly everyone's lives.

I can't explain it, except to offer the theory that maybe emotions are contagious. Why shouldn't they be? If your best friend comes to you, bursting with joy, you're bound to get swept up in it as well.

The mood at the palace shifted. Everyone was snappish and short-tempered. Before long, we were all arguing over petty things. Being hypercritical. Refusing to find satisfaction in things that normally made us happy.

I'd like to say that's what catalyzed the rift between Minura and me, but the truth is, it would have happened regardless.

It started with Duro. No surprise there. It irritated me that she'd basically commanded me to break things off with him. First of all, there wasn't anything to break off. Not really. Second, she shouldn't have pressured me to do anything. It was inappropriate. Heavy-handed.

It got me to thinking. Especially late at night, when I couldn't fall asleep, which was pretty much all the time in those days. I was too stressed, too agitated. I couldn't relax. So I lay there, wondering why Minura was so concerned with Duro.

It was obvious, really. She wanted me to let him go so she could have him.

That profound thought came to me shortly before dawn one day. I hadn't slept at all, which probably explains why I believed it was profound. I dragged myself out of bed, quickly dressed, and marched straight to her house. I was about to bang on the door when I realized that I'd be waking her entire family.

I'd like to say I didn't want to disturb them, but the truth was, I didn't want to make myself look bad. Like the impetuous, thoughtless woman I was being. So I sat down, right outside the door, and waited for it to open. The sun was rising now, so it wouldn't be long before someone in the family came out.

Long enough, though, for my brain to come up with about a thousand ridiculous ways to convince myself that Minura was manipulating me. Amazing the mental acrobatics we'll employ to avoid blaming ourselves for bad behavior.

Her father opened the door. I leapt up and told him I was looking for Minura. He greeted me, then called to his daughter inside.

How I wish I hadn't gone there that day.

She came out.

I did my best impression of one of the Furies. Remember those Roman goddesses? Vengeful. Spiteful. All-around nasty. I berated her for trying to control me. I accused her of wanting Duro for herself. I demanded she explain and then immediately stated that no explanation could be sufficient.

I told her I never wanted to speak to her again. I didn't let her finish a single sentence.

Then I stalked off.

I wasn't supposed to be in charge of the sheep that day, but before I got halfway back to my own house, I knew I'd made a complete fool of myself. Nothing appealed to me more than holing up with livestock until the storm I'd started calmed. Yes, we'd all been testy lately. Yes, I was short of sleep. Guess what? Those explanations weren't sufficient.

I was mortified.

A smart person would've turned right back around and apologized.

I'm not a smart person.

I slunk into our house, told my mother I didn't want breakfast and that I would tend the sheep. My younger sister could do something else. I grabbed my Ovid scrolls and started for the meadow.

I didn't go there. Instead, I turned on the road that led to Gaius's villa. The work was nearly complete now, and he'd already moved in. I wanted to be with someone who valued me for me. Who didn't want me to change. Who cared about the things I did.

I hesitated before knocking on the door. Why did I care if Minura wanted Duro? I didn't love him, did I? I hadn't decided to marry him. I hadn't sought out his company since the day he'd kissed me. Yet something tugged at me. It was what he'd said about making it his mission to figure what it would take to bring me happiness in marriage. I wanted to know what he'd try. Wanted to see if he actually cared enough to do anything.

A smart person would've gone to the village, found Duro, and told him their feelings.

I already said I'm not a smart person.

41

London

"Boudica?" I asked. "You claim to have found Boudica's tomb? When did you develop an interest in archaeology?"

"You wound me," Sebastian said. "I'm a man of many interests. Leonardo himself was not half the Renaissance man as I. It's true I've not before engaged in menial labor—I prefer to avoid getting dirty—but some things are irresistible. I should've thought you'd be delighted. I'm not stealing anything."

"If you don't have permission to dig, you're as good as stealing," Colin said. "Further, items of historical importance shouldn't belong to the random individual who finds them."

"I don't write the laws, Hargreaves. Of course, I don't exactly obey them either, but that's beside the point. In this case, I'm doing nothing illegal. You ought to find that refreshing."

"Why are you here?" my husband asked.

"I do apologize for showing up in such a state, but I thought our dear Emily would want to be the first to hear about my discovery. Also, I needed to get away from the aforementioned bobby and your house was the nearest sanctuary I could think of."

"Nearest? If you did find Boudica's tomb, it wouldn't be in Mayfair," I said. "So far as we know, she razed Londinium and Verulamium and then went on to fight another battle, somewhere west of Birmingham. She was defeated and died shortly thereafter. Why would the Iceni have taken her body for burial back to a destroyed city?"

"Well, I wasn't there when it happened, was I? Who knows what these Celtic tribesmen had on their minds? It's not for me to explain, only to report on what I've found."

"And what, exactly, is that?" Colin asked.

"So far, skeletal remains and a bronze mirror. There were some beads as well, but they're not interesting. The excavation is not complete."

"What about any of that screams Boudica?" I asked.

"Londinium was the location of one of her great victories. Why not bury her there? The mirror dates from the middle of the first century and is clearly Celtic. It would've belonged to an important, wealthy person. She fits the bill."

"Hardly ironclad proof of identity," Colin said.

"Where have you been digging?" I asked. I had no interest in watching them snipe at each other.

"Near Ludgate Hill Road. That's all you need to know for the moment. Despite your unenthusiastic reaction to my news, I shall continue to keep you updated."

"You're generosity itself," I said. Davis appeared with a single cup of tea and handed it to Sebastian.

"Not even a biscuit to go with it?" Sebastian looked rather put out.

"Madam requested tea for you. She mentioned nothing else." Davis bowed to me and left the room.

"I don't think he likes you," Colin said.

"After the shabby treatment he's given me, the feeling is mutual."

"I won't detail his valid reasons for disliking you. At the same time, I admit to being not entirely distressed to see you," I said. "We now know all about Boudica's Sisters, including the identities of all of the members, so you have no need to hide anything about them from us. Do you have any reason to believe Miss Goldsborough's death had something to do with the group? Is it possible she and Miss Price had a falling-out? Or that her fiancé learned of her involvement and became irrationally angry?"

"No." He spoke with conviction. "Victoria and Frances never disagreed. As for her darling marquess, the man may not be a complete imbecile, but neither is he particularly observant. He sees what he wants. It never would've occurred to him that he might have fallen in love with a suffragette and she took great lengths to ensure he'd never find out."

"What about the other members of the group?" Colin asked.

"Innocuous, as I'm sure you noticed when you spoke to them. They were chosen with an extraordinary amount of care. Frances was especially adamant that they needed girls of a specific temperament. They had to be open-minded, malleable, and prone to liberal ideas. On top of this, they must be attractive enough to entice the right eligible bachelors."

"Their recruits all came from wealthy families," Colin said.

"Yes. They didn't want anyone whose status might make a family object to them. You must own it's a clever scheme."

"It is," Colin said. "However, despite its noble intentions, it's also underhanded and built on deception."

"*The strong do what they can, the weak suffer what they must,*" Sebastian replied. "That's Thucydides, the Greek historian, writing about the siege of Melos."

"δυνατὰ δ' ἐξ ὧν ἑκάτεροι ἀληθῶς φρονοῦμεν διαπράσσεσθαι, ἐπισταμένους πρὸς εἰδότας ὅτι δίκαια μὲν ἐν τῷ ἀνθρωπείῳ λόγῳ ἀπὸ τῆς ἴσης ἀνάγκης κρίνεται, δυνατὰ δὲ οἱ προύχοντες πράσσουσι καὶ οἱ ἀσθενεῖς ξυγχωροῦσιν," Colin recited in ancient Greek. "I read Greats, Capet, I know Thucydides."

There was no sense in letting them continue to bicker. "Who did you meet that night, trying to get inside to deliver an invitation to join the group?" I asked. "Victoria or Frances?"

"Victoria," he said.

This surprised me. I didn't think she was so daring. "How long have you been digging at your site?" I asked. "Did you start before or after Miss Goldsborough's murder?"

"You know the pace at which archaeology moves," Sebastian said. "I've been at it for more than a month. Considerably more."

"Were Victoria and Frances aware of what you were doing?" I asked.

"They were. Aside from the obvious use to them my specialized skills provided, it made including me in their organization all the more appealing. Boudica is, after all, their inspiration."

"Why did you want to be appealing to them?" Colin asked.

"Well, Hargreaves, if I prove instrumental in gaining women the right to vote, surely that will endear me to Emily. What further motivation would any man need?"

"I shan't address such nonsense," I said. "Does anyone else know what you're doing? In terms of the dig?"

"There are a smattering of individuals whom I've told. Not details, of course. I've dropped hints as to what I've found, but I've been careful to reveal nothing that might lead to someone else marching in and stealing the site from me."

"So where is it?" Colin asked. "Specifically. It's obviously not in plain view or the world would already know."

"It's in the cellar of a private building. I won't tell you more."

"You are, I hope, maintaining the best scientific practices?" Colin asked. His tone had changed. He was no longer being adversarial.

"What do you take me for?"

"Someone who prioritizes objects over provenance and scientific records," I said.

"I'm not a savage. I have a trained archaeologist working for me. We have a long-standing connection."

"Did he dig at Knossos, by any chance?" I asked.

"I can't put anything past you, can I? Yes, he was there with Arthur Evans."

"What is his name?"

"James Loxton."

"Will you allow him to give me a tour of the site?" I asked.

"Heavens, no, but if you'd like to speak to him about it, I can arrange that."

"Excellent," Colin said. "Bring him round tomorrow afternoon."

"I got the amphora from him," Sebastian said. "It was one of the objects Evans was allowed to keep. He presented it to my friend in thanks for his work. I paid him a fair price for it."

"Be that as it may, I cannot accept it," I said. "Do please take it with you when you go."

"You punish us both." He rose from his seat, picked up the amphora, and flounced out of the room.

"I shouldn't be surprised if his friend worked with Evans in

Aylesford," Colin said when he'd gone. "He excavated an Iron Age cemetery there."

"It's appalling that a trained archaeologist would involve himself with Sebastian."

"Ethics in that field are not always what they might be. Think of Wallace Budge of the British Museum illegally removing things from Egypt."

"Quite," I said. "It sounds as if Sebastian has been rather loose-lipped about his so-called tomb. I wonder if it might have anything to do with the murders?"

"Unlikely. For that to be the case, we'd need something to tie Miss Wright to it. Nothing we've learned about her suggests she had an interest in history."

"Yes, but I just can't shake the feeling that we're missing something."

"If we weren't, we'd already have solved the case," he said. "I think the best thing we can do now is focus our attention elsewhere. There comes a point when it is no longer fruitful to ruminate over facts. The right sort of distraction will occupy us and give our brains the freedom to work in the background."

"What do you suggest?"

He crossed to me, knelt down, and took my hand, his dark eyes boring into mine. "We could play chess."

"We could," I said. "It's a most diverting game."

He raised my hand to his lips. He paused there for what felt like an eternity and then turned my hand over and kissed the palm. "If we can't think of anything else, I'd say it's our only option."

"It's a pity you've no other ideas."

"Forgive me, I'd try to resist, but it's impossible." He rose to his feet, scooped me up, and carried me to our bedroom.

"I don't think you tried at all to resist," I said, as he lowered me gently onto the bed.

"Not exactly, no, but I was trying to take things more slowly."

"Don't," I said.

He didn't.

42

Britannia

One of Gaius's slaves opened the door. I gave him my name and asked for his master. The man's eyebrows shot up almost to his hairline.

"He's not yet awake."

"Then let me in. I'll wait for him."

"I'm not in the habit of admitting strange young women to the house."

"There's a first time for everything," I said and shoved past him. I walked to the corridor that ran along the courtyard. The slave was close on my heels.

"I must ask you to leave."

"Keep talking and you'll disturb Gaius. If he's tired and cranky it will be your fault, not mine. I can be quiet as anything." I kept my voice low to demonstrate the point.

"Wait in there." He opened the door to the room where, on my earlier visit, the artist was laying the mosaic floor. It was complete now, and the bold black-and-white geometric pattern reminded me of a maze. I sat on a stool, impatient, afraid I would lose my nerve.

Gaius came to me after only a few minutes. His hair was rumpled, his face unshaven, and he was wearing a wrinkled tunic.

"Come straight out of bed, have you?" I asked.

"I assumed anyone rude enough to show up uninvited this early couldn't have high standards for etiquette."

"Sounds like an apt description of me. How do you feel about going straight back to bed?"

Really good. At least that's how his subsequent actions made it seem he felt about it.

And just like that, my life became a riot of chaos and confusion.

43

London

The next morning, a stiff breeze scattered the clouds from the sky and the sun shone bright. Colin and I lingered over breakfast longer than strictly necessary, neither of us in any hurry to part company. But part we must, him to gather handwriting samples, me to talk to Frances Price and Portia Goldsborough.

I penned a message to the latter, asking her to come to me that afternoon, and then set off for Bayswater. Frances was the only member of her family at home. She looked extremely tense when she sat down in the drawing room with me.

"Has something else happened?" she asked.

"Do you expect something to?"

"No, but given you've already accused me of murdering Cressida, I find myself perpetually braced for bad news."

"I didn't accuse you," I said, "only pointed out that you might have motive for the crime."

"I would've had plenty of other options if Oscar had decided to propose to her."

"Has he proposed to you?"

"No." She frowned. "I'm beginning to consider those other options. With Victoria gone, it's more critical than ever that I make a good match as quickly as possible."

"I've been speaking to our mutual acquaintance Sebastian Capet. He reiterated that you've been selective about the young ladies you admit to your circle. You're particularly keen on ensuring nothing about their families would put off prospective grooms. Yet surely your own family raises flags in that regard. Their political beliefs are as well-known as they are controversial."

"Yes, but I've made a point of publicly displaying my own, distinct point of view," she said. "While Victoria presented as the perfect Establishment girl, I'm someone who will attract the right sort of gentleman because I've been exposed to radical ideas and rejected them."

"What do you think about Mr. Capet's claim that he's found Boudica's tomb?"

"It's the most exciting thing I've ever heard. He suspected it from the beginning, of course, given all the evidence, but finding incontrovertible proof would be extraordinary. It would bring the warrior queen back to the forefront of conversation, which could only be good for our cause."

"I've always thought it ironic that the government holds her up as a shining example while at the same time refusing to give women the rights they deserve," I said.

"I hope this discovery brings more attention to the issue and starts to turn the tide of public sentiment."

I had far less faith in Sebastian and his discovery than she did, but then, I knew him better. No part of me believed he'd found Boudica. The world at large, however, rarely cared about the actual truth. If they were told it was Boudica, often and loudly enough, they'd accept it. They would make it true.

"To return to our previous subject, it sounds as if you've lost faith in Mr. Tenley's interest," I said.

"I think that, given what happened to Victoria, he's unlikely to pursue an engagement to me or anyone else. His best friend's fiancée is dead and he's bound to be more focused on Peregrine than his own romantic pursuits."

"Was he close to Victoria?"

"Not as such," she said, "but it would be rather insensitive for him to be announcing an engagement in the circumstances."

"He could keep the news quiet until a more appropriate time. That sort of thing isn't unheard of."

"No, but it's possible he doesn't feel strongly enough for me. He's guaranteed to run if word of Victoria's political views come out."

"At the moment, there's no reason to think they will."

"It's probably best that I move on. We've already lost significant time."

"Surely you must have some feelings for Mr. Tenley, or you wouldn't have set your sights on him."

"None at all," she said. "My decision to pursue him was wholly cynical, based only on what I believe he can do for our cause. Nothing personal entered into it."

"That can't be entirely true. For example, you needed to not find him physically repulsive."

"Women have tolerated worse. I'm prepared to do what I must."

"So who will you try for next?" I asked.

"I'm not going to tell you that," she said. "You might warn him off."

"I'd do nothing of the sort. I don't agree with your methods, but I do respect what you're trying to do. I only wish you would consider marrying someone you wouldn't have to deceive. There are influential men who are sympathetic to the cause, but who need to be brought further along in their support for it."

"Gentlemen who are already supporters wouldn't make nearly the difference that a single Establishment stalwart could. There's no point trying to dissuade me. I know the best way to achieve my goals."

Stubbornness was evident both in her voice and her rigid posture. "Who chose a potential husband first? You or Victoria?" I asked.

"We together settled on Peregrine. He's a marquess, after all. Oscar was the natural next choice, given their friendship."

"How did you decide which of you would go after each?"

"We didn't. Instead, we put ourselves in front of them as often as possible and watched their behavior. When it became clear Peregrine was attracted to Victoria, we knew he would be hers."

"Did that leave you with the harder job, then? Or was it evident Oscar was amenable to you?"

She pressed her lips together. "I won't lie, it's been harder for me. There's less of a natural connection between Oscar and myself, but we'd hardly be the first couple to marry who wasn't madly in love. Most men would be delighted to have their wife's best friend married to their own closest mate. It would've made the task easier for Victoria and me as well. The road may be more complicated now, but that doesn't put me off. I'm the one who came up with this scheme and I will see it through to the finish."

"Did it hurt, just a little, that Lord Harrington didn't want you?"

"Not in the least. I didn't care who he wanted, just that he'd fall for one of us."

"Yes, but it stings to be passed over."

"Perhaps if I were the sort of person who cared about all this Society nonsense it would've, but given that I've never attached my self-worth to what vapid twits think, it was all irrelevant so far as I'm concerned."

"You're more thick-skinned than most people," I said.

"This isn't personal, Lady Emily. It's about something vitally important to every woman in Britain and beyond. We must do whatever is necessary to gain the rights we're owed. Nothing matters more. Anyone who could let insignificant slights draw them off course is of no use to me."

"You certainly possess a stronger personality than Victoria," I said. "Did it ever bother her that you fit naturally into the role of leader?"

"We led together. That was essential to us both."

After I left her, I considered all she'd said as I made my way back through the park toward Park Lane. There was something in Frances's tone that struck me. It wasn't quite arrogance, but it approached that. Further, the way she spoke about her plans seemed proprietary. I wasn't convinced she'd been delighted not to have had the lead role in the first engagement they'd managed to secure.

While I didn't doubt that both she and Victoria shared their goals, Frances struck me as a born iconoclast. Victoria might have needed longer to come to her more radical views, not because of some inherent character flaw but as a result of her upbringing. Perhaps they didn't disagree, let alone argue, but I had the distinct impression Frances was the one truly in charge.

I didn't believe she killed her best friend, but it was not outside the realm of possibility. Someone so passionate about her beliefs might come to decide she should have sole control over bringing about the changes in Society she so desperately wanted.

There was no chance each member of Boudica's Sisters would ever be as committed as Frances. They would be hurt by social slights. They might not have the fortitude to stand up to their husbands. A great deal of disappointment could well lie in the group's future.

All of these thoughts led me to adopt a different approach to my conversation with Portia. When she arrived at the house, I brought her out to the garden. The day was fine, so we sat on a bench surrounded by beds of dark purple irises, their grapelike scent perfuming the air. Portia looked much better than she had the last time I'd seen her. A measure of brightness had returned to her eyes and her skin was no longer so sallow.

"It's good to see you," I said. "How are you managing?"

"Better than I ought, which fills me with guilt and sets me to feeling awful again."

"You've nothing to be guilty about."

"You can only say that because you don't know what I've done," she said. "I can't begin to tell you how I rejoiced when I got your note. I've been desperate to share my news with someone, but most people would judge me so harshly. You, however, are less tied to the conventions of Society. . . ."

"You can tell me anything."

"One shouldn't have any happiness so soon after such a tragedy, but when something is meant to be, how can one deny it?"

"What's happened?" I asked.

She met my gaze, then looked away. "I hope you won't despise me."

"I won't. I've known you since you were a baby."

"Yes, but not well enough that I can take your friendship for granted." She drew a deep breath before continuing. "Oscar Tenley has asked me to do him the honor of becoming his wife. I accepted his proposal."

This would be a blow to Frances. "Portia, that's wonderful. I wish you all the best."

Her shoulders relaxed and she unclenched her hands, which had been balled in fists. "The timing is appalling, I'm aware of that. It's why he hasn't yet spoken to my grandmother. He wanted to know my feelings before he sought her permission."

"A very reasonable strategy whatever the circumstance," I said. It infuriated me that men thought it more important to see if a girl's father approved of an engagement before they knew if she did. "I'm delighted for you. I didn't realize the two of you had an attachment."

"It's been growing slowly since we became better acquainted after Victoria's engagement. He and Peregrine are best friends, you see, so it was only natural that we were much thrown together. It does make the current situation all the more delicate, as we neither of us want to cause Peregrine further pain."

"I'm sure he'll understand."

"I do hope so. It's Grandmama about whom I worry the most, though. She does like things to be done properly. We thought we wouldn't tell her until after you've brought your inquiry to a close. Do you think you'll find him soon? The man who did this to Victoria? And Cressida as well. It's all so awful."

"We're continuing to gather evidence and hope it won't take too much longer to have the proof we need."

"That's a relief," she said. "I don't like being dishonest. It's horrible to have to hide something so important. In another time, it would've brought all my family such joy."

"I understand. The reason I asked to see you today is that I have some questions that may help us get to the bottom of things. Did you ever notice tension between your sister and Frances Price?"

"Heavens, no. I think Victoria liked her better even than she did me. They gave each other unwavering solace and support. Frances needed that, given her family situation, but so did my sister. Grandmama can be overbearing."

"In light of your engagement, this question may seem impertinent. I apologize if that's the case. Were you aware that Frances and Mr. Tenley had an attachment of sorts? No doubt this was before the two of you became involved."

She rolled her eyes. "Oh, that was nothing," she said. "Frances could be a dreadful flirt when she wanted to, and for a while she had Oscar in her sights. There never was anything serious between them, at least so far as he was concerned."

"They were alone in the garden together at Harrington House the night Victoria died."

"Yes, Oscar told me all about it. We want no secrets between us, you see. It was quite awkward. He'd taken her there to explain to her there could be nothing between them because of his feelings for me. She was taken aback and . . . well . . . there's no point hiding the truth. She did what she could to try to persuade him to choose her instead. Suffice it to say, he was not enticed."

"What did she try?"

"She kissed him." She leaned closer to me on the bench. "I won't hide that he was shocked by her forwardness. That's not the sort of behavior he would ever tolerate in a young lady. At any rate, it went nowhere and now we're engaged. All is as it should be. I won't ever hold Frances's actions against her. She has a tendency to be a bit pushy in social situations. I never would've said so to Victoria, but I'm sure you've noticed it."

"Mr. Tenley is a most eligible bachelor," I said. "I understand Cressida Wright was interested in him as well."

"Was she? How odd, given the purported strength of her feelings for Peregrine. It doesn't matter now, though."

She was awfully quick to dismiss this information, and despite her presenting as unaffected, I wasn't convinced.

"Did I tell you Oscar has a ring for me? He's keeping it until he gets Grandmama's permission. So please, Emily, please do hurry and solve these wretched murders! Waiting is unbearable."

44

Britannia

I never claimed my morals aren't questionable. Doing what I did was not the world's greatest idea. More like it was stupid. Reckless. Impetuous. Asking for trouble.

I relished every minute of it.

Gaius was an attentive lover. Not that I had anyone to compare him to. The point is I had nothing to complain about. It was delicious. *The spirit captains look for in a soldier / A pretty girl will look for in her man.* Afterward, we had breakfast. He whispered poetry to me in Greek. I'd never heard the language before. Its music seduced me. We went back to bed. Then he had to go to work.

"You can stay here until I return if you'd like," he said. "Unless you've got things to do. I'll be late. I'm dining with friends tonight."

"I don't have to stay."

"I didn't expect this to happen. I hope you're all right. I shouldn't have—"

"It's okay. I'm fine."

"I'm glad it happened," he said. "I would never have presumed—"

"We Iceni know what we want. I wasn't going to wait for you forever." My heart was beating too fast. What would happen now? Soldiers didn't marry local girls. I wasn't stupid enough to think they did. They might live with them, but they weren't going to take them back to Rome at the end of their deployment.

I was still lying on his bed. He bent over and kissed me. "I must be off. If you're here when I return, I'll be glad. If you're not, I'll look forward to our next meeting."

My stomach churned as I watched him go. My confidence vanished. What had I done? What was I thinking? What did I want? I waited until I'd heard the door to the house slam to drag myself out of the bed. I got dressed. I decided to leave, but I didn't want to see the slave again. So I waited for a while. Waited for what? Nothing, of course. It's not like the slave was going anywhere. And it's not like he was the only one in the house.

I plaited my hair. I paced. I accepted the inevitable. The sheep were waiting. I couldn't hide here forever.

45

London

"Portia Goldsborough is engaged to Oscar Tenley?" Colin was all astonishment. "Were you aware of any attachment between them?"

"No," I said.

"The man certainly does get around. We ought to speak to him." We were back in the library. "I've the results from the handwriting samples. Harrington did not write the notes given to Miss Goldsborough and Miss Wright. Morgan's potential to have done so is not altogether clear. Scotland Yard's expert deemed it's possible he penned the note and tried to disguise his handwriting."

"If he were concerned about it being recognizably his hand, wouldn't he have made a greater effort to differentiate it?"

"Arguably, yes, but this outcome allows for the possibility that someone is framing him."

"Have they finished analyzing the stain on the handkerchief?"

"It's from ordinary black tea. None of this clears Morgan, but neither does it remove suspicion from him. We still don't know how Miss Goldsborough came to have a handkerchief that belonged to him. I called in at his house and showed it to the maid. She confirmed it was his."

"Did you see him as well?"

"He wasn't home," Colin said. "I'd like you to speak with the girl. She's called Maeve and has worked for Morgan for only a few months. There's something about the situation that's most concerning. I noticed a bruise on her wrist."

"Like we're told Ida had."

"Precisely. I asked Maeve about it, but she brushed it off as nothing. Said she'd banged it when she tripped and fell down the stairs."

"Why is that always the excuse?" I asked.

"Because we all have the potential to fall down the stairs. I pressed her a bit, but she grew so agitated, I stopped. Fear. It was writ all over her face."

"Maybe we were too quick to dismiss Mr. Morgan as someone who wouldn't play a long game."

"That's precisely what I'm afraid of," Colin said. "If he did attack Ida, it's possible Victoria knew, but we have no reason to think Cressida would have, too."

"She was friends with Mr. Morgan. Victoria knew that," I said. "Even if she and Victoria weren't close, Victoria could well have decided to warn her if she knew what he'd done to Ida."

I considered what might have happened. "The trouble is, Frances stated unequivocally that Victoria didn't know the identity of Ida's attacker. Surely if Victoria revealed it to Cressida, she would've told her best friend as well."

"Would she have done? She was brought up to avoid scandal

at all cost. She wouldn't have wanted the general public to find out what a member of her household had suffered. We all know how quickly salacious gossip spreads."

"Victoria didn't keep it quiet," I said. "She told both Frances and Frances's parents."

"Only in the hope that Mr. and Mrs. Price might be able to offer Ida assistance. Sharing the identity of the perpetrator would've been another matter. The Prices might well have insisted on notifying the police, and that would've dragged Victoria into any inquiries they made."

"An excellent point," I said. "Yet we have no way of proving what Victoria actually knew."

"Or Ida." Colin was pacing. "They could've decided together it was best to keep his identity hidden."

"If Mr. Morgan is brutalizing Maeve, there's a fair chance he's been doing it for a while. I want to speak with her at a time when there's no chance that he can interrupt us."

"I'll invite him to lunch with me at my club tomorrow. You can go to his house and assure her he won't come home and interrupt."

"I hate the thought of waiting so long," I said. "If she's in trouble, I want her removed from his employment immediately. We can give her a job. Davis could sort it out."

"You could send for her right now on some pretense, but that runs the risk of Morgan getting suspicious. We don't want her in a situation where he decides she's a threat, especially if he's our murderer. Tomorrow would be safer."

He was right. It would be better to wait.

Sebastian and his archaeologist were due soon. I doubted their presence would distract me from worrying about Maeve. Mr. Loxton arrived first. This took me aback. I shouldn't have thought Sebastian would want to give us any opportunity of speaking to him alone. Mr. Loxton was of average height and build, wore moustaches that would've been the height of fashion in the middle of the previous century, and gave every appearance of being wretchedly nervous.

"It's very good of you to have me round," he said, accepting a whisky from my husband. "Forgive me, I—I hardly know what to say. It's all rather awkward. Yes, awkward."

"The dig is illegal?" Colin asked.

"Not—not as such. The owner of the property has given us full permission. Even so, I would feel better if it weren't being kept secret."

"Sebastian likes his secrets," I said. "You've known him long?"

"Yes, yes. Our paths crossed some years back in Greece. He was looking for someone to excavate for him. I wasn't the man for the job, and the less said about it all the better, but we've stayed in contact ever since."

"He's a most diverting man," Colin said.

This seemed to put him a little more at ease and signaled to me that Mr. Loxton knew a great deal about Sebastian's true character. "I'm surprised you're not still in Crete with Mr. Evans," I said.

"I plan on returning as soon as I'm finished here. Evans couldn't very well object to me dipping out to work on Boudica."

"He knows about your discovery?" Colin asked.

"I was clear with Capet that I would have to inform him. Evans understands the need for discretion."

"Do you have evidence that what you've found actually relates to Boudica?" I asked.

"Precise evidence is often tricky," he said. "The Iceni didn't leave written records. None of the tribes did in Iron Age Britain. We do, however, know from Roman sources the date of Boudica's rebellion, as well as the general shape of the ensuing battles. The objects we've uncovered so far tell me the time period is correct, as does the thick layer of soot and ash covering them. It's red and black, which is typical for areas destroyed when Boudica burned Londinium. The skeletal remains are of a full-grown female, and her possessions suggest she was wealthy and important."

"Cassius Dio wrote that Boudica received a burial commensurate to her royal status," I said. "Does what you've found measure up to that?"

"Cassius Dio was writing long after her funeral took place," Mr. Loxton said. "He says she died from illness shortly after her final battle. Tacitus, whose father-in-law served in Britannia during her rebellion, claims she committed suicide."

"An honorable death so far as the Romans were concerned," Colin said. "An argument could be made that both authors were concerned more with criticizing the empire as it stood in their time than in recording the truth."

"Quite, quite," Mr. Loxton said. "I agree it will be difficult to prove the identity of our body. The truth is, I'm not convinced it's a tomb at all, but rather a hasty burial, if it was even a burial. It might just be a victim of the battle who was covered by debris where she fell."

"Yet you would stake your professional reputation on claiming the occupant is Boudica?" I asked.

"Do you truly believe Heinrich Schliemann found Priam's treasure at Troy? That the jewelry he photographed his wife wearing belonged to Helen? Archaeology as a science is relatively young. In the early days, monuments and tombs were destroyed by treasure hunters. Now, we know better how to record our finds. How to analyze them. At the same time, we can't deny it's an expensive pursuit.

Historically significant discoveries will draw in patrons who can fund long digs."

"Patrons who don't know enough to recognize disingenuous claims," I said.

"Yes, that's also true. However, they're the sort of people who've always believed what they want. Who am I to disabuse them of the habit of a lifetime?"

"You can see why Loxton and I get along so famously." Sebastian did not enter the room through the door. Instead, he stepped through one of the windows. In one hand, he held a velvet box; in the other, a Brownie camera. "Prepare yourself, Emily, for what I have to present you is like nothing the world has ever seen."

He crossed to me, knelt down, and gave me the box. "I'm not in the habit of accepting jewelry from men who are not my husband."

"It's not yours to keep," he said, "only to model. I want a picture of you wearing it, à la Schliemann and his wife. Open it."

Curious, I did as he asked. Inside the box was a heavy torc, more than half an inch thick, constructed of two gold ropes twisted together, and a matching brooch.

"ἦν δὲ καὶ τὸ σῶμα μεγίστη καὶ τὸ εἶδος βλοσυρωτάτη τό τε βλέμμα δριμυτάτη, καὶ τὸ φθέγμα τραχὺ εἶχε, τήν τε κόμην πλείστην τε καὶ ξανθοτάτην οὖσαν μέχρι τῶν γλουτῶν καθεῖτο, καὶ στρεπτὸν μέγαν χρυσοῦν ἐφόρει, χιτῶνά τε παμποίκιλον ἐνεκεκόλπωτο, καὶ χλαμύδα ἐπ᾽ 3 αὐτῷ παχεῖαν ἐνεπεπόρπητο. οὕτω μὲν ἀεὶ ἐνεσκευάζετο·." Sebastian looked directly at Colin. "I, too, can recite Greek."

"*In stature she was very tall, in appearance most terrifying, in the glance of her eye most fierce, and her voice was harsh; a great mass of the tawniest hair fell to her hips; around her neck was a large golden necklace; and she wore a tunic of divers colors over which a thick mantle was fastened with a brooch. This was her invariable attire,*" I translated.

"It's obviously hers, Boudica's," Sebastian said. He grabbed the box back from me, removed the torc, and moved toward my neck.

"No one should be wearing this," I said. "It's more than a thousand years old."

"It's perfectly fine. Loxton gave it the once-over. It's not about to disintegrate."

Mr. Loxton stammered. "I—I . . . yes, I confirmed that it's in remarkable condition, but, even so, I didn't mean to suggest that—"

"Oh, do put it on, Emily," Sebastian said. "Your neck is slender. You won't have to bend it."

I never should've done it, but I couldn't resist. I took the torc from him and slipped it onto my neck. My skin tingled. All reason vanished from my head. What if it had belonged to Boudica? Could she have worn it into battle? I could almost convince myself I felt heat pulsing from it. I took the brooch and clasped it to the bodice of my gown.

"Emily, I don't think this is a good idea," Colin said.

"Do be quiet, Hargreaves. I don't need you interfering. Stand just as you are, Emily, and be still." He raised the camera and took several pictures of me.

"Which paper do you plan to sell them to?" Colin asked. "I won't have my wife on display as your—"

I marched forward and grabbed the camera from Sebastian. "I'll keep this until the film is developed. You're not publishing these anywhere."

"I had no intention of doing anything of the sort. What do you take me for?"

"A man of dubious character, utterly devoid of morals," Colin said. "A thief."

"Always getting caught up in details, that husband of yours."

Sebastian said, flinging himself onto a chair. "Might I please have some whisky?"

"Get it yourself," Colin said, then thought the better of it. "No, don't." He poured him a glass.

"It suits you, Emily," Sebastian said, smiling as he looked at me. "You'd have made a capital warrior queen."

I removed the jewelry and returned it to the box, which I then handed to Mr. Loxton. "Keep it safe," I directed him.

"Of course, Lady Emily, of course."

"When did you find it?" I asked.

"This afternoon," Mr. Loxton said. "It was some distance from the skeleton. Closer to the mirror, which suggests to me that she wasn't wearing it when she was buried."

"You've got to report this," I said. "Even if it didn't belong to Boudica, it's a significant discovery."

"That it is," Sebastian said. "I find myself rather taken with archaeology. Perhaps I shall redirect my efforts in that direction."

"You'd be dirty all the time," I said. "You hate that."

He sighed. "You know me too well."

"You do realize you can't keep the objects you find," I said. "Strictly speaking, they're the property of whoever owns the building. That person ought to donate them to a museum. Now that you've shown them to us, you can't claim they don't exist."

"I never planned to," he said. "Iron Age Britain isn't a particular interest of mine, although I would like to see Frances Price leading a suffragette march wearing Boudica's torc."

"According to what you told us before, marches were never part of her plan," Colin said. "Who owns the building?"

"The truth is, I'm not entirely sure. I'm acquainted with the solicitor who represents the owner. He turned to me for advice after the tenant found some scraps of Roman pottery in the cellar. I told him if he secured permission from the owner, I would conduct a thorough excavation."

"Why would any legitimate solicitor entrust you with such a task?" I asked.

"The owner wants to maximize the profits from whatever we uncover. I have a certain reputation for being good with that sort of thing. I told the solicitor the discoveries might bring attention to a new group of young suffragettes. That appealed to him, although he admitted it wouldn't be wise to let the owner know."

"So much for being discreet about Boudica's Sisters," I said.

"I didn't reveal any specific information about them," Sebastian said. "I'm a man who always knows his audience and never gives up more than I must."

"We'll need the name of the solicitor," Colin said.

"Cecil Cooke."

Mr. Cooke would be having an interesting conversation tomorrow.

46

Britannia

I promised chaos, didn't I?

That's exactly what I found when I returned to the village from Gaius's home. Prasutagus was dead.

I went straight to Boudica.

"It happened so quickly," she said. We had retreated to her bedroom so we'd be left alone. "One minute, he was holding an audience, the next, he'd fallen to the ground. He was gone."

"What now?" I asked.

"He'd made his new will. Half our kingdom is now a possession of the emperor."

"What does that mean? Will he physically divide it? Or continue to allow us to rule ourselves and pay him even more tribute?"

"Can you envision a scenario where he'd be content with only half? No. He'll demand everything. Of that I have no doubt."

For a few weeks, nothing happened. To the Iceni, that is. I wasn't so lucky.

"I know what you did." Minura was waiting for me when I went to feed our pigs one morning. "I followed you after you left our house when you were done abusing me the day Prasutagus died. I could easily let Duro know, too."

"You'll do what you want. I can't stop you."

"You should watch yourself, Vatta," she said. "Things are changing here. Without Prasutagus to pacify the Romans, I doubt they'll be our friends for much longer. You can be sure Boudica will distance herself from anyone close to them. You're in a dangerous situation."

"What do you want? For me to thank you for the warning?"

She smiled a wicked smile. "I don't care what you do."

I didn't much care what she did.

I'd only seen Gaius once since that morning, at the palace. Boudica was sitting in Prasutagus's seat, holding the audiences he would've if he'd still been alive. He didn't acknowledge me. Didn't even look at me. He handed her a letter from the emperor.

She read it and then stood up, directly in front of him.

"The Iceni will never be subjects of the Romans," she said. "My husband was recognized as a sovereign ruler."

"Your husband is dead. Any understandings between him and the emperor are no longer relevant. Your daughters will, of course, be treated with the utmost respect, as will you, but the governing of this land is now in the hands of Rome. There's nothing further to be said on the matter." He marched out of the room.

A silence descended on us all. I felt like everyone was staring at me. Like they knew I was his lover. That's the way people work, isn't it? Always convinced they're at the center of the universe, everything revolving around them. The truth was, I didn't even know if Minura had told anyone what I'd done. Even if she had, in that moment, no one cared about me. All they wanted to know was what would happen next.

"We can't submit to them," Boudica told me that evening. I'd dined with her, alone. She needed a confidante now that Prasutagus was gone. "I've told all my advisers that, but I don't know if they agree."

"They're willing to give up?" I asked. "To become Roman?"

"Many of them are content to do so. They believe it will enhance their wealth. They're fools. It will mean more taxes, more tribute. They're already demanding a fortune. They say they loaned it to us and want repayment without delay."

"When did they ever make us a loan?"

"When Prasutagus became a client king," she said. "We thought they were making a gift. The emperor sees it differently."

"So what will you do?"

"Repay them what I can."

"If wasn't a loan in the first place—"

"I don't know what it was," she said, "but I'm beginning to suspect Prasutagus didn't tell me everything. My guess is that's why he wanted to leave half the kingdom to Rome. To pay back his debt and keep our sovereignty. Of course, now they say that's not enough."

"Did Duro ever give you his battle plan?" I asked.

"He has not. I need you to remind him that I still want it."

So I did, on my way home from the palace. It was late, but the moon was full and its light was almost as bright as the sun. A rare, clear night. I took it as a good omen.

"So she sent you," Duro observed after I told him why I'd come.

I couldn't tell if he was pleased to see me; I told him as much.

"You've been hard to find lately," he said. "I'm told there's other company you prefer."

"I've been wondering if you were ever going to make good on your promise to figure out what would make marriage worthwhile to me."

"Maybe I decided it shouldn't be so hard."

"Maybe you're right," I said.

"When I see you, though . . ." He stepped closer to me and put his hands on my cheeks.

I pulled away. "Don't."

"It's true then," he said. "You're all but a Roman."

"I'm not."

"Too Roman for me." He shoved me, so hard I fell to the ground. "Minura was right. You're not to be trusted."

47

London

Before we visited Mr. Cooke's offices the next morning, Colin researched the man's practice. The bulk of his clients were slumlords. It may be wrong to judge based solely on appearance, but in this case, Mr. Cooke's greasy hair and slickly expensive suit formed a perfect picture of a solicitor of dubious morals. Thus, it came as no surprise he was hesitant to discuss the goings-on at the property in Ludgate Hill.

"Not everyone is happy to have their private business transactions laid public for all to view," he said. "The property is owned by an anonymous trust, not an individual."

"We're in the midst of a murder inquiry," Colin said.

"I appreciate that, but a handful of Roman ruins can hardly bear upon it. My client demands discretion. There's nothing more I can say."

"I don't understand the need for privacy," I said.

"My client is in a somewhat precarious financial situation. The objects being excavated at Ludgate Hill may prove a way out of these difficulties." He spoke so quickly it was as if he hoped we wouldn't be able to understand his words. "As a result, we would all prefer to draw no attention to the site until the dig is complete. I don't want to invite the notice of treasure hunters."

"Do you believe it's reasonable to expect the sale of the objects will bring your client back from the brink of financial ruin?" Colin asked.

"I never mentioned ruin," Mr. Cooke said. "Difficulties are one thing, ruin another. However, if the treasure belonged to Boudica, then, yes, it could rescue one even from that."

"What if the connection to Boudica can't be proved?" I asked.

"I have every faith in Mr. Capet. It's why I brought him in on the project."

I longed to accuse him of being careless with the truth, but realized it would not help my cause. The fact was, unless we could link the murder to the excavations, we couldn't force him to tell us more. We thanked him and left his office. My plan was to walk with my husband to the Reform Club and then wait down the block in Berry Bros. for him to send word that Mr. Morgan had arrived for lunch. I would then take a cab to Knightsbridge and talk to Maeve.

"It's all very dodgy, this excavation," Colin said, "even if it is strictly legal."

"Until they start lying about Boudica. Surely the law doesn't allow for that."

"Cooke won't let them make oversized claims. He'll insist on language that doesn't get them in trouble. There are plenty of collectors who would be thrilled to overpay for something that Boudica *might* have worn."

"What about the remains themselves?"

"They're likely to wind up on display in the British Museum if there's a meaningful link to the warrior queen. Otherwise, my guess is they'll be remanded to storage."

"The poor girl," I said. "I don't believe she's Boudica, but whoever she was, she deserves a decent burial."

"Quite." We'd reached his club. "We mustn't let it distract us, however. I don't see how any of it connects to the murders."

"Mr. Morgan isn't bankrupt. He may own some property. Perhaps the building in Ludgate Hill belongs to him."

"I shall see what I can learn." He gave me a quick kiss and disappeared inside. I retreated to Berry Bros., where, while I waited for confirmation that it was safe to continue on to Knightsbridge, I ordered a not insignificant amount of port to be laid down for me.

Maeve answered the door when I arrived at Mr. Morgan's house. The bruising on her wrist was still visible. She started to shake when I told her I'd come to speak to her.

"I'm sorry, madam," she said. "I'd like to be of help, of course, but there's a great deal of work to be done this afternoon, and I can't shirk my duties."

"I know about Mr. Morgan. What he's done to you."

"I'm sure I've no idea what you're talking about." She stepped onto the stoop and closed the door behind her. "I'm very happy with my position."

"It's not the only one in London," I said. "I'm in need of a parlormaid myself."

For the flash of an instant I saw something in her eyes. Hope, maybe. It vanished as quickly as it came. "I wish you the best of luck in finding a suitable candidate. Now, I must return to work or I'll be in trouble."

"Maeve, I have reason to believe Mr. Morgan trifled with another girl before you came into his employ. She had bruises just like you do. She's dead now."

"Mr. Morgan would never—"

"Wouldn't he?" I asked. "You fought back, didn't you? That's why he had a bruise on his face when I called on him the other day. You must be a very strong girl to have managed that."

"He never told you I did it. I'm going to get into trouble. Please leave."

"My husband is with him right now, lunching, to give us the opportunity to speak. You're safe."

"I'm not safe," she said. "I'm never safe."

"He's hurting you, isn't he?" She nodded. "Right. Go inside and collect your things. Tell no one where you're going or why. You're coming home with me and will never face Mr. Morgan again. As I said, I'm in need of a parlormaid."

She did as I asked. Back at Park Lane, she confessed all Mr. Morgan had done to her. "He's that sort of man," she said. "There are many of them. They've been taught to take what they want and don't see anything wrong with it."

"There's plenty wrong with it and being badly brought up doesn't excuse that sort of behavior."

"You told me there was another girl. That was Ida, wasn't it?"

"Ida Davies," I said. "You know her name? Were you acquainted?"

"Ida. He told me about her. Told me he wasn't going to make the mistake of trying to help a girl get above her station again."

"He admitted to you what he did to her?" I was aghast.

"No, not exactly. He told me he was fond of girls like me and that I reminded him of a former friend of his. Her name was Ida.

He'd taken good care of her, he said, but she'd treated him badly in the end. That's why he wouldn't take me out walking in the park. He'd learned his lesson, he said."

"She did nothing to him," I said. "He seduced her, then abandoned her. When she found out she was with child, she killed herself."

She shuddered. "You won't tell the butler or housekeeper what's been done to me, will you? I wouldn't want anyone to know."

"Then they shan't be told. However, I do hope you'll consider reporting the crime. Mr. Morgan mustn't be allowed to do this again."

"I don't think I could bear to." Her voice was a bare whisper. "It would be like living through it all again but with people mocking me while it's happening. I know how girls who come forward in situations like this get treated."

How I wished I could guarantee her that the police and the courts and the public would be kind. "Mr. Hargreaves and I will support you however you choose to deal with this. It's your decision."

"I'd rather just get down to work, madam," she said. "I'm grateful you've taken me away from Mr. Morgan, but he's your friend, isn't he? Will I have to see him here?"

"I would never consider a man who preys on women a friend. He will not be welcome again in this house. Even so, I don't want you anywhere near him. If it's agreeable to you, I'd like you to take up service on our estate in Derbyshire."

"I would like that, madam. I've never much liked London and don't have any friends or family here. Thank you."

I rang for Davis, who would arrange the details. Colin returned from the Reform Club soon thereafter.

"She doesn't want to go to the police," I said, after briefing him on all that had happened.

"I don't blame her, but it's infuriating that he won't be punished for his crimes."

"Unless we can prove he's guilty of murder. Knowing what he did to Ida solidifies his motive."

"It would if we could prove Miss Goldsborough knew what he'd done and threatened to expose him," Colin said. "The same goes for Miss Wright. All of our evidence is circumstantial."

"Did you find out anything about the building in Ludgate Hill Road?"

"He's not the owner. We had a lengthy discussion about his finances. He doesn't even own the house in which he lives. It belongs to his father and will be inherited by his brother. They're both aware that he ought not be in control of property or capital. That said, even if he owns the building, there's still no connection to the murders."

"Not one we've yet found, but I'm convinced there's something."

"You're letting your flair for fiction and your love of archaeology distract you."

"No, my instinct is telling me there's something there," I said. "Mark my words, I shall find it."

I couldn't sleep that night. When I heard the hall clock chime three o'clock, I gave up, slipped out of bed, and went down to the library, where I spent hours debating the merits of two separate theories. I was still there, wide awake at my desk, when Colin found me the next morning. By then, I'd settled on the more likely of the two.

"I wonder if we're on the wrong track altogether," I said. "Perhaps we haven't given enough thought to cui bono."

"So who do you think benefits from these deaths?"

"Portia is newly engaged to Oscar Tenley. Cressida's murder eliminated her as a rival."

"Yes, but Portia would hardly have killed her own sister," Colin said.

"I'd like to think not, but she's the one who brought us the diary that so neatly hammered home Victoria's image as a traditional girl who'd never support suffrage. What if Portia had learned about Boudica's Sisters? Had Victoria's role in the group become public, it would've undermined Portia's relationship with Mr. Tenley."

"Making sure the diary was in evidence didn't stop us from discovering Miss Goldsborough's role in the organization."

"No, but Portia's so sheltered she might not have anticipated that. If she felt betrayed by her sister and vulnerable in her hopes for marriage, she might've lashed out. She easily could've given Victoria the poison before they left for the ball."

"The exposure of her sister as a suffragette would've harmed her chances on the Marriage Market. Not only with Tenley."

"A young lady convinced there is no hope for her future can be dangerous," I said. "Frances has admitted she knew things might not work out for her with Mr. Tenley. Cressida told us she'd opened her heart to him."

"Prompting Portia to act again." He shook his head. "I'm not wholly convinced. She hasn't been out in Society since her sister's death. How would she know about Miss Wright's change of feelings?"

"Mr. Tenley might've told her. I want to speak to the Wrights' butler and Hazel, Cressida's maid, again and then to Portia. I also think it's important to find out who's behind the trust that owns the property in Ludgate Hill. There's a chance that Mr. Morgan's father set it up on his son's behalf."

"A valid point," Colin said. "It may take some time, but I can get to the bottom of that. I'm still not convinced it's got anything to do with the murders, but if it turns out to be connected to his family, that would change everything."

48

Britannia

The next day, Duro gave his battle plan to Boudica. She didn't share the details with me. Did she no longer want to confide in me? What had he said to her? Maybe I was being paranoid. Maybe I'd let Minura get in my head. After all, I was no military genius. Why should she tell me?

Three days after that, I was off with the sheep, so disheartened I hadn't even brought Ovid with me. I was being tugged between two worlds, and right now, I didn't much like either of them. I'd been a fool to have gone to Gaius. That much was obvious. He'd has his fun and lost all interest. I hadn't seen or heard from him since that day.

Until I was making my way back home and someone grabbed me from behind. Gaius.

"Quiet," he said, pulling me off the path and into a small copse. "You and your family are in a great deal of danger. Leave the village at once. Take what you can carry, but draw no attention to yourselves. Don't tell anyone what you're doing."

"Why would I believe you?"

"You're angry I've ignored you. I understand that. It was wrong of me. I can offer excuses, but they don't suffice. Now, though, you must listen. I'm trying to help you."

"What's going on?"

"Your queen is refusing to give the emperor what he demands. What's rightfully his. This won't be tolerated."

"Half of our kingdom isn't enough?" I asked. "She's honoring the terms of Prasutagus's will. A Roman will, at that. He followed the form of your people."

"Half doesn't repay what he owes Rome. When you borrow money, eventually you've got to give it back. The emperor has no interest in renegotiating terms with the king's daughters. His agreement was with Prasutagus." He took me by the shoulders. "Look, Vatta, I haven't been trifling with you. I care about you. That's why I'm warning you. Leave the village immediately."

"And go where?"

"Anywhere that is not here. Camulodunum would do."

"That's more than fifty miles away."

"You'll want the distance. I can't say more but beg you to trust me." He looked into my eyes. "I hope to see you again."

He didn't walk with me back to the village. I don't know where he went. Home, I suppose, to his comfortable villa. I headed straight for the palace. Boudica was outside, with her horses.

"I've had a strange conversation," I said and repeated Gaius's warning.

She looked skeptical but concerned. "Do you believe there's something to fear? Or is this a way of him manipulating you? If he

THE SISTERHOOD

gets you and your family out of the village, will he then offer you some sort of assistance so that he has control over you?"

"I don't know why he'd bother. He's already got what he wanted."

"Yes, I've heard. Minura told everyone. Duro's disappointed."

"He'll get over it," I said. "I don't know that I trust Gaius, but can't see him gaining anything by lying about this. Do you trust the Romans?"

"They want more from us. I'll do my best to negotiate with them—"

"Will they let you? They're used to taking what they want."

"There's always been respect between us," she said. "Even after the rebellion, they allowed Prasutagus to maintain our independence. I'll stay on alert, but I'm not worried."

She should have been.

No more than a handful of days later, the Romans swarmed the village. They stormed the palace. It wasn't only soldiers, but slaves, too, making the attack. They dragged Boudica and her daughters into the street. The girls were violated; their mother, flogged.

We were sovereign no more.

49

London

My conversations with the Wrights' servants proved fruitless. The butler was certain Portia hadn't called on Cressida after Victoria's death, and Hazel had no memory of Cressida ever mentioning Portia. I continued on to the Goldsboroughs, more confounded than ever. Nothing about this case was coalescing the way I expected it to. Every time I thought I could grasp the solution, it slipped away.

The sun was so hot as I made my way to Berkeley Square that I nearly opened my parasol, but didn't. It would be damp and cold soon enough and I'd regret not having basked in the warmth while I could. The moment I entered the square, I saw my mother stepping out of her open carriage in front of the Goldsboroughs' house. I stopped walking, thinking it would be better not to call when she was there. Unfortunately, however, she looked in my direction and motioned for me to come to her. There was no point in avoiding the confrontation.

She immediately admonished me. "Parasols were invented to prevent unsightly harm to the skin. You will come to regret abstaining from their use."

"I presume we're both here to call on the Goldsboroughs," I said. I wasn't about to argue with her.

"Have you any notion how rude it is to ignore one's mother?" She huffed. "The fact that I somehow manage to maintain even a veneer of civility when you behave like this is a testament to my strength of character." She snapped her own parasol shut and rapped on the door with its handle. The butler took us to the sitting room, where Lady Goldsborough and all three of her surviving granddaughters were gathered.

"What a delightful surprise to have you both here together," she said. "Do sit. I'll call for tea."

"None for me, please." I remained standing. "I'd like to have a word with Portia in private."

Lady Goldsborough sighed. "Will this investigation never end? It's bad enough to have lost our dear Victoria, but now it seems all hope of a peaceful household is gone as well."

"I'm hopeful that if she can shed light on one or two things for me, we may be at the end of our inquiry."

She perked up and smiled at my mother before turning back to me. "Considering what I brought to you last time we met, I think I know what you mean. Do what you must to prove his guilt."

"And do it quickly, Emily," my mother said. "It's high time you stop tormenting this family."

Portia and I retreated to the music room. "It pains me to see the piano," she said, resting a hand on the instrument as she stood next to it. "No one will ever use it again now that Victoria's gone. We should get rid of it."

"Eventually, you may welcome the memories it evokes. You'll never stop grieving your sister, but time will alter the shape of your feelings."

"I do hope you're right. Why did you pull me away from the others? Is it to talk about Oscar? Or does it really have to do with the murders?"

Her tone was so cheerful, it was hard to reconcile with her comment about the piano. "I need you to tell me the truth, no matter whom you think it might hurt. This is crucial, Portia. Did you have any knowledge of Victoria's involvement with Boudica's Sisters?"

"Victoria abhorred them," she said. "You read her diary. She was no suffragette."

"You never heard her mention anything to do with Boudica in a positive light?"

"Not in reference to the suffragettes, but to the queen, yes. She has that painting of her in her room, but you already know that. Frances gave it to her." She stopped and put a finger on her lips. "In fact, now that I think about it, I do remember something. We were all in the sitting room one afternoon. It was a vile day. Driving rain. Victoria and Frances were bent together in conversation, saying something about mud and how it was lucky the archaeologists weren't working outside. Victoria said she doubted Boudica would like to know she'd been buried in someone's cellar. I had no idea what that meant, so I asked her; and she replied that there was a great discovery being made in the City, not far from St. Paul's. Apparently, someone has discovered the queen's tomb."

"When was this?"

"Not terribly long before she died. Remember how horrid the weather had been? Relentless rain."

"Was there any further discussion of the subject?"

"Grandmama said she didn't believe it. Why would Boudica be buried in London when she'd died elsewhere?" She crinkled her nose. "Where did she die? I can't remember. I suppose it doesn't matter. Frances said there was incontrovertible proof and that it would be announced in the next few weeks."

"Did Victoria say anything else?"

"No, but they were both giggling over it until Grandmama told them to behave with decorum. I don't really understand why they were so excited, but it certainly wasn't because of Boudica's Sisters. That, I can guarantee you."

I did not doubt she believed her words. There was no hint, either in her tone or her expression, to suggest she was lying.

"There's one other thing," I said. "It's to do with Mr. Tenley. Last time we spoke, you gave me the impression you hadn't been aware of Cressida's involvement with him. Cressida saved her dance cards. Given how frequently he partnered her, surely you noticed."

She pursed her lips and chewed on the inside of her cheek. "I did, and I admit to having been ever so slightly jealous. After all, she had a fortune, while my grandmother will barely be able to scrape together a dowry for me. In the end, though, it didn't matter to Oscar, did it? I'm the one he proposed to."

"After Cressida died."

"Yes, but that—Heavens, Emily, you cannot be suggesting that you think I killed her?"

I studied the expression on her face, a mixture of naïveté and horror. "No, I don't mean to suggest that. I only want to get the timing correct. It could prove important."

"Yes, it was after she . . . It's all so awful. These things that should bring such great joy tainted by endless sorrow."

"Have you stuck to your decision not to tell your grandmother about your engagement yet?" I asked.

"Yes. Once the murder inquiry is closed, we can all start again anew."

The door to the room opened and Colin apologized for interrupting. "I need a quick moment with my wife," he said. "We'll meet you back in the sitting room."

Portia squeezed my hand on her way out and smiled.

"She's chipper," Colin said. "Did you learn what you needed to?"

"Yes, but it wasn't at all what I expected. I had a strange idea late last night that I rejected. It relied even more than usual on speculation, but now I'm beginning to think it's the only way to explain everything."

"See if this supports it." He handed me a sheet of paper listing the details of Mr. Cooke's mysterious trust.

"It does." I frowned. "There's one more thing I want to check."

We slipped downstairs and spoke to three of the footmen. Colin easily convinced them they had much to risk if they weren't candid with us.

"We ought to tell the family," he said when we were done. "You should do the honors. If you hadn't pressed for this"—he motioned to the paper and shook his head—"I don't know that we ever would've uncovered the truth. Further, there are questions I still don't know how to answer."

"I do," I said, feeling suddenly confident.

We went to the sitting room, where the mood was notably more jovial than it had been when I arrived. Portia was laughing with her little sisters. My mother was detailing for Lady Goldsborough something she'd seen in the park that morning.

"That she would even consider wearing a dress like that," she said. "Can you imagine?"

"The impropriety exhibited by ladies this Season has sunk to new lows." Lady Goldsborough shook her head. "It's appalling."

"I couldn't agree more," I said, coming to stand in front of them. "The wrong gown is bad enough, but murder is something else altogether."

"Quite right," Lady Goldsborough said. "Dare I hope you've learned what you needed to?"

"In fact, I have. This case puzzled us from the start and only grew more complicated with time. Particularly after Cressida Wright's death. There seemed to be no connection between her and Victoria, and, as it turned out, there wasn't."

"No?" Lady Goldsborough asked, startled. "You can't mean there are two murderers?"

"It would be best if I start at the beginning," I said.

"Winnie, Seraphina, do go upstairs," my mother said. "This isn't fit conversation for young girls."

"Yes, you're quite right, Catherine," Lady Goldsborough said. "I nearly forgot myself. I've been waiting for this news for so long. Portia, go with them. You, too, ought to be spared the details."

"Grandmama, I'd rather stay," she said. "Victoria was my sister."

"As are Winnie and Seraphina. Take care of them for the moment, and I'll—"

"Portia ought to stay," I said.

"Emily, it is not your place—"

"It is my place, Mother. She needs to be here."

"The governess can look after them, Catherine," Lady Goldsborough said. "Portia is grown now and ought to be included."

The governess was summoned and the girls taken away.

"I believe you meant to start at the beginning, Emily," my mother said. "How much longer do you plan to keep us waiting? Are there any other household arrangements in which you'd like to interfere before commencing?"

"Victoria's Season was what every debutante dreams of," I said. "She captivated all of Society from the first and made a spectacular match more quickly than anyone could've anticipated."

"Catching a marquess before Ascot is unheard of," my mother said. "Show me another girl who's managed that."

"I can't think of anyone," Lady Goldsborough said, "although you know a certain lady of our acquaintance had aspirations for her eldest daughter."

"That girl never had a chance—"

"May I continue?" I asked. "Or would you prefer to finish gossiping first?"

"Forgive us, we let emotion carry us away," Lady Goldsborough said.

"From the outside, it seemed as if nothing could go wrong for Victoria. Those on the inside, however, saw something different altogether. Victoria and her dearest friend founded Boudica's Sisters in an attempt to start changing the beliefs held by the most eligible gentlemen in Society. It was an ambitious goal and a dangerous one, for it threatened the very fabric that the Establishment believes holds our world together."

Portia looked stunned. My mother gave every appearance of taking the news in stride; I assumed Lady Goldsborough had already told her.

"I'm not here for a lecture, Emily," my mother said. "If you'd like to rhapsodize on the subject of suffrage, perhaps you should see if Mrs. Pankhurst could organize a rally for you or lend you the use of a balcony. Are you ever going to get to the bit where you tell us who has committed these vile murders?"

"If you'd let me continue without interruption, we'd get there more quickly." I couldn't rush through this. There was too much at stake.

50

Britannia

I took Boudica and her daughters to my parents' house, so my mother and I could nurse their physical wounds. As for the emotional, there was little we could do. At first, shock kept them silent, and they all disappeared into shells of themselves.

The flogging had torn thick chunks of Boudica's flesh from her back, but the horror of seeing her daughters publicly brutalized and humiliated left a greater mark. Before her skin could tolerate the weight of fabric, she sent Duro to the leaders of the Trinovantes, a neighboring tribe. The Romans had taken their land and built their most important city, Camulodunum, on it. Through her messenger, she implored them to join the Iceni in fighting their common enemy. Rome would no longer take whatever it wanted from the Britons.

Duro had identified Camulodunum as the primary target in his battle plan. I knew nothing more than that.

"I trust you, Vatta, I do," Boudica said. In the weeks that had passed, she'd healed enough to return to her ransacked palace. Gone were all the gold and silver objects. The Romans had stolen everything of value. "The trouble is, the rest of the tribe doesn't. They know about your connection to Gaius. They wonder why you read Latin poetry. They remember your brother fights in the army of our enemy."

"No one objected to Solinus joining them when he left."

"Back then, no one thought it would come to this. The best thing you can do now is keep quiet and stay out of the way. Don't think I'm walking away from our friendship. I still value it, but I can't show that to the world right now."

So now my own people were rejecting me. As if it wasn't bad enough that Gaius had done it. This stung more and I wasn't going to stand for it. I would fight for my place in the tribe.

I packed supplies, mounted Aesu, and rode the long distance toward Camulodunum. It took two days. Even before I arrived, I could see all was not well. As I approached the estuary, I saw eerie images of a city that wasn't there, glowing with an evil light, and shapes like corpses on the damp ground where the tide had receded. Positive omens, I thought. I rode on.

Once inside Camulodunum, I met a barrage of noise, women wailing and keening, warning of imminent destruction. Disembodied voices laughing and shouting in an unknown language came from the senate house and the theater. I took note of it all, but it had little effect on me. I was there with a purpose.

The general state of hysteria in the place meant I could move around without drawing attention to myself. I drew maps and recorded the location of the only garrison in the town as well as other buildings that could be used for defense. I counted the soldiers.

Then, as I prepared to go home, I witnessed one final omen: the city's statue of Victory tumbled to the ground. It was time for the Iceni to attack.

The ride back to Venta Icenorum felt like it took years. I hadn't been gone that long, but I hardly recognized the place when I returned. It was heaving with warriors. Not just the Iceni, but the Trinovantes, who had agreed to Boudica's alliance.

From what I could see, the alliance didn't specify much beyond combining forces. Loud arguments raged as to when they should attack, and not everyone accepted Duro's strategic plans.

That's where I came in. I approached Boudica quietly, without drawing attention to myself. That's a pretty way of saying I sneaked into the palace in the middle of the night. This should've been challenging. She was under guard, after all, but men don't recognize the threat women can be. I pulled a shawl over my head so it disguised my face, carried a jug of ale, and told them the queen was thirsty. They let me in without even asking my name.

"You shouldn't be here," she said. That was the last objection I heard from her. My maps and my report about the state of things in Camulodunum gave her all the ammunition she needed to convince her allies the time was right to attack. Just like that, I was no longer a pariah. I'd proven my loyalty.

When our army mustered for the march, Boudica ordered me next to her in front, both of us in our wicker chariots. No other exhilaration could compare. We set off with a roar of battle cries and the sound of hooves and stomping feet. The size of our force alone made it unthinkable victory wouldn't come easily.

A seasoned soldier would tell you it did come easily. For me, who had never before seen such violence, a different word would fit better. It's just I had no idea what that word was.

The city had no walls. We surrounded it and moved in, burning everything in our way. The air, acrid with thick black smoke, burned my lungs. Although it had taken us days to reach Camulodunum, long enough to give the Romans plenty of notice, they hadn't bothered to evacuate. Women, children, the old, and infirm, were all still there. They fled in front of us, but had nowhere to go. They raced to the Temple of Claudius, an enormous stone building, its roof supported by rows of columns, and locked themselves inside.

The few Roman soldiers on hand fought hard, but were no match for us. Eventually, they, too, sought shelter in the temple. For two days we laid siege to them there. Two days of listening to their cries and lamentations.

Then, we arranged logs around the base of the temple. We filled it in with tinder and kindling. We lit a fire. We flung torches onto the roof. Soon, the building was engulfed in flames.

The sounds from inside grew louder and more desperate, mirroring what I'd heard from Boudica and her daughters when they were attacked. Never again would the Romans act with such savagery.

At least that's what I thought then, before I understood that evil begets revenge which begets revenge which begets revenge. Why would the cycle ever end?

51

London

"The primary difficulty with this case is that there was no obvious connection between the two victims," I said. "Once we discovered the truth about Boudica's Sisters, it made sense Victoria's murderer might be motivated by anti-suffragette sentiments. Lord Harrington fit the bill in that regard, but he would've been more likely to end the engagement than to kill the woman he gave every appearance of loving."

"Of course it was him," my mother said. "Only imagine the mortification he would have suffered if Victoria's association with that horrid little group came out."

"I'm not sure embarrassment is sufficient motivation for murder, Catherine," Lady Goldsborough said. "I'd like to believe his character is stronger than that."

"If it's not, your family can rejoice at having avoided a bad match," my mother said. "Losing Victoria is painful enough without having to face the knowledge her fiancé was a murderer."

"Yes, well, we can all take comfort in that, Mother," I said, astonished at her insensitivity. Her friend didn't seem to notice it. "The trouble is, why would he have wanted Cressida Wright dead, too?"

"She was a terrible pest," Lady Goldsborough said. "One doesn't expect a gentleman to become violent in the face of a flirt of the worst kind, but one can only tolerate so much. Even so, I can't believe he would've killed either of them."

"I quite agree," Colin said. "We needed to find something to tie the two young ladies together. Harrington wasn't enough of a connection."

"While looking into Victoria's life, we learned Ida Davies's tragic story," I said. "A book Frances Price gave her led us to discover Victoria's role in founding Boudica's Sisters, but Ida also showed us a possible link between our two victims."

"I knew that would be the way," Lady Goldsborough said. "The instant I found the handkerchief, I saw it all."

"What handkerchief?" my mother asked.

"One belonging to Lionel Morgan," I said. "It was in Victoria's coat pocket. Mr. Morgan is in a great deal of debt. His friend, Lord Harrington, loaned him money."

"Victoria never would've allowed that to continue," Lady Goldsborough said, "and dear Peregrine would never disappoint her."

"He also received money from Cressida Wright," Colin said.

"Who wouldn't have let herself become a private bank," my mother said. "He proposed to her, you know? She refused him, of course. I've no doubt this is why. One wonders if it was a good decision, though. If she'd accepted him, she'd still be alive."

"Yes, but she'd be married to a murderer," Lady Goldsborough said.

"At least she'd have been married." My mother sighed. "What a tragedy for the poor girl."

"There's more to it than just the money," I said. "Mr. Morgan has a history of brutalizing female maids, and not only those in his own household. He was responsible for the attack on Ida Davies."

"Good heavens," my mother said. "The poor thing may have died by her own hand, but I'd argue he killed her, just as he did Victoria and Cressida."

"I agree he as good as murdered her," Colin said.

"Do please tell me he's already in police custody." Lady Goldsborough was all outrage.

"He will be dealt with," I said.

"You've tied it all up so neatly, Mr. Hargreaves," my mother said.

"Not quite," my husband replied. "Emily, you're the one who figured out the rest. Do please continue."

"There's more?" Lady Goldsborough asked.

"It all felt rather too neat," I said, "and we weren't convinced his financial situation was enough to prompt him to kill Cressida. She'd already given him money. Why eliminate the possibility of getting more from her?"

"Surely she wouldn't have given him more after turning down his proposal," my mother said.

"There was another wrinkle as well," I said. "According to Lord Harrington, Victoria had no knowledge of his having loaned money to his friend."

"Thus his motives vanish," my mother said. "I must say, Allegra, I never thought Mr. Morgan displayed signs of a murderous character. He's always been perfectly charming to me."

"Yes, but remember what he did to the maid," Lady Goldsborough said. "That shows an entirely different side of him, one that would make it unsurprising to find him guilty of two different types of heinous crimes."

"Our suspicions of him, in regard to the murders, didn't stand up to scrutiny, so we continued our search for evidence," I said. "Before her death, Cressida Wright admitted to us it was time she gave up on Lord Harrington. She could see how happily matched he was with Victoria and there was no longer any hope he might turn to her instead. In her words, she decided to open her heart to Oscar Tenley."

"Everyone knew that," my mother said. "It was old news weeks ago."

"I don't see how this is pertinent," Portia said, her eyes wide. The color drained from her face.

"We didn't either, until you shared your news with us."

"Emily, you promised not to—"

Her grandmother interrupted. "Not to what?"

"Your relationship with Mr. Tenley showed us the way to the truth," I said.

"What relationship is that?" my mother asked.

Portia sat very still, very silent.

"If you'd prefer I tell them, I will," I said.

"Mr. Tenley and I are engaged." She spat out the words.

"Oh, what a delightful development in the midst of so much horror," her grandmother said. "Why would you hide this from me?"

"I didn't think it was appropriate to announce so soon after Victoria's death."

"What a dear girl she is," my mother said. "To be so concerned about propriety shows the depth of her character. You brought her up well."

"I couldn't agree more," Lady Goldsborough said. "We of course won't tell the general public until the correct amount of time has passed, but this is nothing to be ashamed of. It's all I could've hoped for."

"Precisely," I said. "Which is why it's what allowed us to make the final connection between the two murders."

"I don't see what Mr. Tenley has to do with any of it," my mother said, "unless you're trying to take the wind out of Portia's sails by implying she was his second choice."

"Of course she wasn't his second choice," Lady Goldsborough said. "She's a far superior—"

"That's not what I meant at all," I said. "Victoria's killer acted for a very specific reason: to ensure that three other young ladies would have the chance to make good marriages."

"Why on earth would Mr. Morgan care so deeply for three other young ladies?" my mother asked.

"Mr. Morgan didn't kill anyone," I said and turned to her friend. "You did, Lady Goldsborough."

Portia gasped.

"I shall not tolerate being accused of such an atrocity." She shot to her feet, the veins on her neck throbbing. "No one could believe me capable of harming my own granddaughter."

"When you discovered Victoria's involvement with Boudica's Sisters, you feared she would be exposed. No gossip that salacious could be kept quiet forever, and while it might be possible to get Portia married before it came out, there would be no hope for Winnie and Seraphina if Society knew what Victoria had done."

"Even if she were part of that ridiculous group, she hadn't yet acted on her misguided impulses," my mother said.

"Other than manipulating Lord Harrington into an engagement

based on lies," I said. "The murderer struck before she could implement the rest of her plan. She and Frances Wright set a scheme in motion to marry themselves and other select girls to influential bachelors of rank and fortune. Once the weddings were over, they would do whatever was necessary to force their husbands to support suffrage."

"How on earth would such a thing be possible?" my mother asked.

"I'm certain you'd prefer not to know the details, but if you must, read Aristophanes' *Lysistrata*."

"I've no interest in any of your ridiculous Greek literature," she said.

"Whether they would've succeeded, we'll never know," I said, "but Lady Goldsborough wasn't willing to bet against it. She sacrificed one granddaughter to save the other three."

"I did nothing of the sort," Lady Goldsborough said. She'd sat back down, but her hands were shaking. "You'll stand in court accused of slander, Emily. You cannot prove any of this."

"In fact we can. It's all here." I waved the paper Colin had brought in front of me, then handed it to him. He folded it and put it in his interior jacket pocket. "You keep a footman stationed overnight in the corridor outside the girls' bedrooms. The pretense was they were guarding against intruders."

"A wise precaution," my mother said. "Look what happened to the dowager marchioness's tiara."

"They were also instructed to follow them if they left their rooms, as Victoria did one night," I said. "The night she met a man called Sebastian Capet. They discussed Boudica's Sisters. Your footman told you everything."

Lady Goldsborough said nothing, but clenched her fists.

"You knew then what you were up against. The day of the

Harringtons' ball, you gave Victoria a drink poisoned with yew while her maid struggled to secure her tiara. Your back garden is full of yew hedges. We all know what happened next. As Colin and I began our inquiries, you became afraid that we, too, would find out the truth about Boudica's Sisters. If we did, and exposed Victoria's involvement, your efforts would be for naught. You needed a second murder, one that couldn't be connected to suffragettes.

"The solution presented itself," I continued. "Like everyone else in Society, you'd heard the rumor that Cressida Wright was expecting a proposal from Mr. Tenley, a gentleman you might have hoped would marry Portia. By eliminating Cressida, you could misdirect the investigation and secure your granddaughter's happiness."

"This is absurd," Lady Goldsborough said. "How could I have got her to drink poison?"

"You sent her a message, signed *A Friend Who Cares*, telling her that there was hope for her and Lord Harrington," I said. "It instructed her to meet you in Grosvenor Square, not long before she was set to leave for the Trumbles' ball. She might have tried to open her heart to Oscar, but it always belonged to Lord Harrington."

"We have the note. The handwriting matches the one you told us you found in Victoria's gabardine coat," Colin said. "Your attempt at making it look as if Morgan had written it was well done, but won't fool Scotland Yard's experts."

"When you met her, you brought with you a flask filled with poison and somehow enticed her to drink from it," I said. "We were still confused by Ida Davies's role in all this. I've known you all my life and had always considered you an ethical person. That's what made it all clear. You knew what Ida had suffered and you knew the identity of her attacker. She confided in you, did she not?"

"She did," Lady Goldsborough said, "in the hope I would ban

him from the house. I told her I would ensure he never troubled her again and made her promise to reveal his identity to no one else. I did not know about her delicate condition, however. That, she hid from me."

"I presume you framed Mr. Morgan because you didn't want to run the risk of an innocent person being charged with your crimes," I said. "His acts were utterly vile, but of a sort that rarely end in conviction. He deserved punishment and you couldn't rely on the law to command it. Why should he get away with so brutally abusing a young woman? It wasn't fair, and you had it in your power to correct a great injustice."

"I did, indeed," she said, "and I don't apologize for having done it. He deserves to be found guilty."

"Of grievously harming Ida Davies, yes," Colin said, "but not of committing murder."

"You've admitted to framing a man for murder," I said. "Do the right thing and confess the rest."

"I've nothing to say." She folded her arms.

"We've the testimony of your footman and will soon have confirmation from Scotland Yard that you wrote the notes," Colin said. "Further, there is this." He pulled the paper back out of his pocket.

"There is an archaeological dig taking place in a cellar near St. Paul's," I said. "It's uncovered objects purported to belong to Boudica, the British queen who led her army to slaughter scores of Romans after they'd violated her daughters and savagely flogged her. The same queen who inspired Victoria and Frances. I believe you heard them discussing it here in this very room, did you not, Lady Goldsborough?"

"Yes, I did," she said. "What does it matter?"

"An anonymous trust owns the property in question," I said.

"Your solicitor was careful not to reveal your name. He did, however, admit to having told the owner, who he knows is desperate for money, about the artifacts discovered. Their sale would help you immensely, but their existence being made public could also increase gossip about Boudica's Sisters. This sent you into a panic. You had to act at once, so that Victoria would not be exposed as a member."

"Once she was gone, if they were exposed there would've been no reason for her name to be mentioned in connection with them," Lady Goldsborough said. "It forced me to act so that my other granddaughters wouldn't be tainted by association."

"Grandmama, this can't be true," Portia said. Lady Goldsborough neither looked at her, nor replied, so I continued.

"The irony is that they wanted no attention. Their goal was to catalyze change from within. Secrecy was critical to their mission. Had you done nothing, it's likely that, yes, they would've been exposed. Victoria's marriage would've been called off, but she'd still be alive."

"And ruined," Lady Goldsborough spat. "And her sisters along with her. No decent family would have formed an alliance with any of them. My income isn't sufficient to support four spinsters, even if the dig is as profitable as I hope. I did what I must to ensure the girls' futures. You can understand, Mr. Hargreaves. The decision I made was what generals do whenever they go into battle. You sacrifice one unit to save the rest. It wasn't easy, but it had to be done."

52

Britannia

Our victory was complete, if brutal. That's what battles are like. Or so the warriors claimed. Except that they didn't. Not exactly. No one expressed regret or remorse, but neither did they celebrate the deaths of women and children. They believed it was justified, given what the Romans had done to Boudica and her daughters. We'd done what had to be done.

We weren't finished. We marched on, following our retreating enemies toward Londinium, a growing but unfortified city on the River Thames. My reconnaissance of Camulodunum had guided our every step and had proved flawless. I'd been correct about the number of soldiers we would face. About the best approaches into the city. I'd even identified the Temple of Claudius as the place the Romans would try to defend.

I'd stayed next to Boudica, each of us in our chariots, the entire time. My bravery and my loyalty would never again be questioned. For the first time, I felt like I belonged. Truly belonged.

As we approached Londinium, I could see it was no military enclave, just a motley collection of people engaged in trade. The army wasn't there. The Roman army, that is. Ours had other ideas.

Drunk on our earlier victory, we stormed the city, our desire for revenge not yet sated. This time, I hung back, slowing my chariot. Boudica shouted for me to catch up, but I pretended not to hear. We weren't fighting an army. Not even the remains of one. There were no Roman soldiers to be found.

That didn't matter to my tribesmen. All they saw were Romans. They took no notice of their gender, age, or occupation. They brutalized everyone and showed no mercy. The wholesale slaughter sickened me. I directed my horses away from it all, stopping when I was close to the river. I vomited, over and over, until there was nothing left in my body.

Then I wept. I wanted to hide, to escape, but there was nowhere to go. All that remained of the city was steaming ash. The only people left were my own.

"I was afraid you'd been killed."

It was Boudica, coming up behind me. I was still on the riverbank.

"No. I'm alive, for what that's worth," I said.

"They won't come for us again," she said. "Not after this. Now they know our strength and will leave us alone."

"Do you really believe that?"

"I do. They'll not have seen destruction like this before. Sometimes, brutality is the only way to preserve peace."

I knew she wasn't right. I'd read Caesar. I knew what Rome had suffered in Gaul. It hadn't daunted them. If anything, it spurred them on, just like the Roman attack on Boudica and her daughters had done to us.

Did I tell her any of this? No. I could see in her eyes that she'd never believe me. That she'd view it as proof I was more Roman than Iceni. So I followed her, out of Londinium to Verulamium, where our warriors did it all again.

Then we marched on. And on. And on.

"Where's the Roman army?" I saw Duro ahead of me and urged my chariot forward to catch him.

"Running scared," he said. "They won't be able to flee forever."

I searched the land ahead of us. They'd be there, somewhere, hidden, waiting. We wouldn't be able to march, unmolested, forever.

"Why continue on?" I asked Boudica that night, when we'd stopped to camp. "We've destroyed them. Can't we go home now? You said after all we've done, they'll leave us alone."

"They will," she said, "once our work is done. We still need to defeat their army."

I began to wonder if it would ever end. She was right, of course. Killing civilians sends a message. Defeating an army hammers it home. If we turned back now, they would follow. We couldn't avoid the inevitable battle.

It came the next day. We saw them, in a defile, a line of trees protecting them from behind. There was nothing to do but march forward and give ourselves over to fate. Looking around, I saw no one hesitate. Boudica stood at the front.

"We know what is at stake here," she said to her assembled troops. "Death or slavery, which do you prefer? We gave them the chance for peace. We paid them tribute. We did their bidding. And to what end? My back bears the scars that prove what life will be like for us if we lose today.

"Our enemy looks formidable," she continued. "Yet are they? We don't need chain mail and plate armor to protect ourselves from them. We don't need earthworks and fortifications to hide behind. They are soft where we are strong. They are scared where we are courageous. They are the rabbits, we are the wolves."

Roman javelins filled the air. The battle had begun.

Our numbers were much greater than theirs, but ours included our families, women and children hanging back with our wagons and supplies. We fought valiantly, but they broke through and began to push us back.

I don't know if it was tactics or weaponry or the gods, but we no longer had the upper hand. All was chaos now. All was blood and gore and death. Like us, the Romans spared no one, showed no mercy.

We were all the same.

I stayed at Boudica's side to the end, but it was to no avail. When we knew there was no hope, we drove away from the other straggling survivors to a spot hidden by trees.

"I won't be a slave and I won't march through Rome in chains," she said. She held up a small vial. "Poison. Will you join me?"

Join her? I didn't know what to say. So I nodded. She drank first. I watched her die, racked by convulsions.

"It's not a pleasant way to go." Gaius was standing behind me. "No one else knows you're here. Don't follow her lead."

"Become a slave instead?" I asked. "I'd rather die."

"I'd rather you didn't," he said, "and slavery isn't your only option. Leave this place. Start over somewhere new. You don't belong with these people."

"I don't belong with the Romans either."

"Nor do I when they kill women and children. Come with me."

"And do what? I'm not going back to your villa."

"My villa was razed," he said. "I can leave the army. Go somewhere else. Build a little farm."

"Every legionary's dream."

"No, they dream of a farm in Italy."

"You'd hate farming."

"Probably."

"I'm not going with you. Not after all this." The air was thick with the smell of death.

"Then flee. Promise me. Ride as fast as you can and disappear." He unhitched Aesu from my chariot. "Don't look back. Here there's nothing but death or slavery. You don't deserve either."

I could hear more soldiers approaching.

"You don't have much time. Please, Vatta, go. I'll distract them."

The poison was still in my hand. I looked at Boudica's motionless body. I listened to the soldiers' hobnailed sandals hit the ground. I met Gaius's eyes, just for a second.

"I could've loved you, you know," I said.

"You can do better."

"She deserves a royal burial."

"I'll see to it her body is returned to your people. I promise you that."

Somehow, I knew I could trust him. It was something in the tone of his voice, the seriousness in his eyes. The way he touched my cheek as he spoke. I reached down and removed Boudica's torc from around her neck. I took the matching brooch from her cloak. Without another word, I mounted Aesu and urged him forward. I heard Gaius shouting behind me.

"Their queen is here, dead, and with her all the hopes of the Iceni. Take her body to her people for burial. Our victory is complete."

I felt sick as I fled back down the road we'd marched from Londinium. The ruinous state of the town made it a good place for me to disappear. No one knew who I was, or where I'd come from. I could reinvent myself.

Or, even better, just be myself, with no external pressure from people who didn't understand me. Maybe, like my brother, I'd finally found my true place. I put Boudica's torc around my neck and fastened her brooch onto my cloak. I'd wear both pieces for the rest of my life, in memory of my friend.

53

London

After remanding Lady Goldsborough to the care of the police, Colin and I retired to Park Lane. My mother insisted on accompanying us. She stunned and impressed me by vowing to help Portia and her sisters in every way possible. Difficult though it would be to rehabilitate them socially after what their grandmother had done, at least they would have nothing to worry about financially, and if anyone could bend Society to her will, it was my mother. The warm feelings I had for her in the moment did not last. She quickly directed her ire to me.

"As I told you at the beginning of this mess, it's all your fault, Emily," she said. "Someone of Lady Goldsborough's character would never have stooped to such heinous crimes if she'd not been exposed to villains and miscreants through this dreadful work you insist on doing. You tarnish us all."

"I've hardly paraded hosts of criminals through her house," I said. "Your accusations are wholly unfair."

"All I've done since the day you were born is try to protect you. Your obstinacy and stubbornness have made it impossible for me to succeed."

"Perhaps, Lady Bromley, you ought to abandon your efforts," Colin said. "Emily is my wife, and, as such, it's my job to look after her. Let me remove your burden."

"A pretty idea, Mr. Hargreaves, but you've failed to rein her in for more than a decade. I fear you're not up to the task."

The door to the sitting room opened. "Lord Bromley, sir, madam," Davis announced as my father entered.

"Catherine, it's time to go home," he said. He glowered at her, then came to me and patted me on the shoulder. "I'm prodigiously proud of you, Emily. Another meschant put away. It's quite an accomplishment."

"Samuel, I made it clear when I summoned you here that I required reinforcements. Our daughter is wholly out of control."

"I'd have her no other way." He took his wife by the arm and led her out of the house.

Sebastian stepped out from behind a curtain. "I didn't want to make my presence known until she was gone. Is it safe?"

"How long have you been there?" I asked.

"Does it matter?"

"It most certainly does," Colin said.

"I wanted to let you both know that, given Lady Goldsborough's unfortunate actions, I can no longer leave Boudica's treasures in her hands. Fear not, I'll keep them safe. Unless you'd like them for yourself, Emily."

"What do you mean, you'll keep them safe?"

"Unfortunately, it will soon be discovered that the site was burgled last night. Gold has a tendency to attract the criminal element. Knowing your desire to see the remains get a decent burial, I've boxed up the bones and sent them to your estate in Derbyshire. Perhaps you could build a little mound for her or whatever would be appropriate for an Iceni warrior."

"Does this mean you're abandoning your archaeological adventures?" I asked.

"Yes, they proved rather disappointing in the end. Loxton convinced me we couldn't go public with claims that the body is Boudica. It was too far above the layer of ash from her destruction of Londinium. He's convinced whoever it belongs to was alive through the rebuilding of the city. While the jewelry initially excited me, it turns out to be no better than most Iron Age pieces. I've released Loxton back to Crete."

"What about Lady Harrington's tiara?" Colin asked.

"That, my dear man, is long gone. I shall, however, give you a glimpse of Pompadour's necklace when it's restored."

"I can have you arrested."

"Hargreaves, we both know you don't have the evidence to convict me. I'll be out of sight before you could take me into custody. Kallista, my darling, it has been, as always, a pleasure." He kissed my hand, opened a window, and stepped through it.

"Should you stop him?" I asked.

"He's clever enough to avoid conviction and, frankly, Lady Harrington doesn't care much about that jewelry. It's why she was willing to give it to Miss Goldsborough. I've always admired Madame de Pompadour and can't say I object to seeing her necklace restored."

"I'm all astonishment," I said.

"Sometimes it's best to turn a blind eye, but I don't plan on making a habit of it."

A knock sounded on the door. Davis was back, a decanter of port and a glass on his silver tray.

"Don't think, madam, this signifies a change in my opinion regarding ladies and this particular beverage," he said. "However, you've had a trying time of late, and a spot of port might be in order. Please don't make a habit of it."

Author's Note

Given how large Boudica looms in the collective imagination, it's shocking to discover how little we actually know about her. The Roman historians Tacitus and Cassius Dio are our only sources. Tacitus' father-in-law served in Britannia during his years in the army and likely would have shared stories with his son-in-law, but long after the battles took place. Dio wrote 140 years after Boudica's revolt. Both men had their own agendas. Tacitus suggests the decadence endemic in Rome during Nero's reign made the greatest army in the world susceptible to a barbarian woman, while Dio implies Boudica is more noble than the Romans, who had strayed from their ideas of virtue. As a result, both of their accounts may be more accurate in showing the authors' views on their present-day Rome than in the specific details of what happened when the Iceni revolted.

We cannot say with confidence that the woman leading the charge was named Boudica; the word, which comes from a precursor to Gaelic and means *victory*, may be an epithet. *Boudega*, which is probably what her soldiers chanted marching into battle, means *she*

Author's Note

who brings victory. Regardless, for centuries *Boadicea* was the accepted spelling, the result of a medieval monk incorrectly copying a Tacitus manuscript in which the historian recorded her name as *Boudicca*. Sloppy handwriting sure makes a difference. At present, scholars believe *Boudica* to be the best spelling. The Romans, after all, would only have heard the word, not seen it written.

The town of Venta Icenorum was established by the Romans in the 70s AD after Boudica's defeat. I have chosen to adopt the name for her village as we have no record of what the Iceni called it. To date, no archaeological evidence directly related to the great warrior queen has been found.

Paul Poiret published a book in 1908 featuring drawings of his Hellenistic-inspired dresses. He'd started producing gowns in the style a few years earlier, and I'm certain Emily would have been an early adopter.

Sources

A Pictorial and Descriptive Guide to London and Its Environs. 1911. 36th ed. London: Ward, Lock.

Allason-Jones, Lindsay. 2008. *Daily Life in Roman Britain*. Oxford: Greenwood World Publishing.

Barnstone, Willis, trans. 2009. *The Complete Poems of Sappho*. Boulder, CO: Shambhala.

Blair, Peter Hunter. 1963. *Roman Britain and Early England 55 B.C.–A.D. 871*. New York: W. W. Norton.

Clark, John. 1983. "New Troy to Lake Village—The Legend of Prehistoric London." *London Archaeologist* 4 (11): 292–96. London Archaeologist Association.

Dio Cassius. n.d. *Roman History Books LXI-LXX*. Jeffrey Henderson, ed.; Earnest Cary, trans. Cambridge, MA: Harvard University Press.

Edmonds, John Maxwell, trans. 1955. *Some Greek Poems of Love and Nature*. Cambridge, MA: Deighton Bell.

Ehrlich, Eugene. *Veni, Vidi, Vici*. New York: Harper Perennial, 1995.

Fraser, Antonia. 1990. *The Warrior Queens*. New York: Anchor.

Hingley, Richard, and Christina Unwin. 2006. *Boudica: Iron Age Warrior Queen*. London: Continuum.

Langman, Loralie J., and Bhushan M. Kapur. 2006. "Toxicology: Then and Now." *Clinical Biochemistry* 39 (5): 498–510.

Mackay, Duncan. 2023. *Echolands*. London: Hodder & Stoughton.

Ovid. 2008. *The Love Poems*. A. D. Melville and E. J. Kenney, trans. Oxford: Oxford University Press.

Philodemus. 2006. *Acts of Love: Ancient Greek Poetry from Aphrodite's Garden*. George Economou, trans. New York: Modern Library.

Sproule, Anna. 1978. *The Social Calendar*. Poole, Dorset, UK: Blandford.

Tacitus, Publius Cornelius. (1956) 1996. *The Annals of Imperial Rome*. Betty Radice, ed.; Michael Grant, trans. London: Penguin.

Wallace, Lacey M. 2014. *The Origin of Roman London*. Cambridge, UK: Cambridge University Press.

Watson, Katherine D. 2020. "Poisoning Crimes and Forensic Toxicology Since the 18th Century." *Academic Forensic Pathology* 10 (1): 35–46.

Webster, Graham. 1999. *Boudica: The British Revolt against Rome AD 60*. 2nd ed. London: Routledge.

Whitmarsh, Tim. 2021. "Less Care, More Stress: A Rhythmic Poem from the Roman Empire." *The Cambridge Classical Journal* 67 (August): 135–63.

Wood, Michael. (1981) 2023. *In Search of the Dark Ages*. 40th anniversary ed. London: BBC Books.

Acknowledgments

Myriad thanks to . . .

Charlie Spicer, a joy to work with.

Hannah Pierdolla, Andy Martin, Sarah Melnyk, Sara Beth Haring, Kelley Ragland, and David Rotstein.

Anne Hawkins. I wouldn't have wanted to do twenty years plus with anyone else.

Brett Battles, Laura Bradford, Christina Chen, Jon Clinch, Elizabeth Letts, Lara Matthys, Carrie Medders, Erica Ruth Neubauer, Missy Rightley, and Renee Rosen.

Alexander, Katie, and Jess.

My parents.

About the Author

Charles Osgood

Tasha Alexander is the author of the *New York Times* bestselling Lady Emily Mystery series. The daughter of two philosophy professors, she studied English literature and medieval history at the University of Notre Dame. She and her husband, novelist Andrew Child, live on a ranch in southeastern Wyoming.